It's two o'clock in the morning, and all is <u>not</u> well.

Something was occurring in the apartment.

There was no sound at all. Yet there had to have been something, some tinkle of a sound, some stir of movement. Mady could not have simply leaped out of a very tired sleep for nothing.

She wouldn't be easy in her mind until she had at least looked out into the living room, called Lettie, discovered—oh, something, she thought vaguely, but with mandatory urgency. She had brought a dressing gown and she slid into it and bedroom slippers; she padded across to the door. Just before she opened it she was assailed with terror.

She couldn't breathe. She couldn't stop her heart's pounding. If I don't open that door now I never will, she thought wildly, and made herself turn the knob and open the door . . .

"New and diverting."   —*Publishers Weekly*

"A smooth whodunit."   —*Buffalo News*

"Fast-paced and riveting."   —*Booklist*

Also by
MIGNON G. EBERHART

Another Man's Murder

Family Affair

Hunt with the Hounds

Murder in Waiting

Postmark Murder

Unidentified Woman

Witness at Large

Wolf in Man's Clothing

Published by
WARNER BOOKS

MIGNON G. EBERHART
NEXT OF KIN

WARNER BOOKS

A Warner Communications Company

All the persons and events in this are entirely imaginary.
Nothing in it derives from anything that ever happened.

WARNER BOOKS EDITION

This Warner Books Edition is published by arrangement with Random House, Inc., 201 East 50 Street, New York, N.Y. 10022

Warner Books, Inc.
666 Fifth Avenue
New York, N.Y. 10103

 A Warner Communications Company

Printed in the United States of America

First Warner Books Printing: December, 1984

10 9 8 7 6 5 4 3 2 1

One

The snow began at noon. By four o'clock the New York streets were a tangled mass of automobiles, pedestrians, trucks and men shoveling the sidewalks. There was very little result of all this labor, for the snow was proving itself too heavy and too resistant. As soon as a path along a sidewalk was half-cleared, the beginning of it was covered with white again. People scurried along, bumping into one another for their heads and faces were muffled up and their haste was as defeating as the snow that tripped them, baffled their sense of direction, took their breath away, caused them to slip and slide and had swiftly become a blinding, invincible, almost frightening world of cold and white.

Mady felt that her eyelashes were stuck together; her gloved hand was clumsy with cold when she paid the taxi driver who took the money without any thanks for the too-generous tip and grumbled through a kind of woolly helmet he had on that he was going home and nobody need try to flag him down because that was that. He accelerated the motor and the orange taxi vanished behind white curtains of snow.

But 21 was as always cheerful and quietly ignored the carryings on of nature. "He's over there—" said a waiter in reply to Mady's question and nodded toward the man sitting at a table, eyeing a glass before him rather seriously.

"Chan!"

1

He rose, his face clearing, and pulled out her chair. "Mady! There's snow in your hair—" He brushed at it lightly and she gave a small shriek. "Don't touch!"

"Why not?" He looked surprised.

"Because I've just come from the hairdresser, that's why. Never mind, you didn't ruin Monsieur Raldo's symphony. I'm not too sure I like it anyway."

The waiter said, "Yes, Mr. Channing?"

Chan paused. "What about it, Mady?"

"I'm cold enough already without a cold drink—"

"A hot toddy," the waiter suggested, smiling.

"Go ahead." Chan took his seat. "It can't hurt you. Not the smooth way they make it."

"But I'll have to drink at Lettie's."

Chan laughed. "Make it extra mild—" he said to the waiter. He leaned his elbows on the table and surveyed Mady. "Why in the world did you go to the hairdresser? Your hair is always just right as it is."

"Chan, it's just hair. The fact is I am trying to put my best foot forward."

"At *Lettie's?* Why?"

"Oh, Chan, you know! I want to impress your brother, the senator. I mean the former senator now to be in the Cabinet."

His dark eyes were serious again. "Why on earth do you want to impress Stu?"

"I want to work for him."

He stared at her. "Work for Stu?"

"Yes, certainly."

"But Mady—" He fumbled with his glass, took several hasty swallows and said, "You never mentioned it this morning when I phoned you and asked you to meet me here, and you said you would—"

"I'm meeting you." That morning over the telephone he had sounded different, very intent somehow. She had had a swift notion that, just perhaps, his intentions might be honorable. She grinned a little wryly to herself; probably he had no such intentions after all. If she could get the job with his brother, the one-time senator now to be a Cabinet member, at least she would be nearer Chan. Ballantry College was not far from Washington. The little silence was broken by people coming, shaking off snow, laughing. One group settled at the next table, shed coats, ordered drinks. There was the usual pleasant, busy hub-bub of the before-dinner hours all around them.

She said at last, "Of course, I realize that he'll have a whole corps of office workers—"

"He may not go to Washington."

"But it's been in the papers. Everybody knows—"

Chan frowned. "Oh, yes. It's a great honor. He talked to me this morning about it. Seemed to be pleased. Told me about the Valentine party this afternoon. That's when I called you. But I'd intended to come here anyway—"

The party at the next table was hilarious over some joke. Chan glowered at them. Mady said mischievously, "That's nothing to the noise at the party where we are going."

His gaze returned to her. "You really mean to ask Stu for a job?"

"If I can get up my courage. That's why I had to have my hair done. False courage. And now you don't like it."

He eyed her hair. The waiter put a barely steaming mug in front of her, which did have a most delicious smell.

Chan said absently. "Napoleon would have liked it."

"Liked my *hair?*" Even after years she didn't really understand Hill Channing. She guessed his reactions sometimes; she never quite knew what he might say or do. "What has Napoleon got to do with it?"

His eyes had a serious but still-absent look. "Oh, bees."

"Talk sense."

"That is sense. His emblem was a bee. Usually made of gold. Your hair looks like a golden beehive. I mean—well, anyway, it just reminded me."

"You do come out with the damnedest things."

He returned from idle speculation. "Your stepfather wouldn't like to hear you say damned," he said severely.

"He'd be surprised that I could relax to that extent. He thinks I'm a cruel tyrant."

"Dear me!" Chan grinned.

"And I am! Sometimes. You know him."

"Well," said Chan cautiously. "He means well."

"Oh," she said in exasperation. "Everything just rolls off his back like—like water off a duck. He doesn't even stop to shake, just goes on and spends more money."

"There's plenty to spend," Chan said dryly. "Drink your drink while it's hot."

"I'm not a Scrooge," she said crossly. "I just don't like to see money wasted. My mother told me to look out for him, but I can't watch him all the time."

"You control the purse strings, don't you?"

"Well, with the bank."

"You're a funny kind of rich girl," Chan said, still in an absent way as if he were thinking of something else. "Taking a secretarial course—"

"I had to do something. Seeing to Clarence is not really a fulltime job. At least not always." And I'd like to see you more often, she thought.

There was another burst of hilarity from the next table.

Chan said, "You like Clarence, though."

"Yes, I do," she admitted rather reluctantly. "My mother adored him. But she knew him, too! That's why she asked me to do my best to see to him. I am not always successful." She sighed as she sipped the toddy, thinking of Clarence's latest hobby, which was auction rooms and, unfortunately, also bidding. Still she realized that much of Clarence's frenzied pursuit of hobbies was due to loneliness.

"But there are other ways to spend your time."

"I'm not that fond of bridge," she said shortly. "Or acting as a volunteer for every available cause. Or getting up charity shows or—"

"You might marry."

Marry? Her heart gave a great plunge. Was he by any chance working around to the thing she wanted him to say?

No. He was quietly finishing his drink, not even looking at her to see how she took the suggestion.

He said, eyeing the glass he put down on the table, "Or are you just bored?"

"No, Professor Channing, I am not bored! I just want to—" she paused and ended feebly, "—do something."

The party at the next table supplied too much laughter and talk. Chan was making circles on their table with his glass. She felt she must say something, anything. "When you phoned me this morning from Princeton, you said you wanted to see me—"

"Yes, certainly. I wish they'd shut up!" He cast a venomous glance toward the nearby table.

"What were you doing in Princeton?"

"Stopped to see a friend at the physics lab there. Let's get out of here—"

She finished the toddy quickly and then moved her head unintentionally and caught a glimpse of herself in a mirror. "Oh, heavens, Chan! You are perfectly right. My hair looks terrible. I'll try to fix it while you get a taxi. If you can. We must get off to Lettie's. We are late and the traffic is terrible—" She was out of her chair, clutching her handbag as Chan rose.

In the ladies' room she dug out the tiny comb in her handbag and worked resolutely on her hair. Chan could always make her feel like the most backward student in any of his classes. No, lately he called them seminars: only a few graduate students now, he'd said, not boasting but merely stating a fact as he always did, even an unpalatable one. Beehive indeed!

That morning there had been something in his voice that suggested a change. But clearly he hadn't changed. It seemed that their long-time friendship must merely continue contentedly. She thought dismally of something that someone sometime had said to her: "The relationship between a man and a woman does not stand still; it either advances or retreats."

But if she was in Washington near his university and actually working for his brother, then just perhaps—she caught a snarl in her hair so viciously that she stopped thinking useless thoughts and put her mind on her hair. When it was smoother, calmer, less frenzied, she touched her mouth with lipstick, felt pleasantly aglow from the hot toddy, and went to join Chan, who was standing at the door, overcoat lapels turned up. "It's all right. The doorman has a magnet that draws in taxis."

He held her coat for her and, she thought, gave her hair a glance of approval as he tucked the fur collar around her throat. The snow flew in their faces as they ran across the sidewalk and got into the cab. Its headlights turned the flying snow into almost hypnotic swirls of white. She wished she dared snuggle her hand into the curve of Chan's arm.

If she did he would merely turn to her and ask if she were cold and—it was not improbable—pull gloves out from some pocket and offer them to her. No flirtatious gesture ever made the slightest impression upon Chan; at least he certainly seemed unaware of its implications. Most young men recognized a gesture when they saw one.

She sighed. Chan did hear that. "Scared? It's not slippery yet—I guess." Since the taxi did slide them together, jolting, at that moment, he said, "Sorry, my mistake," but didn't put his arm around her. There had been the barest, briefest contact with him, close enough and hard enough to feel his strength and warmth. Then he very kindly (*kindly*, she thought crossly) helped her sit erect on the seat beside him. "It's not getting any better." He leaned forward to the taxi driver and shouted. "Shouldn't we miss that snowplow on the next block?"

She could see, too, the whirling fan of snow from the lighted, plunging snowplow.

The driver seemed to debate. Then he shouted back, "No chance. They're all over. We'll just have to take it easy—"

So he took it easy, skidding now and then and taking what Mady felt were hairbreadth chances with pedestrians who insisted upon battling their way across the avenue, clutching scarves over mouths and eyes, and never looking at anything, especially taxis.

"We'll be very late," she said once when they were obliged to wait, engine panting, while a snow-laden truck pushed its slow way ahead of them.

"We were late before we started. You took too long at your fancy hairdresser's." Chan said. "Never mind. We'll get there."

Eventually, get there they did and came to a throbbing, wheezing halt before lighted doors. "This the place?" the taxi driver asked.

This was the place, an elegant apartment house in, naturally, as good a location as there was in town. Chan put out his hand to assist her from the cab. He shoved the money in the other hand at the driver and said to her, "Why, Mady—you're shivering."

"There's Lettie," Mady said. "The party must be over."

The door thrust open, a doorman stuck his head out from some sheltered booth inside the foyer and Lettie herself, a flying figure wrapped in chinchilla and carrying, of all things, a large grocery bag, whirled out from the snow and cried, "Oh! Chan! Mady! You finally got here!"

She leaned a warm cheek for Mady to brush with her own in the customary New York kiss, which is not a kiss at all. No woman who has spent hours, or even moments, in front of her dressing table really likes a destructive touch to her make-up. Lettie was breathless. "Such a storm! Come along, you two. The party is over, but there is still food and drink."

In the elevator, Lettie ran on breathlessly, "A wonderful

party really. I'm sorry you missed it. It was all on the spur of the moment. But I had to celebrate the senator's new appointment somehow. We had the very best caterers. They managed to come even at the last moment. Nadine phoned for them yesterday. But then they're the ones I always use. Nobody in town better." She clutched the grocery bag closer under one arm and a huge red handbag under the other. Her lovely face with its delicate charm had a touch of pink in the cheeks. Her soft brown eyes were animated, almost excited. Her short, brown-auburn curls made a cap over her head. All she ever did was push a comb casually through the curls. Mady had seen her do it often and always for a second hated her; Mady's own hair required a certain discipline. A whiff of the scent Lettie used came from the open collar of her coat, which showed her lovely white throat and a necklace set with emeralds and diamonds.

Chan eyed the grocery bag. "Your guests must have liked your caterer, too. Is that for home supper?"

"What? Oh, that?" She glanced down at the grocery bag. "The senator likes plain food as you know. I just ran out—" The elevator door moved silently open and they moved into the small outer entrance hall for the apartment. The door was ajar and Lettie waved them in toward the larger hall and a coatroom.

Beyond the coatroom there was a most elegantly equipped washroom. The door from the inner hall was usually closed, but now it was wide open. From where Mady and Chan stood there was a full view of the main rooms, which were lovely, sparkling with light and color and just then amazingly disheveled. Empty glasses, plates and small red paper hearts from some kind of decoration lay everywhere; cigarette trays were full and smelly. Red roses in the shape of an enormous heart on the large table in the dining room were drooping slightly. The long living room had dazzling lights, soft colors of pastel blues, pinks and yellows, cushioned sofas and graceful chairs; a handsome piano was set at an angle.

"The detritus of a cocktail party," Chan said idly. "Never attractive. Still, there must be some food left on the table. Better take off your coat, Mady."

He took it from her, but dropped it on a handsome Chinese Chippendale chair, which Mady recognized as such because recently her step-father had bid for two such chairs, brought them home and then decided he didn't like them. It had been rather a problem inducing the small gallery to take them back. Most of her education about antiques, she thought briefly, had been by way of Clarence, so perhaps she ought to thank him for that, although it had been a rather expensive education. She wondered briefly what he had been about that day when, owing to the snow, the auction rooms of the big galleries would not have been as fully populated as usual and consequently smaller bids might have been accepted.

Chan went into the dining room and returned with a tray. "Have some caviar." He offered her a generously heaped slice of rye bread. "Also," he flourished a glass that he had apparently whisked from the long buffet which had been used as a bar, judging by the debris of glasses, decanters, a tall, crystal martini mixer, olives, tiny onions. "Martini?" He had one for himself and sipped it appreciatively. "Chilled just right. I wonder who mixed it. One of these admirable caterers, I suppose. I wonder where they are—"

A loud sound like a shot came from somewhere. Chan jerked up his head. Mady said, laughing, "She's giving us champagne."

Chan was already at the door leading to the pantry. Mady, glass in hand, followed him.

It was a long narrow pantry, with a door leading to the front hall, another to the dining room and another to the glittering modern kitchen with every appliance known as yet to inventive manufacturers. Lettie was there, her chinchilla coat tossed on a stool. She was laughing and closing the door to one of three refrigerators. "Sorry. Did it scare you? Heavens, now what happened to the cork! It just flew. Anyway, here's champagne. I thought you'd like some. Maybe we can get the senator to venture out now that everybody is gone. That is—have they all gone?" Lettie and many people always called Stuart the senator, although he was now a former senator, Mady thought on a tangent. Clarence had said once that they always would call him the senator; it was the way once a judge, always a judge, retired or not.

"Looks like it." Chan picked up the chinchilla coat, which had slid to the floor. He put it neatly over a chair. "I'll get some glasses." He went into the pantry.

There was the debris of a party in the kitchen, too. Lettie thrust a hand across her shining curls, eyed the litter of boxes, trays, plates, napkins, and said helplessly, "These caterers never clean up. I'm supposed to have somebody else on tap to do that. I don't, not today. Gretchen usually helps out, but she was afraid to come on account of the weather. She lives in New Jersey. I suppose she was right. But what a mess—"

Chan returned with three glasses. "These right?"

"Oh, yes. The tulip glasses. Would you believe it, Mady, I went to a party last week and they were still using those silly flat glasses? What's the matter, Chan?" Chan was pouring champagne carefully. He said, "Doesn't Stu come out for parties?"

"Oh," Lettie sighed. "He was on the phone when the guests began to arrive and said he'd be here as soon as he could. But I suppose there were calls from Washington and—oh, I don't know. Chan, do go and dig him out. He's in his study, I think." She glanced around her, said again, "What a mess," and sank down on another kitchen stool. Her white silk dress clung to her in graceful lines; the emerald-and-diamond necklace glittered in the overhead lights. She wore on her left breast a large red paper heart.

She caught Mady's glance at it and said, "Valentine. I thought I'd make it a Valentine party and—oh, Mady, don't look so upset about the mess. The glasses can go in the dishwasher in the pantry. There's another bigger one there. And anyway I'll just stack up things I can't fit into a dishwasher and maybe Gretchen can get here by morning—what's that?"

She jerked around as Chan came in hurriedly from the pantry, his footsteps loud and sharp. "Stuart seems to have locked himself in—"

"Oh, he often does that. Especially if there are people—"

"But he doesn't answer me. I knocked and I called him and—"

Lettie slid off the stool and ran toward the study, Chan after her. Mady put down her champagne. The hot toddy, the martini and now champagne! Certainly all that was why something in Chan's voice and face had made her feel so very—very odd, she thought, and followed Lettie and Chan who were in the long corridor on the far side of the splendid living room.

She passed open doors to a library and three bedrooms. The senator's study was at the very end of the corridor and both Chan and Lettie were calling him, but there was no reply.

Chan shook the door, pushed, calling "Stu—Stu—"

"The key," Lettie cried. "Wait. I think there's an extra one in the library—"

"Never mind." Chan snatched out his own keyring and quickly selected a key. "I've always had this. Stu gave it to me—"

The door opened. Chan burst into the room first, then Lettie and Mady. Chan ran to the man, who sagged like an empty sack in the armchair beside a long writing table. He leaned over him and looked and listened and put a hand on the dangling wrist. The room was suffocatingly hot. Waves of heat surged over them.

Mady stumbled over something, caught herself and

glanced down at a gun that lay on the rug not far from the door, gleaming in the desk light. A key lay near it. "Chan! Look—there's the key! And a gun—" She stopped, foolishly intending to pick it up. Chan stopped her. "*Don't! Mady— don't touch that!* Get out. Both of you. I mean it, Lettie."

"But Chan! A doctor—surely a doctor." Lettie tried to bend over the senator, and Chan shouldered her away.

"It's too late, Lettie. He is dead. Shot."

Lettie put both her hands on Chan's arm. "Chan, you must let me see! You must—I'll call the doctor."

Mady could see only a dark, wet stain on the back of a gray tweed jacket.

"*Mady,*" Chan spoke to her over his shoulder. "Call the police—*Now*. Lettie! Do as I say."

Two

He literally pushed them both into the hall. Then he closed the door with a thud.

"Doctor—" Lettie ran for the library.

"Chan said police—"

Lettie whirled into the library. A telephone stood on a table and she began to dial. "Yes—yes. It's Mrs. Channing. Doctor—the senator's been hurt. Oh, I don't know. Chan, I mean his brother, says he's dead—Yes. Oh, hurry." She put down the telephone and sank back into a sofa.

Mady said blankly, "The police. Chan said—" She took up the telephone herself. Oddly, she remembered the famous number and dialed it but when someone answered could only say that a man had been shot and that it was Senator Channing and gave the address.

The voice livened up. "Yes, Ma'am! I've got the address. Don't do anything—"

Do anything? Mady thought. I couldn't possibly do anything. I don't see how I had whatever it took to lift the receiver, let alone make my fingers dial.

She was sitting in a leather-covered chair, very comfortable and deep, near the small table where the telephone stood. Books lined the walls, although there was a portrait of a darkly handsome, decisive-looking man hanging above the mantel of the fireplace, which actually was laid with real birch logs, unlike most New York City fireplaces. The man in the portrait seemed to look at her as firmly and yet as kindly as Chan sometimes eyed her, and with a certain guarded restraint. He was, she knew, Chan's and the senator's father, now gone for many years. The senator and probably Chan had read and read and read those books; law books for the most part, those would have interested Stuart, but perhaps not Chan, although one could never be sure. There were novels also, and books of biography and poetry and—my head is swimming, she thought. A hot toddy, a martini and then champagne! She thought wildly, I'll be completely out of my head! Maybe I *am* out of my head this minute. Maybe the senator wasn't shot! Maybe I just passed out and dreamed it!

Lettie leaned her head back; her face was so pale that the touches of blue eye shadow she had used looked like ugly bruises. "You called the police?"

So Lettie could whisper. Mady didn't trust herself to speak again; she nodded.

"They said they are coming?"

"Yes. The man at the phone—he said somebody would be here."

Lettie seemed to listen as if for a bell; she rose, moved slowly like a sleepwalker to the window, drew aside the heavy drapery and looked out and down. Her face was mirrored in the black glass with its flying white particles. After a moment she dropped the drapery and turned. "I don't know—" she said as if to herself, "I don't understand!"

Chan came in. He was so white that his firmly drawn chin and nose and mouth seemed as if they were carved in stone. All of us, Mady thought vaguely, all of us have been turned to stone. No feeling, nothing, just stone. "Are the police coming, Mady?"

She nodded. They were acting like zombies, she thought, and knew she was more than half touched by the alcohol she had consumed. But how did one act in the face of—of that?

The men in blue would come any minute, she thought, still fuzzily.

Actually, they were not in blue when they came, at least the first contingent, who arrived on the heels of a doorbell ringing and a house telephone buzzing at the same time.

Chan let them in.

There was a jumble of voices. Chan's voice came clearly through the lovely, disorderly living and dining rooms. "In his study. I'll show you—this way."

Lettie had moved to the door of the library. She said again in a whisper, "But they are not in uniform. Mady, are you sure it was the police you phoned?"

"Yes—"

"Oh. Detectives, I suppose. Yes—"

There was the steady tramp of feet in the apartment.

Mady wanted to join Lettie at the door where she could see down the narrow corridor, but she couldn't move. The house bell buzzed again, urgently. Almost at once the doorbell began to ring, in short, sharp peals. "I'll answer." Lettie disappeared.

These men were in uniform.

In Mady's memory, the inquiry into the shocking death of former Senator Stuart Channing always began with the ringing of the doorbell and the sound of feet along the narrow corridor to the senator's study.

It was cold in the library in spite of the heavy brown

draperies. It was a man's room, thick brown rugs on a polished floor, deep leather-covered chairs and a sofa that looked worn at each end as if tall men had used it for hurried naps. There was nothing feminine in the room; Lettie's exquisite taste had obviously ordered the huge living room and lovely dining room and big entrance hall. Valentine's Day, Mady thought. She wondered dimly what the policeman thought of all the after-party litter. Probably that someone had had too much to drink and shot the senator in a drunken rage.

That reflection brought her at least halfway to her senses with a jolt. That would be murder.

Yet in her heart hadn't she been sure from the first shocking instant that Stuart Channing was not a man to kill himself?

And especially at the very zenith of a brilliant career! But then the chilling fact was that she had had a terrible glimpse of his slumped back and the stained tweed jacket. So it was murder. Chan had leaped to that conclusion at once. A man can't shoot himself in the back. So Chan had said, "Police."

Murder?

She stared at the rug below her feet and tried to face the dreadful word, a word for headlines, for news items, nothing one would normally see, or experience, or know anything about at all.

A wave of unreality, something fantastically disturbing, caught her like a sudden mist.

Lettie had quietly disappeared; she came back, huddled now in the chinchilla coat she had tossed down somewhere— oh, yes, in the pantry as Mady and Chan arrived. "It's cold here." Lettie clutched her coat around her white silk dress with its red paper heart still plastered at one shoulder. She had removed her emerald necklace. Mady wondered vaguely why. "I turned up the thermostat for this room just now." Lettie added, "Each room has its own, you know. Oh, Mady, *what happened?*"

"What happened? Good Heavens, Lettie!"

"I know. I know—that is, I don't know. Somebody must have gotten into his study and shot him but—Mady, he promised to come out for the party, just as soon as he finished some phoning he said he had to do. In connection with this appointment, I thought. Oh, Mady, now he can't—" she put her hands over her face and then reached down to clutch the furs higher.

Mady thought, I'm still fogged. But she heard herself say, "He was shot. Chan said he was shot. Didn't you hear it?"

"Hear—no, no!" Lettie put her hands over her face. "But during the party—there is always so much noise. It had to happen then—oh, Mady, what can I do!"

"Dear Lettie—try to—" Try to what? Mady stopped as feet came toward the library and yet more feet came in through the entrance hall and trudged back along the corridor.

There was another buzz at the door near the elevator and this time a real policeman, clad in blue, came heavily across the living room and into the library. He towed with him a small man, with a Van Dyke beard and an agitated manner. "Doctor Lorsome, he says he is," said the policeman.

Lettie cried, "Oh, doctor. Stuart—"

"They told me downstairs. It's all right, officer," the doctor said to the policeman, who looked around slowly, then took himself off. Lettie clung to the doctor's hand. "Chan thinks his brother was murdered, but he can't have been, doctor."

The doctor patted her hand and looked unhappily down the hall. "Perhaps—that is, there will be a medical examiner—"

"No, doctor, please go—please see—you know the way—"

"Certainly, Mrs. Channing." He took himself, half trotting, yet with an air of reluctance, down the corridor and out of sight. It seemed only a moment before he returned. "Dear me—oh, my dear Mrs. Channing—now, now, I'm sorry but—" He seemed to pull himself together with difficulty and assumed an authoritative air. "Now then, I am sorry. There is nothing I can do, you know. But now, Mrs. Channing, you must—you must really take it easy. You really must. Take two of these. Here—" He had a small black bag, which he whisked open; he withdrew some capsules neatly and held them toward Lettie, who just looked at him as if she didn't see him or the capsules. After a moment, he put them down on a table and said, "Now then—now then—can't tell you how sorry—call me if—at any time—yes, yes—"

He departed as another man entered and stood looking at them. He was tall, well-built, with smooth brown hair and kind yet extremely observant brown eyes. He wore a plain business suit of dark gray, a black pullover sweater, white shirt and an air of quiet, watchful ease. "My name is McEvor—Mrs. Channing?" He looked at Lettie, who nodded like a mechanical doll. He said, "Homicide. Captain McEvor. And Lieutenant Swain—" he added as another man, dark, bony but also with an air of cautious ease, entered.

Lettie made some kind of motion with her lovely auburn-brown curls and nodded. Each man cast a rather swift, yet not unobserving, glance at Mady. Then McEvor said, "Mind if we sit down—thank you. Now then, Mrs. Channing, this is only a—call it a preliminary kind of survey. But I must warn you that a record will be made of anything you say, so—"

Lettie's brown eyes were pansy soft but steady. "You mean he *was* murdered."

There was a slight pause as if the men communicated without speaking. Then McEvor said, "Well, it looks that way, Mrs. Channing. I'm sorry, but—you see he was shot in the back. The gun was over near the door. So his brother tells us. Not close beside him. And further—oh, we're not sure of anything just now."

"Except he was shot," said Swain morosely and jerked at his collar.

"Yes," Lettie said.

"We only want to make some inquiries now, but the record—"

"Oh, I know." Lettie lifted her chin. "I know, the Miranda warning. I can only tell you what I know."

"Excellent," said McEvor. "Good," said Swain, but as if he preferred to say "Bad." He nodded toward another man, very young but with a balding head sparsely trimmed with long red hair, who appeared in the doorway. "The sergeant here will take notes but—just remember you have been warned not to incriminate yourself, Mrs. Channing."

"I can only tell you what I know."

Captain McEvor said pleasantly, "All right. Now then, I understand you had a party."

Lettie's head moved. "Valentine's Day," she said stiffly. "Just an informal little party."

McEvor seemed to be the spokesman. "Seems to me that I read about your husband when he was senator. Two terms, but he didn't run again last fall. Why not?"

"He decided to enter a law firm."

"Couldn't have been in some law firm very long before he was elected to the Senate," said McEvor thoughtfully. "How old was he?"

"He is—" Lettie seemed to start to amend the verb and didn't. "Thirty-two, the first term."

"Youngest senator for a long time. Right?"

"So now he was forty-four."

Lettie merely nodded but something in her manner implied that anybody could add.

McEvor's eyes were patient but watchful.

Suddenly Lettie decided to speak. "I believe I should have a lawyer."

Neither detective seemed taken aback. McEvor said at once, agreeably, "Certainly. Shall I phone him or will you?"

"Well, I—the fact is I don't really have a lawyer. But there's a friend. His name is Larry Todd." She paused and as an after-thought said, "He may not be at home yet. He was here, you see. At the party."

Mady was not surprised. Larry Todd was a long time friend. Younger than the senator, older than Chan, he was still youthful in appearance, a popular bachelor seen everywhere. Mady liked him, but couldn't help feeling that just possibly he enjoyed his position as an eligible young man about town too much. For a second her mind flashed back to the years when Lettie had often stayed at her home, when Chan and Larry had been in a way their special escorts; and then during his first term the senator had come home, met Lettie and, instantly it seemed now, fallen in love with her.

McEvor said without a flicker, "I'll phone to him just in the event he's at home. I expect you have his number, Mrs. Channing."

"Oh, yes—here—" Lettie picked up the note pad, which lay, complete with pencil, beside the telephone, and scribbled a number. She lifted her questioning gaze to the detective. "I think that is it. Is it really all right to call him? Somebody—somewhere I heard that that was the thing to do whenever—"

"Certainly, Mrs. Channing. Perfectly all right. Good idea, in fact. Now then—"

Beyond the slight click of the dial Mady could hear a distant murmur of men's voices and the tread of two more men coming through the living room and down the corridor.

But the telephone merely buzzed until McEvor put it down. "Doesn't seem to be at home. Now if you prefer to wait until we can get hold of him before talking to you, it's all right, you know."

"Oh, no. No. Ask anything you like." Lettie leaned back in the sofa, pushing her coat aside so her white dress shone against the brown leather. Her curls were for once disheveled, the blue shadows on her eyelids and soft pink lipstick on her mouth stood out against the pallor of her face.

"Good. Your brother-in-law—the man who let us in—"

"Chan. That is, his name is Hill Channing."

"Now then, he wasn't at this party."

"Yes—that is, no. He and Mady—Miss Smith here—came in just as everybody had gone."

McEvor transferred his caramel-brown gaze to Mady. "Late, were you?"

She moistened her lips. "The storm. Traffic—"

"But you did arrive."

"Yes. We were too late, though. The storm and the traffic and—guests had gone when Chan and I—I mean Hill and I—arrived."

"Mrs. Channing, can you give us the guest list?"

Lettie opened her mouth twice before clear words came out. "I'm not sure I have a complete list. You see, this was all impromptu. I began phoning people yesterday and then again this morning. It was—well, it was like that."

"I am sure you'll remember who was here. We'll just make a little list—" He drew out a pad of paper and a pencil. "Just put down the names as you think of them."

"All right," said Lettie and then caught her breath. "I forgot. Nadine will know exactly. She called the caterers for me yesterday and made some of the phone calls and ordered the flowers—"

"Nadine?" said McEvor politely.

"My husband's secretary. I mean, his—his head secretary, since he was in the Senate. She does everything like that."

It seemed to Mady that both detectives' faces altered just slightly as if each were saying to himself: What did *you* do, Mrs. Channing? They didn't understand Lettie or the pressures of the life she led so efficiently. There was no better hostess anywhere and certainly few as beautiful. Mady said, a little indignantly, "Mrs. Channing has a great deal to see to, you know. Nadine, I mean Miss Hallowell, is always a help and glad to be."

Both men looked at her thoughtfully. McEvor said after a moment, "Well, then, this Nadine—I expect she was at the party."

"No," Lettie said, "she wasn't. She was welcome, naturally. She is always welcome at any time, anywhere. But this morning she said she was taking a plane to Washington. You see—" her voice wobbled, "—my husband's new—new appointment—there would be so much to do and arrange, and Nadine—"

She stopped and put one hand to her throat.

McEvor glanced at the bald young sergeant with the notebook. "Get this Nadine's address in Washington—" he turned to Lettie. "I suppose she has an address there."

"She did have during my husband's term in the Senate, but last fall she came to New York in order to continue to work for him. She couldn't find an apartment she liked so she's been staying with a friend, Adrienne Nichols. On Sutton Place—"

"Phone number?" McEvor said shortly, and nodded to the bald young man who scribbled the number that Lettie gave them.

"Try her there," said McEvor. The young man walked over to the phone and started dialing. Lettie said, "But she must be in Washington by now."

"All right. Now then. The guests had gone. But your husband still hadn't come from his study. Is that right?"

"Yes. He told me he'd come in later, but first he had some telephoning to do."

"But he didn't leave his study."

"No. That is, I didn't see him if he came in to the party. I'm sure I would have known it."

"I understand you went out just as the party was breaking up."

"Yes, I did. I met Chan—I mean Hill and Miss Smith—" She nodded at Mady without looking at her. "They were arriving just as I returned."

"Where did you go?"

"To get some things for my husband to eat tonight. He never liked party leftovers. Besides," she added flatly. "There wasn't much left. I could see that."

"Where did you go?"

"A little delicatessen off Seventy-second Street."

"You met your brother-in-law and Miss—" he seemed to reach back in his memory. "—Miss Smith as you returned."

"We met at the door. My brother-in-law must have told you."

McEvor transferred his attention to Mady. "That right, Miss Smith?"

"Yes."

"How'd you get here, Miss Smith?" That was the other detective, Lieutenant Swain.

"We came by taxi. The traffic delayed us. We didn't mean to be so late."

"Where did you two meet?"

Chan, of course, had probably told them; not that it mattered. "At Twenty-one. We had a drink. Talked awhile. Then got a taxi. And the traffic—"

"Yes, we know." This was McEvor again. The young man at the telephone put it down. "She's not there. Miss Nichols said she'd gone to Washington today."

"Ah," Swain said morosely, as if it indicated guilt on Nadine's part.

McEvor turned to Lettie again. "Now, Mrs. Channing. If you'll give me as many names as you can—your guests, I mean—and also, do you have any idea where this Nadine was going to stay in Washington?"

"At the Mayflower, I think. But really—oh, yes, she'll help."

The bald young man suddenly slid to a table near Mady and plucked out a thick Washington telephone book. "I'll find it. Mayflower you said, Mrs. Channing?"

Lettie nodded. "But I don't see how—oh, yes, she may

remember most of the guests. But I think I can be fairly accurate—''

Chan came abruptly into the room, brushed past McEvor and Swain and then turned to close the door. He stood against it. "Sorry, Lettie."

Lettie sprang up. "They're taking him away—"

"Yes, Lettie. Have to. The medical examiner—"

"Oh, Chan!" She went to him and put her head against his shoulder, hiding her face. "Oh, Chan—"

"There, there, Lettie—"

McEvor cleared his throat. Swain coughed. The bald young sergeant scribbled something in his notebook and returned the telephone directory to its shelf.

There was again the sound of men's feet tramping along the corridor, but this time it was a heavier, more measured, tramp and Mady sickly knew why.

She had known Stuart, as she had known Larry Todd and Chan, it seemed to her now, almost all her life. The difference in their ages had never seemed important, although after Stu had entered politics and (unexpectedly, even to himself, she thought), had succeeded in his first race and become a senator, she had found herself a little in awe of him. During his second term he and Lettie had been married and as one of Lettie's friends she had seen, or at least heard, much of him. She tried to think of the former senator as he had been when a rather serious young man, over twenty years older than she, but always agreeable, always pleasant, always thoughtful—and always adamant about truth, as his father must have been.

No, she had never felt really close to him as she did to Chan, but she did feel an enormous sense of tragedy and loss as she heard the heavy, careful footsteps. Chan had revered his older brother, although he hadn't always agreed with him. They were both men of strong wills and serious determinations. Naturally, sometimes their opinions clashed. But in fact, since there was a ten-year difference in their ages, Stu had rather taken the place of a father after the old, but still handsome, Professor Channing died.

Chan was stony white, so that his black hair and eyebrows seemed very marked and his firm chin and mouth were set, even as he patted Lettie's arm.

The heavy tramp went on; now the men were in the living room with its heaps of wilting roses and emptied glasses and full ashtrays and general air of raffishness, then the dining room, toward the wide back elevator.

Then Senator Channing had gone for the last time from that luxurious, beautiful apartment.

"Now, Lettie—" Chan said. "We'll get Nadine to stay with you—"

Lettie held Chan closer and began to cry at last.

He looked over her shoulder at Mady. "Try to find Nadine—"

The bald young man was dialing earnestly and then speaking into the telephone. "Nadine Hallowell. That's right. Arrived this afternoon—I think—" he shot an inquiring glance toward Lettie, who did not see it since her face was against Chan's shoulder.

"But you can't stay alone—" Chan began when a commotion arose somewhere in the living room—no, it was in the front entrance hall. Then Mady heard a high-pitched, pleasant and very familiar voice: "Take it easy, I told you. No, it's not heavy. It's hollow. Yes, I know but—now this way—don't hit the doorway with it—careful now—"

"Clarence!" she cried. And actually, just for an instant, her life seemed to jolt back into a normal sway. "Clarence! What on earth—" she started toward the door into the living room when Clarence appeared, smiling.

"Looks as if you had an orgy here—glasses—everything—" He then saw the detectives and by some instinctive reasoning guessed what they were. His high voice rose higher. "My God, it must have been some orgy if the police took over. What on earth happened? That is, you are policemen, aren't you?—New York's finest—'' He said very politely to the detectives. As no one answered for a second, he went on cheerfully. ''But what happened?''

The uniformed doorman appeared; at least his black-clad back appeared. He seemed to be tugging at something unwieldy. Clarence heard him and whirled around as neatly as a dancer. ''Ah, there you are. We'll just set it up here. Now, upsy-daisy. Hah—'' said Clarence, dusting his gloved hands. ''Isn't it a beauty!''

Chan gave a muffled groan. Mady would have groaned too if she had the strength. The detectives just stared.

''Beautiful,'' said Clarence. ''And it was so stormy today there weren't many people there so I got it dirt cheap. Beautiful.'' He handed a bill to the doorman: a blue-clad policeman looked over his shoulder.

Mady got her breath. ''*Oh, Clarence!*''

It was a huge, wooden Indian, a cigar-store Indian; the paint was worn and chipped here and there, but the blank-faced Indian stared into some remote space. Both doorman and policeman disappeared.

''Clarence!'' Mady cried again. ''How could you? Take it right back.''

''Can't take it back. Had to pay for it then and there. You know these auctions. No return but—such a beauty—'' He fell into an admiring pose; he was a dapper little man with a tiny mustache, pomaded black, black eyebrows and neatly brushed, curly white hair. He got out a pair of spectacles, put them on his straight nose and waved his hands in their lemon-colored gloves. The gloves were a residue of his youth, Mady knew. He ordered them from London by the dozen; some were still in their tissue-paper wrappers in the chest of drawers in the big and handsome corner bedroom, which he had never thought of giving up after her mother's death.

''Don't you agree?'' His bright black eyes swiftly traveled from face to face until Chan said, ''Really, sir—really—''

''Oh, I'm only going to leave it here until I can induce

someone to deliver it home. I knew you wouldn't mind, Lettie dear. You see I couldn't induce a taxi driver to take me and Heap Big Chief here home. He said it was too far and too snowy, and I thought of you within a block or two, so he yielded and brought us here. You don't mind do you, Lettie? I'll take him home as soon as I can."

"Well, anyway he has an alibi," Mady began, without thinking of her own words which came out of the blue. She choked off with a gasp and felt her face grow hot as she met Chan's eyes, which actually had a faraway understanding. It vanished swiftly and he said, "You'll have to go, Clarence. Take that thing with you—"

"He comes to pieces," Clarence continued proudly. "See. Head screws off—" As if mesmerized, all of them watched as Clarence neatly turned the Indian's head, taking it off, holding it for them to see and, triumphantly, clicking it back on again. This time he adjusted the head so the Indian stared blankly at the portrait of old Dr. Channing. "Hollow," said Clarence pleasantly. "All of it comes to pieces, I believe. Interesting—"

Chan's eyes were again a frozen dark gray. "Sometime I may take you to pieces, Clarence. I've often wanted to—"

"Why, Chan! How can you speak like that to me! Why, I knew you two boys and your father—"

Captain McEvor became vocal. "Just a minute, Mr.—"

"Fotheringay," said Clarence blithely. "My stepdaughter insists on keeping her father's name, Smith. So commonplace, now Fotheringay—"

McEvor seemed to swallow rather hard. The bald young man clicked down the telephone and said, "She's not there. Hasn't turned up at all—"

Clarence said, "See here, what *is* going on here? You all look so—"

Lettie tried to cling to Chan, but he disengaged himself and went over to Clarence, taking him by the arm. "Something very serious, Clarence. Now you must take Mady home. That's all right, isn't it?" he asked McEvor.

Lieutenant Swain said, "We have their address—"

McEvor said shortly, "Yes, all right. You can go—"

"But of course I can go. Why not?" Clarence bristled. "I haven't done anything wrong. Just lugging that lovely Indian—"

Chan said, "Now get this in your head, Clarence. The senator was—was shot—"

This did rock Clarence. One lemon-gloved hand went up to his mustache. "*Stuart! You said shot?*"

"Yes. So now—" Chan took Mady's hand and pushed her toward Clarence. "Please, Mady—"

"A woman!" Clarence cried. "A woman! Oh, dear me. Sorry, Lettie—"

"Clarence," said Chan in a voice that permitted no reply as he went back to Lettie. "Just go. Leave your damn wooden junk here, but go. Wrap up, Mady. The doorman will get you a taxi—"

"He didn't shoot himself?" Clarence asked.

"No," said McEvor and added, "Anything you can tell me—"

"Oh, I don't know anything about anybody being shot," Clarence waved both gloved hands. "But I'll bet you *that*—" he waved at the blank-faced Indian. "It's a prize, if only you had the artistic sense to know it—"

McEvor appeared to stifle a slight moan. Swain said savagely, "Get him out of here."

"I'd bet you that Indian it was a woman," Clarence went on. "It was the woman I saw him lunching with today. At the Four Seasons. I don't know who it was but my advice is: *cherchez la femme*, my friends."

Lettie suddenly doubled up in Chan's arms; he lifted her to the sofa. "Brandy, I guess," he said to Mady.

McEvor gave her a swift glance. "It's all right. Go and get the brandy. Or something. Looks as if the liquor supply in this place is pretty adequate."

Mady went past the wooden Indian, wondering in the

back of her mind how she could persuade her stepfather to relinquish this latest acquisition.

But then, she thought, who was the woman the senator was lunching with today? She knew that if Clarence had recognized her he would have no qualms about telling them her name.

The litter in the brilliantly lighted living room, in the glass- and plate-strewn dining room with its chairs all pushed out of their usual stately places, was all of it an ugly contrast to what had really happened. She found a decanter that smelled as if it held brandy. She went into the pantry and took a glass from one of the long chromium-and-glass cabinets along the wall. Her fingers were shaking. She noted that impersonally and held on to the glass.

When she went back into the library, Clarence was sitting with his curly white hair in his hands, still in their lemon-colored gloves. McEvor and Swain were talking to the bald young man at the telephone.

Chan sat on the sofa beside Lettie, who had put her head on his shoulder and was sobbing softly. "You'll stay with me tonight, Chan, won't you? Please. I can't stay here alone."

Three

"But—" Chan said and saw Mady. "Oh, thank you, Mady. Here, Lettie, drink this."

Lettie took the glass. "But that's for wine—"

"Drink it!" Chan pushed her firmly back against the

sofa and rose. "As soon as we find Nadine she'll come and stay with you, Lettie."

Lettie lifted lovely brown eyes toward him. "But Chan—oh, not Nadine! I want you to stay here with me. I tell you I can't stay alone."

"But Lettie—" Chan began.

"There's that little guest room," Lettie said and drank.

Clarence was mumbling behind his hands in a kind of repetitious way as if he had been asked questions and was repeating his answers over and over again stubbornly. "—couldn't see her. One of those tables near the windows. Could see the senator all right. He didn't see me, but I could see him. Couldn't see her. Back turned to me. A woman—some kind of big furry hat—but—" he took his hands down and said brightly, "Good-looking legs! I could see that! Below the table and her chair and—very good looking legs—"

McEvor seemed to hear him and turned. "All right, Mr.—you and your daughter—I mean, your stepdaughter, Miss Smith, can go."

Mady felt that he rather approved of her name Smith. She wondered how he would feel if—or when—he learned her christened name; it wasn't as fancy as Fotheringay but it wasn't Mady; it was Maddox, her mother's family name. Naturally, she had been known all her life as Mady; who is going to call a little girl Maddox? Oh, stop it, she told herself, get Clarence out of here. And yourself—but what about Chan and Lettie?

"Look here," she said to Chan. "You and Lettie have got to eat. It must be very late. I'll fix something—"

"Never mind," Lettie said. "But thank you just the same. Now if you can—" she lifted her eyebrows, indicating Clarence, "take him home. You can leave that—that *thing* there—"

Clarence heard that and jumped up indignantly. "My Indian! *Thing?*"

"All right," Chan said. "I'll phone to you later, Mady.

Now if the police don't need to talk to you any further—"
He looked at McEvor and Swain.

McEvor nodded. "We know where to find Miss Smith."

Chan took Clarence's arm. "Come on—"

Clarence looked up, startled, and sprang to his feet.
"What? Oh! Yes, yes of course. Home! Certainly. Home—"
He darted toward the door, paused, seemed to remember
his manners and bowed politely to the room at large.

Chan took Mady's arm as he led her through the living
room into the entrance hall. In the cloakroom that adjoined
it he found Mady's coat and took it out, shoving her arms
into the sleeves. "Haven't you got any boots or—here, try
these—"

"These" were long, beautiful lizard-skin boots, too
small for Mady. "They belong to Lettie. I can't—"

"Oh! Have the doorman get a taxi. No, I'll ring down.
But now mind me, wait until it arrives. When you get
home change your slippers and oh, dear God—what a
thing this is!"

"Chan, I'm sorry about your brother."

His face hardened. "Yes. He'd hate the—the way he
went. All right, now, Clarence—"

"Oh, I'm fine, my boy. I'm fine. I'll see to Mady.
Don't let them do anything to my Indian—"

Chan's thumb had pressed the elevator button. As the
cage reached their floor, the door opened. Chan leaned
over suddenly and put his hand on Mady's face. "Don't
worry. I'll phone—"

The door moved noiselessly and closed off the view of
Chan's white face and the elegance of the hall's gold-and-
gray striped wallpaper.

"Dear me—" Clarence began, and she must have given
him a silencing look, for he said no more, not even while
they waited in the plant-bedecked foyer with all its mirrors
until a taxi had drawn up at the curb. There were two men
in the foyer, both of whom watched them—one was
certainly a policeman, with an interested but noncommuni-

cative face, the other, the doorman who was obviously bursting with curiosity, and shot excited glances from them to the policeman, but hadn't the courage to ask questions.

Clarence said, "Here's the taxi. Come on now, Mady. If you run fast enough your feet won't get wet."

Snow again, swirling in her face, making little needle pricks of chill. Then the taxi throbbed along. Streetlights were haloed in flying white. Snowplows thudded. Cars were stalled along the street or merely parked and gathering snow. When they turned east, the snowplows were fewer and the street barely traveled.

I don't believe any of it, Mady thought, but of course she had to believe it.

Dear Chan! He had loved Stuart and been very proud of him. She thought that the senator had been proud of Chan, too. She had heard him introduce him as Dr. Hill Channing, and then with a pretense of being jovial (in order to cover his pride) "but not the kind of doctor you're thinking of. He's young but he's a full professor. Fine teacher. Field is nuclear energy." Lately the senator would add, "He says he teaches nuclear fission but works on fusion."

Usually a rather baffled look greeted this explanation.

As they neared home, Mady caught a glimpse of the old Channing house through the curtain of snow. It had been sold long ago, even before Professor Channing had died; even before her mother's marriage to Clarence. Often when she was a child and Chan was in his teens, she and Chan and Larry Todd had been among the children gathering there for birthday parties and Halloween parties and Christmas Eve singing, anything that provided an excuse for youthful festivities. But then all at once the Channings were gone. All of the children were grown up. The senator had turned to politics with unexpected success. Chan had stayed on at Ballantry College, teaching as his father had taught for so many years at Columbia.

She could see them all, as if in a swift little dance— Chan, older than she but always the one she could at least pretend was her very special friend, Larry even then practicing his later career—not as the lawyer which he became, but as a charming and flattering, she thought rather tartly, guest. Stuart, the senator, always seemed to look upon their galas as very, very youthful—but then she had brought Lettie home with her from school. Lettie was a few years older than Mady, but she was always rather childish-looking with her mop of short curls and her delicate beauty. The senator married her almost at once.

And now—Mady was cold, thinking of Lettie, thinking of the senator. But then it was actually cold, even in the heated taxi. She huddled her coat more closely around her. The taxi came to a stop before her own home.

The house was warm. Clarence didn't have money for the taxi. "Spent my last five dollars on the doorman," he said, but not apologetically.

Somehow Mady had her handbag over her arm. Of course, Chan had placed it there; she hadn't noticed. She paid the driver and Clarence bounded up the steps to the door, turned his key in the lock and flung the door wide. "Hurry up, Mady. Can't cool off the whole house. I only hope Mrs. Whatever-her-name-is has left us something to eat. Your mother," said Clarence, holding the door as Mady came in, "your mother had three servants. Living in. Chauffeur and laundress lived out but—"

"But times are different," Mady said wearily. "We are lucky to have Mrs. Baynes. So don't fuss now, Clarence. She'll have left something in the oven."

"What I intend to have now is a drink. All that liquor at Lettie's and nobody so much as offered me a sip of it."

"Get it yourself," Mady said, but Clarence had already slid out of his overcoat and gloves and was prancing toward the liquor cabinet in the first-floor library. Mady dropped her coat and handbag on one of Clarence's least obnoxious acquisitions, which was a Florentine bench (so he said) too big for the tiny entrance hall but not unattractive and certainly useful as a depository.

The house and the former Channing house were of the tall, rather narrow houses which abound in the East Sixties. An area-way, with a door to the kitchen, pantry and dining room, lay below the front steps. Other steps led up past living room and library to bedrooms. Mady's father had bought it; Mady's mother had loved it and continued to live in it during her short widowhood and marriage to Clarence. It had been her Yankee sense of order and her matter-of-fact pride which kept the place in the neatest, trimmest condition throughout. She had willed it to Mady, but with a catch which was a life tenancy for Clarence.

This had not really presented a problem. Clarence had been a loving husband to Mady's mother; never impatient, always gentle in his manner and, Mady had thought, genuinely attached to her mother. It had not been, really, a marriage for money on Clarence's part; it wasn't his fault that Mady's father and his father before him had been remarkably rich; even after inheritance taxes there was plenty of the Amyas Smith money.

Mady's mother had also had Yankee prudence about money; she had made a sensible disposition of the estate her first husband had left her; she had even had her own inherited money to care for, so she was not unschooled as to investments. The result was that Mady—along with the Trust Department of the bank—did indeed, as Chan had said, hold the purse strings. Clarence had a generous allowance and he was grateful for that in a most sincere and touched way when he heard the will. But if money could ever be said truly to go through people's fingers, then Clarence's finely boned and finely manicured fingers had that talent. It didn't matter—much—that he was almost always out of money, as he was a most comfortable, most agreeable housemate. And her mother had contrived to induce in Mady the feeling that Clarence was her charge.

Clarence, just the same, was one of the lilies of the field. Mady often thought, yet not bitterly, that no one expected Clarence to do anything. Sometime or other he had worked in a bank and then in the brokerage firm where Mady's mother had met him. Since his marriage he had been simply, happily content to be Clarence.

Nobody could possibly dislike Clarence; he was never out of sorts, never petulant and also—sometimes regrettably—never without interests in life. He had started harmlessly enough by attending art exhibits; this led, somehow (Clarence being essentially a gregarious and pleasant person), to private viewings and then to auctions where the bidding aroused a dormant instinct of competition beneath Clarence's neat tattersall waistcoats. Mady had been obliged to permit him to hang his first few cautious purchases on any wall of the house where he might feel that, say, a slash of crimson, dotted with yellow and two squares of white (in the dining room at the moment) would be nice to look at. He tired of this, however, and naturally enough drifted to art galleries. The house grew rather crowded with charming music boxes, oddments of sculpture, two or three lovely clocks that wouldn't work and too many bizarre *objets d'art*. It was harmless, but it was expensive even though he spent his own allowance cheerfully. However, he had never before brought home a cigar-store Indian.

If she hadn't been so strangely tired, as if drained of all spirit, she would certainly have made a stand against cigar-store Indians. As it was, she followed Clarence, who had already poured a whiskey and soda for each of them, left a glass for her and departed kitchenward.

He reappeared, his coat off and a frilly pink apron tied around him; he carried a casserole of sorts in both hands. How could she feel irritated and impatient with anybody done up in a frilly apron and taking a happy turn at household chores? The answer was she couldn't. Chan had said it—"You rather like Clarence." Well, why not? Everybody wasn't serious all the time or, as she had always thought about Stuart, ambitious.

She didn't want to think of the senator and couldn't

think of anything else. Clarence deposited his load on the Queen Anne breakfast table in the library which they both preferred to the big, sometimes chilly, dining room downstairs.

"Still hot," he said, having dropped the casserole rather suddenly, sucking at a finger. "Not really burned," he added, inspecting the finger. "I think there's a salad of sorts down there and even a dessert—"

"All right. I'll get them."

The kitchen was shining, clean and warm; the salad was in the refrigerator, properly crisp. There was a baked dessert, a chocolate mousse. Really, Mrs. Bayne was a jewel.

It suddenly occurred to her that she had never wondered just how Clarence would get along if the senator did give her a job in Washington. Anyway, Clarence always got along.

She glanced around at the kitchen, thought rather guiltily of the utter shambles in Lettie's apartment—and thought of what had happened there.

She went back to the library and the table where Clarence had put the casserole. Mrs. Bayne had set the table nicely; good china, good linen, old-fashioned, heavy silver. Mrs. Bayne kept the silver polished. A friend of hers, a cleaning lady, as Mrs. Bayne called her, came to the house twice a week.

It wasn't the way it had been in her mother's time, but what was? They got along very well indeed in what many people would call luxury. Lettie, of course, did not put up with this kind of housekeeping, but then Lettie had so much money now and so enjoyed spending it.

Lettie had had no real home; her father and mother had separated, money had been provided for her education but not much more; Lettie's mother had gone to live in Italy and later her father had died. Lettie had happily come home with Mady for vacations. She had no money and no job to look forward to. She was always beautiful. After marrying Stuart, Lettie had gone happily with him to Washington and for two years they had lived on a senator's salary. But then a faraway uncle of Lettie's had died in Australia and had left all his money to Lettie.

Nobody could blame Lettie, who had been next door to poverty-stricken in her youth, for spending money lavishly now.

Although perhaps, Mady thought, that was why Stuart had decided to leave politics and join one of the big law firms. Lettie had so much money that he might have felt himself in an inferior position. That was only surmise, and now nobody would ever know. She had picked up the glass beside her plate. She set it down with a thump, and Clarence looked up from his steady consumption of chicken casserole. "Don't think about it," he said kindly.

"How can I help it! Clarence, you knew the senator. He couldn't have killed himself—"

"No." Clarence dug up a forkful of chicken.

"But—murder!"

"Of course," Clarence said largely. "I expect the police are obliged to question any fatal—accident or anything of the kind. They'll have a hard time going through Lettie's guest list." His neatly pomaded mustache quivered in a half smile. "She does pick up odd people sometimes."

"Clarence, it *was* murder—"

"Yes, certainly."

"Well, I mean—who—"

"Who didn't like him?" Clarence shrugged. "I told the police. Some woman probably. My guess is the one he was lunching with today. They seemed to be having a—call it a serious conversation. He looked upset."

Mady took up her fork and put it down again. "*How?*"

"How? Dear me, Mady! How does anybody look upset. Not exactly mad at anybody but—upset," said Clarence firmly.

She thought for a moment. "Didn't you see them leave?"

"No. Left first myself. Had to get to this auction. I think that Indian might go in this room." Clarence glanced around at the scenic wallpaper. "Yes—a good place—hills, old churches and old bridges and—and rivers and valleys!" Clarence ran out of words and discovered another with an air of triumph, "And trees! All quite suitable. I thought of it when I bid for him. Seemed just the right thing for this room."

It deflected Mady. "I'm not going to have that—that thing staring blankly at me every time I take a bite!"

"You'll love it," said Clarence happily. "Now don't get that Amyas Smith look about your chin—eyes, too. Really, Mady, you are so lovely when you just let your dear mother's look take over. Mischievous she could be, lovely blond hair, you've got that. Sparkling blue eyes—dark—you've got those, too. She could—I can't describe it, but just something about her was like a honey rose attracting bees. I mean, men. That is, she was always a lady. But there was just something about her that—" He sighed. "She was so dear, even that straight, little nose and her mouth curled up—not as you are looking just now," he said sternly. "Amyas Smith kept his mouth shut tight for fear he'd lose some money, I suppose, although how—but never mind that. Now, Mady." All at once he was coaxing. "Please just look natural. You can be almost as beautiful as your mother—" He looked up at the portrait of Mady's mother above the mantel. He looked a long time and sighed with, Mady was sure, genuine sadness. "She was beautiful. So are you—except when all at once you can turn into old Amyas. Granite! Don't!"

"Really, Clarence—"

"I'll give you some salad."

"You've already given me a scolding—"

"Didn't mean to. Only meant to point out some facts." He started to serve the salad. He was still wearing the frilly pink apron, plus his tattersall waistcoat and a silvery, striped tie at his snowy collar. Gold links held the equally snowy cuffs. Somehow Clarence never seemed so much as touched by New York smog.

Her mother had been happy with him, probably happier than in her first marriage. Mady got herself back on the track: "You keep talking about some woman. I don't think Stu ever looked at anybody but Lettie."

"Oh, don't you!" Clarence said darkly. "More chicken?"

"Now, listen to me. You can't just—just hint like that."

"Can't I? Come on, Mady, use your head." He added severely, "You've had enough to drink today. There at the party—"

"You know we got there late. Everybody had gone."

"Never mind what I know. Eat your dinner."

"Listen," Mady began desperately. "You know Stuart—"

"Knew," Clarence shook his elegant white head.

"All right. And Chan and their father—"

"In a way," Clarence said cautiously. "Met their father at the club sometimes. Nice old duffer." Clarence was in his late sixties. "Played chess with him a time or two. He cheated. That is—it's very hard to cheat at chess," he added almost regretfully, yet she was perfectly sure that Clarence himself would never think of cheating at chess or cards or anything. "But he was all right. Had no money to speak of. Just his income from teaching. Couldn't leave much to the boys. Life insurance, I heard, at the time he popped off. However," his tone became charitable, "he did his best. Teachers weren't paid much then. Both his boys, Stu and your Hill—"

"*My* Hill!"

"Why, of course. Oh, don't try to keep it a secret from me. Hill is why you thought of going to Washington with Stu when he took over this Cabinet post. You wanted to be nearer Hill—well, dear me, a fine thing, young love."

"*Clarence—*"

"Your Hill isn't making much money either. Too bad he decided to teach like his father. But then I expect with your money it doesn't really matter. Dessert?"

"Yes!" said Mady violently.

"Needn't explode." Clarence slid nimbly out of his chair.

"Take the casserole with you. Put it in the fridge."

"Why, certainly." Always good natured, always pleasant!

He was in the kitchen when the doorbell rang loudly, shrilling through the silence of the house. Clarence, magically, reached the door ahead of Mady, and Chan came in along with a burst of cold wind and snow. A taxi stood at the curb, its lights shining through the flying sheets of white.

"Take your coat, dear boy." Clarence reached for it.

"I can't stay. You all right, Mady?"

"Of course she's all right." Clarence had got Chan's coat and was gently shaking off snow. "Come in, my boy. There's still some food. Not precisely hot, but warm."

"No. Mady—it was my gun." He shook snow off his black hair.

Four

Clarence hung up the coat. Mady clutched her napkin so hard that her fingernails dug into her palm. "Your gun! You mean—"

"That's the one. Inside Stu's room. The door locked. But I had a key and opened the door."

Clarence was seriously concerned. "My dear boy, you aren't trying to tell us that the police suspect you—*you!* —of shooting Stuart."

Chan said shortly, "I think they have to suspect everybody. It wasn't suicide. Or an accident."

"But see here, it seems to me it could have been either—"

Chan shook his head. "No. Not shot in the back."

Clarence shook his head, thoughtfully. "Yes—yes, that seems to be proof. After all nobody can walk right up to a man and shoot him. He stops you."

"Not always," Chan said. "This way—"

Clarence broke in, agreeing. "Yes. Looks as if somebody he knew got into the room and got the gun and— Chan, I *am* sorry. Stu wasn't afraid, or taken by surprise, or—a number of explanations. But I can't believe in so serious a quarrel with anybody. Stu wasn't the kind to engage in a quarrel that might bring—that perhaps did bring on his own murder. I mean—"

"I know what you mean!"

"Yes. The senator always kept his head. He had this fine Cabinet appointment right in his lap. No." Clarence shook his white curls. "But if it was murder as everything seems to indicate, believe me, I'm right. A woman."

"See here, Clarence. Who was that woman with him at lunch?"

"I tell you I couldn't see her face."

"But that's not the only way to recognize anyone. There are a hundred ways."

"Maybe," Clarence said doubtfully and considered it. "Yes. You may be right. I'd know you or Mady or almost anybody from—oh, the way you walk or—dozens of ways. But I did not know the woman he lunched with. At the Four Seasons," said Clarence, pinning it down as if it might add authority.

Mady was clinging to the newel post. "Chan, you did have the key. The senator gave it to you, oh, ages ago when Lettie bought that apartment. But how did your gun get there?"

"I lent it to him. I didn't need it. Belonged to our father. Stu was a kind of target in a way. A senator. Lettie, so rich. I said to him once, you ought to have a gun. And he said—'' Chan swallowed hard, "He said he didn't need one. Like a fool, I insisted. If I hadn't—''

"Stop that!" Clarence was intelligent enough when he chose to be. "Come in here now. A drink—something to eat—''

Chan permitted himself to be drawn into the library; Clarence bustled down to the kitchen, pink apron flying and came back with a plate full of chicken casserole. "Better than nothing." He put it down in front of Chan. "Now eat. You've had a drink and you've had a—well, really a terrible shock and—''

Mady said stiffly, "Have they asked you about when and—'' she swallowed hard, "and where we met?''

"Oh, no. That will come. I don't have an alibi if that is what you mean.''

"You were with me. At Twenty-one—''

"That was later. I got to Twenty-one about five-thirty. You came in a little after six. I remember looking at my watch and thinking you were caught in traffic. But as to an alibi, no. I went through Penn Station, how would anybody remember me there? It hadn't started to snow heavily so I walked up to Scribner's bookstore on Fifth Avenue. Then I just—oh, I just wandered around looking at this and that. Suddenly I realized I'd better get over to Twenty-one, and it was about then that the snow began to really come down. I walked. Couldn't get a taxi. But you see it leaves quite a gap. I *could* have gotten into Lettie's apartment. I *could* have shot Stu—oh, for God's sake, me shoot Stu?''

"Eat some more," said Clarence practically.

Mady said slowly, "But the police haven't firmly decided about—about anything.''

"I don't know what they have decided. They turned the place upside down. The preliminary opinion is that probably Stu was shot about five or so, maybe later. The trouble was the room was so hot.''

"I remember," Mady said.

"Each room in the apartment has its own thermostat. Stu liked a cool room. He wouldn't have turned the thermostat up so high. So it's possible that somebody else turned it up. The police seemed to think that the idea was to conceal the time of his death. They can tell something from the condition of the—the body," said Chan, looking sick.

Clarence shook himself as if to induce some order in his thoughts. "But how about fingerprints?"

"Oh, yes, they went all over the place for fingerprints. Most of those in my brother's study were his own, so the police said. Mine, too, naturally. I leaned on the desk for a moment. Lettie's—even some they think are probably Mady's on the door. And my own on the gun but a little smeared."

"As if somebody else had handled it?" Clarence said positively.

"Yes, I think so. Yes."

Mady said slowly, "The door to the senator's study was locked on the inside."

"That's where we found the key. On the floor. Somebody asked me if I could have pushed it out of the keyhole when I put my own key in. Of course, I could have. I don't think I did. I think I'd have noticed it. My own key would have stuck or—oh, I don't know! They asked about the noise the shot had made. Remember, Mady, just as we arrived, Lettie opened some champagne and we heard the pop. It was like a shot—"

"It couldn't have been *that* shot. We saw the champagne." Mady had had a fleeting glimpse of the senator's study, recollection of which now returned. "I remember thinking—I was surprised that Stu's study didn't look like the rest of the place."

"Not at all. Nothing but a writing table, two chairs, filing cabinets, dictating machine. Telephone. Extra bed. Paper shredder. They were dusting everywhere with what looked like a kind of powder puff on a stick. I told you—taking fingerprints and photographs and the whole apartment in an uproar. It looked like a Babylonian orgy."

"What I said when I arrived." Clarence preened himself slightly but then frowned. "But not Babylonian. They had benches, long marble—" His interest in antiques was coming out and nothing would stop it, but Chan interrupted him brusquely.

"Lettie went to bed. The Lorsome doctor came back and made her take a sedative, and now I've got to go back. I told the taxi to wait—"

Clarence slid out of his chair and skipped to the entrance hall. "I'll tell him to wait longer—"

Mady said, "I can't believe it but—Chan, I am so sorry. Whatever it was, I am so sorry."

He put one hand over her own. "I know, Mady. I wish it hadn't been with my gun. I'll always feel guilty about that—"

"You can't. You felt that he needed a gun."

"But I insisted. The fact always is that if there is no gun available there's not much chance of any shooting."

"Chan, if you *had* gone to Lettie's apartment sooner than the time we went there together, somebody would have seen you."

"Probably. The police are questioning everybody. Doorman—two of them really, they change at six o'clock. Elevators are self-service. Back elevators the same. The police have to do a thorough job of it. They are working through the list of guests Lettie could give them when I left. Also busy in Stu's study looking for papers—anything."

"Can't you stay here tonight? You don't have to go back there."

"Thank you, Mady. No."

"But—but the doctor surely can get a nurse for Lettie. Or if not the police can send a policewoman to stay with her?"

"With Lettie?" Chan said simply.

Mady knew defeat; Lettie was a woman who got her

way, gently, quietly, and with almost childlike assurance. "I know. But you—"

"Oh, I expect they want me to stay around anyway—"

Clarence appeared in the doorway; he was wiping his neat hands on the pink apron. "Chan," he said in a shaken voice. "There is a police car out there. They paid the driver and sent the taxi away. Said you could repay them. But they want you back at the apartment."

Chan's face was again white and stony. "All right. Tell them to come in."

Clarence, waving the apron absurdly, disappeared. Chan rose and took Mady's chin in his hand. "Don't worry. I ought not to have told you all this. But I—I had to talk to you."

She nestled her cheek against his hand. "Yes, I know—"

It was the nearest he had ever come to a recognition of a stronger tie between them than merely old friendship. But he had never before said, in so many words, that he needed her.

Without quite intending to, indeed without conscious reasoning, she turned her face upward to meet his face and then, unbelievably, his lips.

It was a kiss, a real kiss, she thought, a kiss . . . Clarence spoke from the doorway, "Sorry. I mean—well, sorry. But they do want you to come with them, Chan. And they say Mady, too. They wouldn't explain why."

Clarence bundled her into her coat. He held Chan's coat when Chan got entangled trying to get the left arm into the right sleeve. "I think I'll just come, too," said Clarence then and by some kind of conjuring act was into his own coat, grasping a fine cashmere scarf and opening the door before either Mady or Chan had moved. Chan looked at her, she thought, very seriously, but with a question in his eyes.

"It's me," she said softly.

"Oh, of course it's you," Chan said shortly, but rather huskily. "Naturally it's you."

Clarence held the door open, and cold and snow swirled in. "Come on, come on. You can do all the carrying-on you want to when the time comes, but now," said Clarence severely, "is not the time."

Somehow Clarence had already wedged himself into the front seat beside the driver. Somehow a second policeman sat between Mady and Chan in the rear seat. Before Mady there rose a kind of heavy wire-mesh partition. The policeman beside her noted her surprise. "That's for voylence, Miss. Drunk and voylent. Or—" he considered, "just voylent."

"Oh," said Mady.

Clarence heard and turned. "You from Brooklyn?" he said chattily.

The policeman grunted proudly.

Chan said in the half-light, half-dusk of the car, "Why are you taking us back to my brother's apartment?"

"Don't have the least idea," said the driver pleasantly.

"We're only patrolmen," the man between Mady and Chan volunteered. "Somebody sent us to pick up youse two—nobody said nothin' about the gent with the white hair."

Clarence stirred at that, his neat white curls rising, but seemed to think better of trying to justify his presence.

Back again across to Park Avenue, up to a cross street above Lettie's apartment, then a few blocks down Fifth, with its one-way traffic. Windows everywhere were still alight. It couldn't be late.

A man in plain clothes waited for them, murmured something to the two patrolmen and politely but firmly guided all three of them into the foyer. He looked a little surprised to see Clarence, but was very polite when he said the elevator was waiting, they were sorry to have been obliged to ask them to return so soon but there were some things—

The elevator gave a dignified hiccup and stopped. The doors opened.

Upstairs, it developed that the homicide detectives, McEvor and Swain, were interested in the exact procedure of their opening the senator's room and would appreciate it if they would go over it again. "Just take the way you went down the corridor and let us see just how you opened the door and—"

"Just anything," said McEvor. "Shaking the door? Calling to your brother? Getting out your own key—"

"Everything," said Swain, as if he expected the worst.

The bald young man was still slumped in the sofa beside the telephone. He had sheets of paper in one hand, on which were scrawled many pencil markings, and he looked not only morose but so tired that he had to pull himself together in order even to look their way as they passed the door. The wooden Indian stared inscrutably at Old Professor Channing, and the bald young man said, "Not a single one of them remembers anything at all about the senator. None of them saw him."

"Sound of a shot?" McEvor also looked very weary.

The young man shook his head. "Some said they had heard champagne corks popping. Nobody heard any sound of a shot. At least, that's what they all say." He wiped his head with a startlingly red and yellow handkerchief, looked at it with a kind of surprise, tucked it away in a hip pocket and sighed.

"This Nadine?" Swain said, morosely. "Still can't find her."

Lettie spoke from behind Mady. "But she's only gone to dinner with somebody in Washington. You'll find her—"

If Lettie had been given a sedative it must have been a very mild one, either that or Lettie was impervious to any kind of medication. She had removed her white silk dress and had wrapped around her an ancient blue wool dressing gown; it was one that she had worn during long-ago school days and it caught at Mady's heart. In the clutch, she thought, Lettie stopped being a rich and fashionable lady and became herself, just Lettie, young and helpless. She put her arm around Lettie, who turned a tear-streaked face to her. "They can't find Nadine," she said. "They seem to think that she shot Stu. And then got away. I didn't see her here. Truly I don't think she was here. I had thanked her and asked her to do one or two errands for me in Washington, nothing important, but you know how very efficient Nadine is. But now nobody can find her and they say—oh, Mady, he was murdered! But Nadine—" She whirled around toward the two detectives, her pretty hands doubled up into fists. "I tell you Nadine would never—*never* have done this—this terrible thing."

Chan said, "Easy, Lettie," and turned to McEvor and Swain. "So it definitely was murder. Who did it?"

The two detectives exchanged a look. The young man at the telephone pulled out his gaudy handkerchief and polished his bald head again exhaustedly. Swain gave his colleague a slight nod and McEvor said, "Yes, Mr. Channing. Couldn't have been anything but murder. But who did it? I can't say yet. You must know, the lab boys went through his study. A rather peculiar thing has developed. Every single used paper has disappeared from your brother's study. There remains only blank notepaper, envelopes, stamps. Not a single piece of personal mail, not even an address book. Nothing."

"But—" Chan began.

"The paper shredder had been used. Nothing is left that can be put together."

"But," Chan began again, thought and said, "that seems natural. He was planning to go into an office at the law firm. He would certainly destroy anything that had anything to do with his terms in the senate."

Neither McEvor nor Swain looked satisfied. McEvor drew a cellophane envelope from his pocket. It contained, unbelievably, a rather large, beige suede glove. "This was found in the washroom off that cloakroom. The laboratory boys say it has been in close contact with a firearm. In short, that someone wearing this glove, fired a gun. The senator was shot in the back, as you know, at close range. The gun—your gun,'' McEvor said dryly, "was on the floor near the door. Near the key that you say you may have pushed out of the keyhole with your own key. This glove yours?'' he said suddenly to Chan.

Chan looked at it soberly. "Not mine—" he spread out his hand, which could never have been fitted by the glove in the envelope, and Clarence said, irrepressibly, "I told you it was a woman. That's a woman's glove.''

Chan walked across to the sofa and sat down. "I don't think a woman shot him. Stu—my brother—was never one to go for women. I mean naturally he liked them—he had a sort of good man's eye for a pretty woman.''

But he was in love with Lettie, Mady knew. He had been in love with Lettie from the first time he had seen her. No other woman could have felt anything but mild gratification if he showed that her face pleased him. Her thoughts flew to Nadine who was as beautiful in her own, tall, sleek and striking way as Lettie with her petite and unassuming beauty.

Lettie's lovely face would bear any inspection, but right now her eyelids were swollen and red. Mady tightened her arm around her friend, who pressed close to her as if for protection.

McEvor cleared his throat. "This glove was used by somebody who fired a gun very recently. Now you said that nobody you knew had reason to shoot your brother. You must have had some knowledge of his friends and enemies—''

Chan said slowly, "I know he had friends—many friends. I suppose he had enemies—''

"Must have had at least one," Swain said sourly.

Chan looked at him. "Yes. I realize that it happened and there must be a reason for it. But as to enemies—''

"He was in public life," McEvor said.

"Yes. He was on one or two quite important committees.''

Stu had, in fact, made himself an expert in international

trade law; it was probably the reason he had been offered the Cabinet post. It was in its way appropriate that both the Channing brothers should take a particularly strong and indeed dedicated interest in their chosen professions; old Professor Channing, looking sternly down now from the mantel, would have permitted nothing else. Mady glanced up at the portrait; he had posed for it in his doctor's gown with its hood fastened neatly below a strong chin. The portrait had been done when he was younger than she remembered him, but it had a kind of stamp of authority and wisdom—tempered, however, with kindness. She wondered for an instant just how Chan would look when he reached the age his father had been when the portrait was painted.

Chan said, "I mean, of course, while he was in the Senate—"

"Yes, yes we know all that. We even know the committees. And," said McEvor, looking disappointed, "we couldn't find anything that might be considered a motive for murder—but then—" His face slightly cleared. "It only happened today. By the way, did you know that your friend Nadine—"

"My brother's secretary," said Chan.

"Yes. Well, did you know that she had a passport?"

Chan was unperturbed. "It seems likely. She did take an occasional vacation, you know."

The young man at the telephone said dourly, "Bet she's on her way now to some place where we have no extradition treaty."

"Have you tried the airlines?" Swain asked.

"Good God," the young man said indignantly. "I've been working over all these people and listening to their yelps and—no, I have not tried the airlines and you can get somebody else to do it." He surged out from the sofa.

McEvor snapped, "Sergeant!"

"I'm thirsty," said the sergeant, yielding reluctantly to authority, and slouched off toward the dining room and kitchen. Swain started after him and McEvor said, "Oh, let him go. He takes this hard. One of the first times—now then, Mr. Channing, will you and Miss—'' He waited a second, as if searching for Mady's name.

Clarence, hovering around the edges like an inquisitive little puppy, supplied it. ''Smith. I told you. Wouldn't take my name. Said Smith was good enough for her. And I must say I admire her for it. Sticking up for her father who—well, in my opinion he was an old pirate. Rich, but a pirate—''

''Thank you, Mr. Fotheringay,'' McEvor said firmly. ''Now then, Miss Smith, will you and Mr. Channing and Mrs. Channing please go through all the actions you took when you went to call the senator. I mean, what you said if anything or—but the main things you did.''

Lettie drew closer to Mady. ''Yes,'' she said. ''Come on, Chan, Mady. First we were talking in—in the kitchen, I think. I had opened some champagne and the guests had all left. Chan said he'd call my husband and we—went down the corridor—''

She started for the long corridor. Mady and Chan fell in with her. Mady tried desperately to remember just where they had stood, what they had said. Chan said, ''I called him and he didn't answer, so I sort of shook the door. It was locked. Then Lettie—I think Lettie said, wait a minute, there's another key—''

''In the library,'' Lettie said. ''But then Chan—''

''I took out my own key ring and shoved it in the keyhole—I must have pushed out the other key—I mean my brother's key because it was on the floor just there beside the door when we noticed it. You were told all that. But I saw only—'' Chan's voice was not quite steady. He took a long breath. ''Just then I only saw my brother. He was sitting in the armchair and I ran to him and his hand was hanging over the arm of the chair and I felt for a pulse, I think—''

''Yes,'' Mady said. ''Yes, you did. I remember that.

And I started forward to you—and that's when I tripped on the gun. It was there on the floor—''

"Where?" said Swain.

"Why—why, right there." She pointed. "Just at the door. Near the key. I started to pick it up—"

"Why?" Swain asked sharply.

"I don't know. Just because it was there. But Chan stopped me. And then he told us both—Lettie and me—to get out and call the police. No, he said to call the police before I stumbled over the gun. Lettie said we should call a doctor—"

Chan took up the short and ugly tale. "I knew he was dead. I knew it should be reported. That kind of wound—in the back. I sent both women out."

Swain did not tire of his repeated question. "Why?"

Chan gave him a cold look. "Because it was no place for either of them. I wanted them to get out, that's all. And I knew we must call the police."

"Because of the nature of the wound," Swain said reflectively. "Then what happened?"

Lettie said forlornly, "Oh, we did what Chan told us to do. Mady called the police. From the phone in the library—"

"You didn't think of using that phone there on the senator's desk?" McEvor said thoughtfully.

Chan said slowly, "No. As a matter of fact, I didn't. I only wanted Lettie and Mady to get out—"

"So we did," Mady said as firmly as her somewhat shaky voice permitted, trying not to look at the chalkmarks on the dark rug around the senator's chair.

"The phone—this one, I mean—was in its cradle?" That was Swain again.

Chan frowned. "Yes, I think so. I'm sure of it. We were all three in a state of shock, you know. But I'd have noticed it, I'm sure, if the phone had been just lying somewhere, as if he'd dropped it. Yes, I'd have seen that."

"Suppose we just go over all this again," Swain said. So they went over it again; discovering nothing new in their fragmentary accounts. They were allowed to return to the library, where the bald young man was recuperating with a glass of something that he thrust behind the sofa as they entered. McEvor now had no pity on him. "You'll have to go over the entire guest list again, sergeant. We need to find the owner of this glove."

"*What!*" The young man stared. "Why didn't you tell me before—"

"Didn't know about it—" said McEvor. "Get busy. And while you're at it, ask every single one if he—she— saw either Mr. Channing here or Miss Smith at the party. Or," he added as if for good measure, "Mr. Fotheringay."

"Oh, Jesus," said the young man dejectedly, and scrabbled together the sheets of paper with names and telephone numbers scrawled upon them. He sank down beside the telephone again, looking completely miserable. "They don't like my calling them, you know," he said feebly. "And every one of them, the women, that is, gave out shrieks when I told them why—and oh, all right, I'll get busy. Gloves for God's sake," he added bitterly.

"I told you it was a woman." Clarence straightened his waistcoat proudly.

Lettie said timidly, "May we sort of clear up the dining room and—and everywhere? I mean, are the police through with things?"

Again McEvor and Swain exchanged a look. Then both nodded.

"But not you, please, Mr. Channing. I'd like to talk to you a little more," Swain began, and Clarence piped, "Not *Mr.* Channing. It's *Dr.* Channing. He teaches fission but works on fusion," he added neatly and disappeared.

Swain looked as blank as the wooden Indian, and Mady said, "Go to bed, Lettie. Clarence and I will straighten things up a bit."

She didn't know then that Clarence's straightening up would uncover an astonishing cache of Lettie's jewels.

Five

Not all her jewels; staring at Clarence's find, Mady knew that a very beautiful emerald necklace and a really stunning bracelet were not among the flashing, softly tinkling jewels that Clarence found in a brown paper bag below cans of tomato soup and packages of frozen foods.

"Very smart of Lettie," said Clarence, looking down at the heap of glittering reds and blues and greens and the brilliance of diamonds.

"Lettie?" Mady was startled.

"Why, of course. Policemen everywhere, going in and out. Can't trust them."

"Clarence!"

"Look here now, Mady. Suppose you worked like a dog—well," Clarence said dreamily. "I can't say I've ever seen a very hardworking dog. Your mother's Peke now—"

"Why can't you trust a policeman? Why should Lettie hide her jewels?"

"Now put yourself in some poor guy's place. Working long, hard hours, putting his life on the line far too many times, maybe a wife and little ones at home, and suppose you just happened to see an unguarded diamond like that one," he pointed a manicured finger at a ring on the table, which didn't actually light up the whole kitchen but seemed to. "—lying around some place. Seems to me it would be natural just to slide it into your pocket and sell it somewhere—a policeman must know of a good wall—"

Mady groped in a dazed way through Clarence's vocabulary. "You mean a fence?"

"That's what I said. Well, can't you see what a temptation it would be?"

"I can't see either Captain McEvor or Lieutenant Swain pocketing some jewelry."

Clarence shrugged. "No," he said thoughtfully, as if considering it very carefully. "No. Can't say I do either. But that's not what Lettie might think. State of shock. Terrified. Strange men all over the place. Hid her jewelry. Exactly what any woman with her wits about her would have done. Good for Lettie! You'd better take them to her now, though. So she'll know we have found them and they're safe."

"Well, I—yes, I suppose so—"

Clarence had found another apron and was wearing it; it was too large so it was wrapped like a sheet around his neat waist. He had shown indeed a most welcome celerity about cleaning up the living room and dining room. More glasses and plates had been adroitly wedged into a dishwasher than Mady would have believed possible and the appliance was by then humming away efficiently. The remaining serving dishes, a tag end of ashtrays, small plates, whatever he couldn't possibly get into the loaded dishwasher, had been rinsed and set in plate racks over one of the chromium sinks. Clarence really had extremely welcome talents. He began to unwrap his apron. "This must belong to Lettie's—oh, cleaning woman, somebody, whoever she had intended to take care of this unsightly mess." He said thoughtfully, "Wonder if Lettie will pay us for doing her work!" He hung the apron over a chair. "Now you go on and give her the jewelry and tell her to put it in a safe if there is one in the house. Can't be too careful," said Clarence darkly, "with all these strange men around."

"Why, that's the grocery bag Lettie had with her when

we met at the door! The senator's supper! She said he couldn't stand party leftovers.''

"Poor man," Clarence said. "Seems—seems—" he stared at the grocery bag. "All right," he said defiantly, as if excusing himself for sentimentality. "That is, it's not all right. It's just too—too dreadful. There was Lettie going to get supper for him, and all the time—" He paused, thought, and added, "Of course, I'm not sure that the police are very certain just when he was killed. Take these —these baubles to Lettie," he said bravely, but eyeing the jewels with admiration. "Stay with her. They're still acting as if somehow, some way, Chan got in here and shot his brother and then met you and—"

"But he had no reason to do such a thing. Nobody can say that he did."

"Anybody," said Clarence pontifically, "can say anything. Of course, proving it is a different affair."

Mady took out the various food containers and shoved the jewels into the brown bag again; easier to carry them like that, she thought briefly; nobody would see them and question her and—she could prove that Chan had been with her at 21. She wished she had looked at the time when she arrived to meet him and when they went out to the taxi and took their crawling way to Lottie's apartment.

She did not have to pass the open door of the library, but as she turned into the long corridor she could hear the mumble of the man at the telephone and the crisp yet also tired voice of—she thought—McEvor. "—anybody see you leave Twenty-one?"

"Oh, yes. The waiter. The doorman." That was Chan. She went on to Lettie's room.

It was the second door on her left, just past the tiny guest room, which had been wedged in-between Lettie's room and the library. It was a really beautiful room, simple in its elegant way and yet luxurious; pale-blue chaise longue, white chair or two, white rug (must be a problem to keep clean in New York soot, Mady thought absently), a glimpse of a marbled bathroom with gold-colored faucets, possibly a coating of real gold.

Lettie was lying face downward across the huge four-poster bed, a small, miserable figure in the shabby dressing gown. She jerked up as Mady knocked lightly and entered without waiting for a reply. She was sobbing wildly and shivering as if she had a chill. She twisted her tear-stained face around to Mady and gulped down a sob. "Oh, it's you."

"You're cold. Here—" Mady put the paper bag down on the dressing table and reached for a blue silk-covered eiderdown, which she huddled around Lettie's shaking figure. "Go ahead and cry. But you've got to get warm—"

Lettie wiped at her eyes with one hand. "What are they doing?"

"Talking to Chan. Lettie, *you* know we arrived at the same time. Surely you can tell them that Chan was not here at all this afternoon."

"Of course he wasn't. Have they found Nadine?"

"I don't know. Here—" She picked up the paper bag and gave it to Lettie. "Clarence said it was very smart and quick of you to hide all of these. Clarence," she said rather dryly, "does not trust policemen. He says neither do you."

"But I—" Lettie opened the bag and let the jewels cascade in glittering colors over the eiderdown. A key fell out with them. "Oh, there's my door key! How quick of Clarence!" She dropped it into the drawer of a bedside table.

"He's quick enough when he wants to be. By the way, he said you'd better put them in a safe."

Lettie looked up at her. "We don't have a safe! I just keep them in that drawer. I do lock it as a rule—here, it's not locked now, I think. Put them away for me, Mady."

Mady scooped up the brilliant heap of color. "Where's your diamond bracelet?"

"I don't know. That is—yes, I remember. The clasp was

broken. Stu said he'd see to it. It must have been in Stu's study.''

Mady thought hard for a moment. The police—some of them, they called them the lab boys, had gone through the study. They didn't mention a diamond bracelet. Could Clarence possibly be right in his dark suspicion of police integrity, she wondered blankly?

Lettie had no such doubt. ''Maybe Stu took it to the jewelers when he went out for lunch. It'll be there—unless—'' She reached out to clutch at Mady's hand. ''Mady! Could the—the—whoever shot him—could he have done it because of the bracelet? To steal the bracelet? To—oh, Mady! Everybody has had so many burglaries! The policemen must be told about this.''

''Yes. But do try to—'' She was going to say calm down, but it seemed wickedly callous. She thrust the eiderdown around Lettie's shaking shoulders. ''Here, try to get warm first. I'll put these away.''

''But my necklace, Mady! I was wearing a necklace and I put it down somewhere—I don't know where—''

''All right, Lettie. We'll find it. Which drawer?''

''That one. The top right. That's it.''

The drawer was deep; the key was there, together with a number of velvet jewelry boxes. Mady couldn't help putting the jewels carefully into their proper containers. Some stones, she thought, do scratch. Lettie gave another desolate sob.

''I'll look for the necklace. It must be somewhere around—in the kitchen or pantry or—oh, somewhere—'' Mady closed the drawer. ''I do hope you have them all insured.''

''Some of them. The senator insisted. While we were in Washington. This rage of thefts began. But then it costs so much to insure everything and really I'd rather take the chance of wearing them and enjoying them and not worrying about insurance. So I dropped the insurance. Do you insure everything you have?''

"Why, I—no."

"But you had so much. Your mother and—for heaven's sake, your grandmother—"

"Oh, those. They're at the bank. Clarence said there was no point in inviting a mugging."

Lettie's pretty lips twitched. "He's right, of course. Stu shot! My bracelet gone! Mady, what is going to happen next? How could anybody have done—that?"

"The police are trying to find out. But it wasn't Chan! Besides he wouldn't want a diamond bracelet!"

"He wasn't here at any time I'm sure of that. The senator went out to lunch. He came back about four. Said he had some phoning to do but he'd certainly—certainly—" Lettie repeated unevenly, "get to the party in time to see everybody."

"Didn't you wonder about it when he didn't come out? Are you perfectly sure that he *didn't* come out of his study at all?"

"Oh, yes, I'm sure. I'd have seen him. You know how people always gather around him. He was that kind. And then everybody had heard of the Cabinet appointment so they would have congratulated him and—" Lettie shook her head sadly. "No. He couldn't have been out of his study at all. I'd have known it."

Mady sat down in a white velvet-covered chair. "This makes no sense but—Lettie, could anyone have come in the back way and then sneaked through the dining room and—"

"Anyone? I don't know. I don't think so. There were the caterers. Somebody would have seen him. Have they questioned the caterers yet?"

"I don't know. I just don't know anything. I'll see what they are doing—"

"Yes. And you might look in—oh, the pantry or the coatroom or somewhere. I know I dropped that necklace, but I can't remember where. That mess out there—"

"Clarence and I cleaned up."

"Really I hated the idea of all that. Thank you."

"Clarence did most of it," Mady said honestly. "It's not quite all done, but the rest of it can keep. All right, I'll see if I can find the necklace." Also, she suddenly felt she must get back to the library and find out what was happening.

Lettie guessed that. "Come back and tell me what they are doing."

"If they'll let me."

"How can anybody keep you away?"

But they can, Mady thought; she said, as cheerfully as she could, "Try to rest, Lettie. Chan said the doctor had given you a sedative."

"Yes. But I just pretended to take it."

"I should think—"

"I have to know what is going on, don't I?"

"I guess so. All right—" She went out, closing the door as carefully as if Lettie were asleep.

She walked rather quickly past the library door this time and again heard a mumble from the sergeant at the telephone. She went on and turned into the entrance hall and the big cloakroom with its small lavatory at one end. There were not many places to search for the diamond-and-emerald necklace. She even upended an ivory-and-gilt box of face tissues and pulled up the heavy top of the toilet trap to peer down into perfectly clear water. No rewarding sparkle greeted her. In the dining room, Clarence was standing at the buffet with a glass in his hand.

"How is Lettie?" he said.

"How do you suppose? What are you doing?"

"Drinking." Clarence raised both jet-black eyebrows. "What else?"

"But just now—"

"Champagne, of course. A little flat, but no use in its going to waste." He put the empty glass down upon the table, carefully snapped off a rose from the great heart-shaped mound of red flowers, pushed it jauntily into the button hole of the coat he had resumed, shot his cuffs and said airily, "So, shall we return to our muttonheads? And when I say muttonheads—" he added with an air of giving credit where credit was due, "I don't really mean those two detectives. They strike me as very intelligent men."

"I hope they are intelligent enough not to think that Chan had anything to do with the senator's—death—"

"Murder," said Clarence. "Not a nice word, I'll grant you. But still—" When they entered the library, Clarence said pleasantly, "Would you gentlemen like say—sandwiches or a drink—or—," a light of inspiration came into his face, "coffee? Yes. I'll make you coffee—"

"Don't bother," said Swain.

McEvor emulated the young man still drearily addressing the telephone and mopped his face, but with a clean white handkerchief. He was polite, however, as he pointed to a neat heap of paper plates and cups. "Thank you. We sent out. Now then, I think you can go back home—both of you—"

"Both—" Mady then permitted herself to look at Chan, who was sitting in the sofa at the other end from the telephone, his dark aquiline face stony.

"I'm staying here," he told her.

"Not—"

"Not because the police asked me to stay. It's Lettie. I promised her."

"But can't somebody else—"

McEvor and Swain simply said nothing. The man at the telephone was talking into the instrument, "I'm sure I didn't want to bother you but—yes, I know it's nearly one o'clock but—oh, all right but it's the police—" He listened for a moment and then put down the receiver. "She hung up."

Clarence tut-tutted. "Too bad. Hard work. I told you so, Mady. The police—however, have you found Nadine?"

Chan replied. "No. They phoned five Washington hotels.

Lettie couldn't remember or never heard precisely where Nadine intended to stay, although she thought it might be the Mayflower. They keep phoning Nadine's friend's apartment here. No Nadine. While we were at your house, they asked Lettie about other friends of Nadine's. Lettie couldn't think of many, but—"

"Everybody out—" McEvor began and Swain said, "Or didn't know anything about this Nadine."

"Well," Clarence caressed his mustache. "Seems peculiar, doesn't it?"

"Does it?" said Swain after a dull silence.

"Yes, I think so. If she was the woman the senator was lunching with, she surely ought to know something of his affairs. Should know quite a bit about his affairs as a matter of fact. She's been his secretary for years—"

"Yes, Mr. Fotheringay, we realize that. Goodnight." Swain glowered.

McEvor eased his belt and straightened his shoulders. "A police car will take you home. It's waiting."

Clarence paused, then put an affectionate hand on the wooden Indian. "I'll just take this fellow with me—"

"Get out!" McEvor shouted, suddenly losing his calm.

"Oh, all right," Clarence said agreeably. "If you insist. But remember it's an old rule. *Cherchez la femme*—" However, Clarence did retire to the entrance hall and drew on his overcoat, adjusting it with care so as not to crush the red rose in his buttonhole.

Chan, though, had gone with them. McEvor said behind him. "Not yet, please, Mr. Channing. I mean—" he became rather heavily sarcastic, "I mean *Dr.* Channing."

"I'm coming back," Chan said over his shoulder. Clarence poked the elevator button and Chan held Mady's coat for her, lingering a little (she thought and hoped), as he held it closely around her.

"Now, Chan," Clarence said pleasantly. "They can't stop you. You just come right along with us."

"You heard the lieutenant. They expect me to stay here. And then Lettie—"

"Yes," Mady said, "of course. You can't leave her alone."

"Bring Lettie," Clarence said brightly. "No sense her staying here."

The elevator came and the doors slid quietly open.

Chan shook his head and gave Mady a thrust into the elevator, but it was a pleasant little thrust, almost a caress. The doors closed and Clarence said petulantly, "I cannot get used to this silent elevator business. Uncanny."

The police car had been simply waiting at the curb for orders. The night doorman stumbled out of some cubbyhole, buttoning his overcoat. "Taxi? Oh, I see, police car." The sleepiness vanished from his eyes, which became intent and curious. "What's going on up there? Anybody arrested yet?"

Clarence said, "Pull your coat around you, Mady."

"Terrible thing." The doorman insisted upon accompanying them to the police car. "Terrible. Always proud of the senator. He was a very good—"

"Goodnight." Clarence smartly shut off the doorman. The two patrolmen were the pair who had brought them and apparently had been ordered to stand by. One of them said over his shoulder. "Same place where we picked you up?"

"Same place." Clarence huddled down in his own heavy coat.

The snow had silenced the whole city by then; streetlights still shone through halos of white; the red and orange and green traffic lights went on, off, on. Actually, the police car seemed to pay little attention to the lights.

Clarence, always mindful of courtesies, thanked the two patrolmen and unlocked the house door.

"Want a nightcap, Mady?"

"No, thank you."

"Hot milk? Anything?"

"No—no."

He locked and bolted the door, left the hall light turned on and followed her lightly up the stairs. As she turned into her own room he said thoughtfully, "You know, Lettie is a very attractive woman."

"Yes."

Clarence yawned largely. "So is Nadine. In a different way. More—" he yawned again. "More impressive or—but as to getting a man, I'd back Lettie any day. Goodnight—"

His bedroom door closed with a bang, leaving Mady standing in the middle of her own room and visited by an extraordinarily vivid picture of Lettie, curls disheveled, little figure forlorn in that shabby blue dressing gown, crying and clinging in Chan's arms.

Six

But that couldn't happen.

Oh, couldn't it, said a jeering inner voice later, much later, in the darkness around her.

It would be natural and kind of Chan, indeed it was mandatory that he show concern for his brother's wife—widow, Mady amended.

Chan was always kind. He had a strong sense of loyalty and plain good sense.

Yes, Chan was always kind. Chan would never put Lettie or any of her wishes aside. Chan had loved the senator.

The nagging little picture, provided unwillingly by her own fancy, kept returning.

She tossed and turned. The eiderdown became too

warm; she shoved it off. Then it was too cold; she reached for the quilt and yanked it up on the bed again. Her pillows were uncomfortable. She turned on the bedside light, and everything was the same and for the moment displaced the unwelcome persistent little picture.

When she turned out the light again it returned. In desperation she reached for the tiny radio on the bed table. Clarence wouldn't hear it; he always slept like a worn-out child. In some ways he was a child, she had often thought, and then at once, but a remarkably resourceful child.

He had always explained his positive talent for domestic affairs. He had been a bachelor until his marriage to Mady's mother. He had lived alone for many years in a tiny apartment with a kitchen; he had often seen to his own cooking and some of the cleaning. That was, he had once told her airily, when he was low in funds and didn't have many invitations. However, he had gone on to say with a pleased air, a single man in New York, reasonably well dressed, reasonably tactful in his manners, really needn't eat a single dinner at home unless, of course, he preferred it.

She believed that. Bachelors and widowers could all but write their own meal tickets. Yet she had always felt Clarence had never thought of a meal ticket when he met her mother and truly fell in love with her. Perhaps the fact that her mother had all the combined Maddox and Smith money didn't precisely weaken his affection, but, to do Clarence justice, Mady could never feel that the money had much to do with his obvious devotion to her mother. For months after her death he had been a tragic little figure, still dapper, still spritely, but with a lost and hurt look in his face—again like a child, but one whose people have betrayed him.

She had been thankful when he began to pay attention to his hobbies; something of his old-time spirit had returned.

But he had never really forgotten her mother. He cherished

her portrait and her memory. He had loved Mady because she was her mother's daughter. She was sufficiently realistic, however, to understand that she gave him a kind of prop and a purpose.

All the same, if she had gotten the job she'd wanted from the senator, she'd have known in her heart that somehow Clarence could get along without her. Not so contentedly, perhaps, but he did have a strong sense of self-preservation. It said much for Clarence's youthful buoyancy and friendliness that even very much younger men, everyone in fact, called him Clarence, never Mr. Fotheringay.

His proclaimed affection for the wooden Indian was surely a bit of a pose. Nobody could want that thing, she thought resentfully, and then the radio stopped some rather dreary music and began with the news and she sat up in bed.

Already Stuart's death was news. And already somebody called it a Valentine murder, because the former senator and Mrs. Channing had been entertaining at a cocktail party—so-and-so and so-and-so were present—the former senator (the news item was repetitious, but meticulous, about Stu's present status) was found in his study—the police did not intend at this point to make statements—the implication was all too clear and the man reading the city news said flatly, "the tragedy of the former senator's murder on the eve of his appointment to the Cabinet—" and in a few words—"irony of guests in the next room at the time when it is supposed the former senator was shot—"

Her hand reached out as if of its own volition to turn off the voice, but then another voice came out of the air. "The police will be grateful if Miss Nadine Hallowell will communicate with them in the hope of facilitating an inquiry into the senator's affairs."

That was all. A dance band came on, and Mady choked off the sound.

The police request had been worded deliberately, carefully, not a word about murder, only his affairs, never by a word indicating any suspicion that Nadine might have known more than she should of the senator's death. One way to put it. *Cherchez la femme,* Clarence had said. But Clarence had to be wrong about Nadine.

She was extremely efficient; she had worked for the senator for—oh, how many years? Mady couldn't remember exactly, certainly the twelve years in the Senate, but that didn't matter. Nadine was like his right arm, she knew that.

Nadine had been frank, friendly, perfectly confident in her relationship with Lettie. Mady had sometimes thought that Lettie expected too much of Nadine. Surely Nadine's duties did not include getting caterers and florists for Lettie's Valentine party. In Washington it was likely that the lists and arrangements for Lettie's many dinners and cocktail parties could have fallen within Nadine's province, for Nadine knew the ins and outs of the political scene and just what guests might have been interested in the senator or (more likely) interested him. During the few years since Lettie had inherited all that money, she had spent it freely, as indeed it was her right to do. Her Sunday-night suppers became, all at once, a Washington institution, something that must have surprised, rather unpleasantly, older and far more experienced hostesses than Lettie.

Lettie had made great strides since she had had so much money to spend, but Nadine had never seemed to begrudge Lettie's beauty or success. It had never once occurred to Mady that Nadine had been—say, too faithful to the senator, too loyal, perhaps (oh, just perhaps), too loving.

"As to getting a man I'd back Lettie any day," Clarence had said.

But Nadine had had her own standards, her own life and purposes. They had certainly included the senator's; Mady suspected that he had been the mainspring of Nadine's existence. Yet Nadine had other interests. She must have had. A woman of such poise and beauty and intelligence!

Perhaps she had been too intelligent. That could happen with a few unlucky women.

Mady thought, rather worriedly, that she didn't know much about Chan's work; in fact, she knew all but nothing about it.

She must have gone to sleep at last, remembering in her sleep the way Chan had kissed her, once only, but a real kiss—and the way he had turned to her certainly at least for sympathy about the terrible problem that had fallen upon them all.

She awoke knowing it was late, seeing the newspaper Clarence had thrust under the door, smelling the coffee Clarence had made.

The snow had stopped, but it was a sullen, threatening day with a heavy gray-white sky as if it might begin snowing again at any moment.

Traffic was still almost at a standstill; snowplows were still ranging the streets, chugging along, sending up great fans of snow. Pedestrians trudged through drifts.

Nobody knew or at least reported anything at all of Nadine.

Clarence was in the tiny library where there was a television set. She took her coffee to the room just in time to catch a fleeting view of, yes, it must be herself. She recognized Clarence and her own coat, escorted out of the apartment house by the doorman into the waiting patrol car. She hadn't known there were reporters and photographers there already. Clarence said, "I saw them! There at the corner. Not," he said disappointedly, "a very good picture of me."

The morning paper's story about the senator's death was worse in a way than the radio coverage, for it was in huge headlines.

Mady had a swift vision of the guests at the party, all reading and exclaiming and telephoning one another—"The senator! Haven't you heard! Yes, murdered! Right while we were there—must have been." And then every one of them: "No! No, I didn't see him at all!"

That was what they had said to the young man at the telephone, poring over his battered lists. "—didn't see him—no, not at all—he wasn't there—"

She wondered about the glove. Too small for Chan, that was good. And it was definitely a woman's glove. Nadine might have worn such a glove, but if she had shot Stu she was far too efficient to leave her own glove to be found and identified.

Strangers, as a rule, don't walk into a man's house (and a thoroughly populated house with a party in full swing) and shoot him.

The senator would not have allowed a stranger to enter his study.

He certainly would not have permitted a known enemy to walk into the room; take his own, or rather Chan's, gun and shoot him in the back.

The *Times* did not release a guest list for Lettie's Valentine party, which must have relieved a great many people.

There was an account, very brief, of Dr. Hill Channing, a distinguished young physicist and expert on nuclear-fusion energy, the senator's brother, arriving moments before the senator's body was found.

Chan wouldn't like that; his work was only a very small part of a team effort, he had told Mady. Indeed, the whole development of fusion energy had to be a united effort. Small commercial firms could undertake the work nowadays, but only if expressly permitted by the government and hedged in by classifications. The results of all those teams of physicists had to be shared by every other team.

There was a final but heartening paragraph in the report of the senator's murder: the police had found that a diamond bracelet belonging to Mrs. Channing had disappeared and there was a strong suggestion to the effect that the police were searching for a robber, someone who could have entered the back way, along with or during the activity of caterers employed for the occasion.

She sat back and took a breath of relief.

She knew precisely what the senator would have done if he had caught sight of a thief or any intruder. He would have gone straight for Chan's gun and held it pointed at the thief—perhaps not intending to shoot, but to frighten the thief or at least to keep him quiet while the senator called the police.

The more she thought of it the more likely and logical it became. There was no way of surmising just how the thief had wrested the gun from the senator, somehow moved behind him and pulled the trigger, but it must have occurred. This was conjecture, but a reasonable conjecture.

Clarence said, "Thief, they say! Very likely! Too much of this breaking into places and stealing going on. Fellow could have slid in the back way and nobody noticed him. Then the senator found him." Clarence was cheered and proved it and his mettle by going about preparing lunch. Mady followed his example, for Mrs. Baynes had been independent from the first and came to work when and if she felt like it. She was, however, very good when she did come. So Mady made beds, aired rooms, dusted, but also listened to the news radio.

The telephone did not ring. Chan did not arrive. No police arrived. And—fortunately, really—no reporters arrived, for Clarence, while happily accepting the notion of a thief, would inevitably have more than hinted that it was peculiar that they couldn't find Nadine and would have added, with his knowing air, *"Cherchez la femme."*

The gray day went grayer with early twilight. Clarence, giving her a rather defiant look, brought out a tray with glasses and decanter. "Early," he said. "Your dear mother didn't approve of early drinking. But in these circumstances—"

"I agree," said Mady.

"I don't believe we should phone Lettie. Do you think—"

"No," she said forcefully.

"Well, but surely Chan—There he is now. Bet you!" Clarence yelped jubilantly as the doorbell rang and he pranced for the door.

It *was* Chan. He came in, saw Mady and put his hands out toward her. "You all right?"

"Oh, yes. Chan, what has happened? What are they doing? Was it a thief? Have they found him or—"

"Or Nadine?" said Clarence. "I'll take your coat—"

Chan was wearing rather shabby tweeds and a pullover sweater. He caught Mady's glance and said, "Friend came up from Ballantry. Brought me some clothes. Lettie told me to use some of Stu's—he wore the same size, but somehow—" his voice was unsteady, "I couldn't."

"Naturally not!" Clarence bustled them back into the room with the decanter on the table. "Now, my boy, lucky I brought out an extra glass. Expecting you, of course. Subconsciously. Very interesting if one has time to explore—"

"Clarence," said Mady tautly.

"What? Oh, yes, certainly. Let Chan tell us—now then—here you are, Chan. Too much water?"

Chan lifted his glass, tasted and winced. "*Some* water, Clarence. Perhaps two drops. Please—"

Clarence obligingly took up the silver pitcher. "Certainly, my dear boy. I just didn't want to drown it. Here you are. Now then, have they found Nadine?"

"No." Chan drank slowly. "No, they haven't found her, and they haven't found anybody who knows anything at all of where she may be. Or at least says so. But the police now are inclined to think it was a burglar—I think." Chan sighed. "Certainly Lettie's bracelet is gone. A burglar could have slipped into the place and nobody noticed. The police have questioned the caterers but they said they were too busy, didn't see anybody strange. If he were dressed just—just like anybody else, he wouldn't have been noticed. Of course, he might have to have known the layout of the apartment. Still, it would be easy enough to find Lettie's room. But the bracelet was in Stu's possession as far as Lettie knew. It needed repair. Stu said he would see to it. So he could have discovered a burglar, remembered my gun, got it—and somehow the fellow got my gun away from Stu.''

"That's what we thought. Think," said Clarence as if making a declaration.

Chan finished his drink and put the glass down. A little color was coming back into his face. "But there's news about the glove—''

Clarence leaned forward; if he had been a terrier he couldn't have appeared more alert. "What? Who owned it?''

Chan looked at him wearily. "Rose Chavez."

"Oh, dear me!" Clarence yelped.

"Says she lost it in the coatroom but didn't realize it until somebody from the police phoned her last night. She took the call herself and said she was too sleepy just then to check. But she looked this morning and one of her gloves was gone, the other still in her coat pocket.''

There was a long, thoughtful silence; they probably shared the same thought.

Rose Chavez was a long-time and loved family friend, both to the Channings and to Mady and Clarence. She was built on majestic and beautiful lines; she was very rich, philanthropic and kind. She had a friendly, happy way of meeting every day and every person with a beaming smile in which complete sincerity was the main ingredient. But she was also shrewdly analytical. Rose Chavez was not the type to shoot anybody.

Chan said, "Even the police don't suspect her. But they do insist that the glove had gunpowder stains on it, which suggests premeditation on the part of the murderer.''

"You mean he—why, he would have had to get into the cloakroom and take Rose's glove to shield his own hand and—''

Chan nodded. "That's what the police say. Also the medical examiner told them that the heat in Stu's study would have altered the state of the—the body," said Chan with difficulty. "Well, anyway, they say that whoever shot him had planned it and had taken Rose's glove, got back to Stu and somehow got his gun—they haven't nailed down that part yet but they think, since he was shot in the back, whoever it was might have known where he kept the gun—"

"Where did he keep it?" Clarence asked.

Chan shook his head. "I don't know. Lettie said she supposed in one of the desk drawers, but hadn't seen it there. The medical examiner and the police say that he must have been murdered during the party after Rose had arrived and left her gloves and coat. According to the police, it doesn't fix the exact time of the shot, but indicates that it happened during the party when there was enough noise, enough hubbub to cover the sound of the shot. Those walls are thick. And Stu's study door was shut. Anyway, nobody apparently heard the shot. The key to the study is a puzzle, yet anybody close to Stu might have known that there was another key in the library. How he got out and left the key inside a locked door—"

"There are ways," Clarence said darkly. "Criminals know—"

Chan sighed. "A criminal at the party?"

Clarence sprang to the attack. "The point is that glove is probably rather large for a woman. Rose likes her gloves loose so she can pull them on easily. Now my mother would work on each finger, tight as gloves could be made. But—oh, here's a catch. A burglar would have had to mingle with the party guests in order to sneak into the coatroom. Rose did leave her coat there?"

Chan nodded.

"So a man could have gotten that glove and worn it. But somebody would have seen him. Still, it's true that one doesn't always know everybody at one of those parties.

As you say, the point is he must have looked—he couldn't have been dressed like a burglar—''

"How do you think a burglar dresses?" Chan had the faintest glimmer of a smile in his eyes.

Clarence fidgeted. "Naturally he dresses—well, he wouldn't dress like a burglar. He'd have to dress," Clarence said triumphantly, "like any party guest. Bankers gray probably, neatly tailored shirt and waistcoat and—''

"Yes, Clarence. But they think they've covered every single guest at the party. Not a single one of them seems at all likely to go about shooting people or stealing diamond bracelets.''

"Never can tell," Clarence said darkly.

"That's what the police seem to believe. I'll have another drink if you please.''

"Oh, dear me," Clarence sprang to his chore, but said, over his shoulder, "Seems peculiar they can't find Nadine. I've said it before and I'll say it again—dear me, what does that remind me of—''

Chan supplied it absently, "I said to Wilbur and I said to Orville, that thing—''

"Will never get off the ground!" Clarence finished happily. "I've been saying to the police, *cherchez la femme*. But they haven't found her.''

"I cannot believe that Nadine killed the senator." Chan took his drink.

"Of course she didn't," Mady said warmly. "Not Nadine!''

Chan shot her one swift look. "Oh! So you saw that, too.''

"Saw—''

"Nadine has been devoted to Stu—I guess—I'm almost sure she's been in love with him ever since she started to work for him. That is—I've got to qualify that. She never told me. She never said a word about it, I mean nothing like that—''

Clarence again pounced like a terrier. "Did they have an affair?"

Chan sighed. "No."

"Well, but how do you know?"

"Same way I knew that Stu never shot himself."

Clarence leaned back in his chair and squinted his eyes ceiling-ward in a very knowing way. "Now just look at it this way. Suppose Nadine and Stu had had—listen to me, Chan—a really long and happy *affaire de coeur*. Don't interrupt. Just suppose that for some reason she didn't want him to return to Washington. Just suppose they had it out—there at the Four Seasons yesterday. While I watched. Little did I think—"

"*Clarence!*" said Chan.

Clarence went on, "Nadine had managed the whole party. She had got the caterers, the florists, all of them knew her or at least knew who she was, and none of them would have thought twice about it if she had turned up quietly in the kitchen or the dining room or for God's sake anywhere in the place."

"They didn't see her."

Clarence paid no attention to that. "But even supposing she wanted Stu to refuse the appointment, she had not induced him to agree with her. So she knew she was licked—although why she wouldn't want him to accept the appointment, naturally I can't begin to surmise—"

"*Clarence!*" said Chan again.

This time Clarence unsquinted his gaze and seemed to see something in Chan's face that strongly recommended silence. He didn't wriggle, but almost. "Oh, all right, Chan, all right. I'm only saying it *could* have happened that way."

"It didn't."

"How do you know? Where is Nadine? Why doesn't she come forward and talk to the police?"

"I don't know. Clarence, will you just shut up for a moment? I want to talk to Mady."

Mady put her hand on his arm. "What else has been happening?

Chan sighed. "Lettie sent out for black clothes, dresses, everything. Wherever she buys her clothes. The services are set for day after tomorrow. *If* the police permit it, as they say they will. Lettie wanted him to be buried at Arlington, but it seems that is not possible. He had had two terms in the Senate and made a brilliant record, but, they pointed out to me tactfully, he wasn't, so to speak, a national hero. Services at St. Ethelbert's. Here. Larry Todd did the obituary, but a eulogy is to be written by somebody at the White House. Larry came in this morning. He'd been out when they tried to reach him yesterday. He is not exactly Lettie's lawyer, but is the nearest thing to it."

Clarence couldn't help breaking in. "Larry, of course, is a partner in the firm Stu was planning to enter?"

Chan nodded. "Stu had made a will, at least Larry had drawn it up for him and had a copy in his office. Originally, Stu was to become a partner in the firm—I think in March. So obviously Stu must have cleared out any personal papers, any records at all before he got news of the Cabinet appointment. That could be why no papers were found in his study—" There was the slightest hint of a question in Chan's voice.

Clarence sensed it. "Seems odd though. I mean, no bank records? No tax records? No personal memos of any kind?"

Chan sighed. "Yes, it does seem unusual. We will open and examine the contents of his safe-deposit box. Larry knew what bank. The police and the tax appraiser will get a look through that when we do. Remember Stu was a very straightforward person. He really had no dark secrets to hide."

"Everybody—" Clarence began skeptically and stopped at Chan's forbidding look.

Chan said, "Lettie made Larry bring Stu's will and read

it then and there. He said he'd rather wait till after the—the services, but Lettie insisted and so he read it. Today. Everything to Lettie, of course—" he paused as if to steady his voice, "except our father's books and a walking stick he always carried—"

"I remember that," Clarence broke in. "Sure. He was always losing it."

"Yes. Oh, and some cufflinks and—"

"No money?" Clarence asked irrepressibly.

"Certainly not. Why should he have left me any money? The police have been busy, of course, asking all sorts of things. Such as, was it Stu's habit to lock his study door?"

"What did Lettie say?" Clarence could not be subdued for long.

"She said not always. Only if there were people—like at that party—who might stray in to talk to him when he was busy. Then they talked again about the key and how it had got to the floor where we found it—I can't be sure that I pushed it out of the keyhole with my own key but that seems reasonable. Their main questions this morning had to do with Nadine—"

"Naturally," said Clarence.

"And the distance from Stu where we found the gun."

"But I told them," Mady said. "It must have been only a few feet from the door. I stumbled over it."

Chan said, "That's what I thought. Lettie thought it lay almost beside Stu. But none of us was in a state to notice or remember—Well, I've got to get back. Lettie's cleaning woman turned up, but she leaves at six and Lettie says she can't be alone there."

Mady took a quick breath and decision. "Of course not. I'm going to stay with her."

"But, Mady, it's not a very pleasant place just now, you know. I'd like Lettie to go to a hotel, but she won't budge—"

"I'll get a few things—toothbrush—slippers—" Mady mumbled, on her way to the door, but she caught a congratulatory murmur from Clarence, clearly meaning, good for you: don't leave him to Lettie's wiles.

Silly, of course. Like Clarence to leap to such a conjecture. Yet perhaps there was a grain of truth in it. Never mind, she told herself, threw a few things in a bag and went down to meet Chan. She thought he was pleased to have her with him; she couldn't be sure. Clarence had already gotten out Mady's favorite coat, woolen, as red as a robin's spring breast; she wrapped it around her and went with Chan to the taxi. They reached Lettie's apartment house and the doorman greeted them as if Chan were an old friend, and said that Mr. Wilkins had just left.

"Mr. Wilkins? Who's that?" Chan asked. The doorman shook his head. "Don't know, I'm sure, sir. But Mrs. Channing wouldn't see him. Oh, yes, I believe he said he was her uncle. Yes."

"Uncle Ernest!" Mady said, stunned. "But he can't be! It's her uncle Ernest Wilkins who died and left all that money to Lettie."

Seven

"You mean—some mistake," Chan said as if the doorman were eavesdropping on every word, as indeed, Mady discovered, glancing at him, he was.

In the elevator, Chan said, "An imposter. People do crawl out of the woodwork when a case like this gets in the news."

"That *was* the name of the uncle who left her all that money! I've heard her say Uncle Ernest many times. How grateful she was to Uncle Ernest for thinking of her! How much she enjoyed spending Uncle Ernest's kind and loving—''

"How often did she see him?"

"Well, never. It just happened that way. He died and she got his estate and—oh, I'm sure she never saw him."

"Then depend upon it, it's some impostor. Trying to engage her interest and—"

"But how would he know they hadn't seen each other? What could he hope to accomplish?"

"I don't know. Several possibilities. One would be—blackmail, I suppose. Yet he'd have to prove that in fact he was her uncle and if Uncle Ernest has been dead for—how long, three years—''

"Nearer four. Lettie will certainly know."

The elevator coughed in its usual suave manner and its doors opened.

Lettie came running to meet them—or rather, Mady couldn't help noting, to meet Chan, her little hands outstretched. "Oh, Chan, I thought you'd never get back. Oh," her voice cooled a little—a very little, Mady told herself. But at once Lettie became warm and friendly. "Dear Mady! How nice of you to come! I could always count on you, no matter what. Let me take your coat. Is it still snowing?"

"No." Chan took Mady's red wool coat into the coatroom and from there his voice came back. "How long has it been since you saw your Uncle Ernest, Lettie?"

"I told you," Mady began but Lettie replied, "My uncle! Why, I never saw him!"

"Not even lately?"

"Lately! Chan, he's dead."

Chan emerged from the coatroom. "There was a man downstairs who said he was Ernest Wilkins."

"Why—but that—that's impossible—"

"The doorman said he phoned up and you said you couldn't see him."

"But—but he couldn't have given his name. Gretchen took the phone messages. But it can't be he—not Uncle Ernest, I tell you—" She moved her pretty hands helplessly. "Why, that's where all my money came from. I mean after he died. And—oh, there's a mistake—"

"Let's see your phone messages. I suppose your Gretchen leaves them."

"Oh, yes. In the library. She always leaves notes at the phone."

In the library a small sheaf of notes lay beside the telephone. Lettie sped to it, Chan at her side. She ruffled through the pages swiftly. "No—no—no—Oh, here's Rose Chavez. Something about her glove—"

"We know about that. I mean the police know. Lettie, here's a Mr.—"

"Let me see." Lettie snatched the paper. "Mr. Williams—"

"Gretchen's version of Wilkins, probably," Chan said.

"It simply can't be! I tell you he's dead! He left me all this money. He can't be—"

"We'll have to report it, I think."

"Report? To the police? Oh, why?"

"Not being your uncle and claiming to be suggests some sort of racket."

"Oh!" Lettie stared at the paper. Black was becoming to her delicate coloring; her newly donned black dress fit every enticing curve and line of her slim figure beautifully. She had put on a tiny string of pearls around her throat and wore only her big wedding ring.

With a feeling that she was being observed, Mady turned away and was surprised to see the back of the wooden Indian's head instead of his blank gaze. Gretchen had apparently turned his head during the cleaning. Mady only hoped that Lettie would remind Clarence of it and that Clarence himself would soon—and forever—forget his admiration for the absurd thing, really grotesque as a bit of home decoration. She must go home very early in the morning, she thought suddenly, with a warning pang.

Usually she watched the notices of auctions at the many art galleries. She made a marginal mental note to remember Clarence as Chan said, "Mady has come to spend the night, Lettie. I think I'd better go to the club. You two will be all right here. Have you heard from Nadine?"

"Nadine! Oh, no! I can't imagine what has happened to her! This just isn't like Nadine. Vanishing like this! Chan, you don't suppose—" Lettie put both her hands at her throat and looked up at Chan. "She couldn't have—she wouldn't have—"

"Shot Stu and then disappeared? No!"

"But I've heard the radio requests for her to get in touch with the police. They have checked the airlines and—and all that. Nobody seems to know anything about her."

"Lettie, I don't mean to hurt your feelings, but do you think that perhaps—just perhaps, Stu and Nadine may have had—"

"An affair going?" Lettie shook her curls. "Now really, Chan!"

"You are sure?"

"Of course I'm sure! You can't hide things like that from a wife. Besides—oh, dear me, Chan, I'm surprised you even think of such a thing."

The telephone rang sharply.

There was a startled silence. Then Chan said, "Answer, Lettie."

She moistened her lips. "But there have been so many—so many—all right." She took up the telephone.

"Yes—why, I—yes—" There was only a distant rumble of a voice, but it sounded like a man's voice. Lettie was white, but steady. "Where? But I don't understand—I see—yes, yes, certainly—yes—wait a minute please—"

She put her hand over the telephone and whispered, "He says—he says his name is Wilkins. He says he is my Uncle Ernest. He says I'm to meet him. Chan, what shall I do?"

Chan waited a second or two, his face hard and thoughtful. "Ask him where to meet him."

"Oh, he said—he said the St. Regis. He said—"

"Tell him you'll be there—"

She spoke into the telephone again. "Yes—hello— hello—"

She put down the telephone. "He hung up."

"Did he say when you were to meet him?"

"No. He said he'd be in this evening—after dinner I think he said. Oh, Chan, I don't understand it! I *can't* understand. Look around you! This apartment—everything in it—my clothes—my jewels—everything has been bought with Uncle Ernest's money. It came to me after Uncle Ernest died! This—this just cannot be—"

"It can be because it is." Chan shoved his hands in his pockets, turned, walked over to the wooden Indian, withdrew one hand in order to give the Indian's decorated breast an idle thump, which gave forth a hollow sound, muttered, "Hollow, all right. So Clarence said," and turned back again. "Lettie, do you have any enemies?"

"Enemies!" Lettie's eyes widened. "What on earth—"

"Enemies. Sure. Somebody who doesn't like you."

"Why—oh, I suppose so. I may have offended somebody, some woman, by not inviting her to a party or—or refusing to act on some silly committee or—but not a real enemy, Chan. No! What do you mean?"

"It only occurred to me that somebody who is particularly nasty might undertake this business of claiming to be your uncle just to—to make you worried and miserable and—"

"Who would do that!"

"All kinds of people would do the strangest things," Chan said in a faraway voice. "Well, then, the other reason for all this business of Ernest Wilkins is, somebody who has gotten hold of his name knows about the money left you and is preparing some kind of racket. Don't ask me what. But we'll send the police to meet him."

"Chan, they'll only say it is some crank. Some crackpot, some—"

"Naturally. And perhaps it is, but certainly there's some motive behind all this attempted impersonation." Chan took the telephone himself.

"Oh, I wish you wouldn't," Lettie cried. "It's all so horrible. This just makes it worse. The police again. They'll be here. They'll question me again. I don't think I can stand it, Chan. Please don't. Mady," Lettie flung herself upon Mady. "Stop him. You can stop him. I just can't have all this—this questioning and—Mady, please!"

It was hard to resist Lettie when she pled. Mady hardened her heart. "I think he must report it. I'm sorry. But I do think that."

Lettie looked at her with the eyes of a spaniel about to be scolded. "I thought you'd understand. You've always understood about me. Ever since we were in school. Why, you—you've done so much for me, always. If it hadn't been for you, I'd have had a miserable time at school. All the other girls had money and clothes and I didn't have anything—only the vacations and the fun you gave me and—why, Mady, I met my darling Stu at your house. All my happiness is due to you—"

Mady said stiffly, "Some of it to Stu and some of it to your—"

"My uncle!" Lettie began to cry. She could cry beautifully, big tears running down her cheeks, no red nose, no anguished face.

"Besides," Mady said, softened in spite of herself. "I think Chan is having a hard time finding one of those two detectives—"

He was having a frustrated, prolonged affair of being sent from one department to another and at last, obliged to leave the message, and Lettie's telephone number with the request that either Captain McEvor or Lieutenant Swain telephone to him as soon as possible.

He dropped the telephone. "Both out. Nobody seems to

know where or when either will be back. But,'' Chan, sometimes infuriatingly, could always see the other fellow's side, ''our problem is not the only one in this city. We can't expect them to concentrate entirely upon this.''

Lettie left Mady and sat down. ''They concentrated last night,'' she said coldly. ''And far too much today. But perhaps it's just as well. This—this impostor is not going to hurt anybody. He's obviously just a—a crackpot, nuisance. I'll forget all about him.''

Chan sat down, too, crossed his knees, surveyed the tip of one shoe and said seriously, ''I don't think I'd quite forget him. Whoever he is, he means mischief of some kind.''

Lettie sighed. ''You know, Chan, I keep feeling that if only Nadine could be found she could explain—not Stu's murder, no! But explain—well, who was the woman Mady's stepfather said he saw lunching with Stu? Probably there are things that Nadine knew about Stu's—his professional life that I didn't know. He may have run up against some very important interests, in his career in the Senate, I mean. So now when he was about to accept the appointment to the Cabinet, whomever it was he had defied came to the conclusion that Stu had to be gotten rid of. You see?''

''I don't think I do,'' Chan said soberly. ''I really don't think he was on any committee that would have affected any one person very much. Any special person—who remember, could get in here, take the gun from Stu, shoot him in the back and get away. That takes us back to square one.''

''You mean the guest list,'' Mady said.

Chan nodded. ''Or uninvited guests. Lettie, I know you told the police that you didn't know anyone in the apartment house—other residents, I mean—but isn't it barely possible that one of them knew Stu and came in and—''

''Shot Stu?'' Lettie shook her head. ''Never. That is just not possible. We haven't lived here long, as you know. We were still in Washington when I—we—bought this place. We've lived here only since last November when we came back from Washington.''

"But still there are twelve apartments altogether in this building—''

"I know. It is a very good building as a matter of fact—''

"It would be," Chan said, but without the slightest tinge of sarcasm; merely a statement of fact.

But Lettie gave him a long, quiet look. "You know that Stu wouldn't have wanted any home that wasn't the kind he liked and felt he would enjoy."

The flicker of a grin touched Chan's mouth. "I understand. Same goes for you—never mind now. You must know some of the other residents."

"Not really. If we happen to meet in the elevator we say good morning. That kind of thing. And when we decided to buy the apartment we were invited to an interview with a sort of committee so they could look us over. Of course, they were very pleased to have Stu."

"They liked you, too!" Mady said.

"They didn't object to me." Lettie sighed. "But it was Stu they were really delighted to accept. I recognize some members of the committee, or board—whatever they call it. But we've lived here such a short time. I never thought of inviting any of them to the party yesterday. We—Nadine and I—we just included old friends, people we'd known here and some who happened to be in town—people from Washington, I mean. No, Chan, if you are thinking that someone living in the apartment house sneaked in here uninvited and—and took my diamond bracelet and shot Stu—you are wrong. I'd have recognized anybody we didn't invite. After all, I do greet people when they come and try to make them enjoy themselves—almost everybody knew everybody else so that wasn't hard. I asked Nadine to stay for the party, but after she had got things together she said she had to get back to Washington so—''

"Yes," Chan said soberly. "*Could* Nadine have lunched with Stu at the Four Seasons?"

Lettie replied steadily. "Good Heavens! Nadine could have lunched with Stu anywhere and certainly has, many times. If you are still thinking of a possible affair between them, forget it. You knew Stu. You know Nadine."

"But all the same, she could have taken a later plane. By the way, when did you last see her?"

"Don't say 'last see her' as if she—" Lettie put her hands together. The charming old-fashioned wedding ring she wore had belonged to Stu and Chan's mother; it was wide and heavy and to Mady's knowledge Lettie had never worn another ring with it. Stu had given her an engagement ring, which, firmly, she usually wore on the right hand.

Chan said, "I don't mean last—that is—I mean when did she leave here?"

"In the morning, of course. After she had done some chores for me. The party was all impromptu. I told you that. A spur of the moment affair. Nadine—" Lettie's voice was a little unsteady. "Nadine stood right there, in the doorway, waiting for the elevator—"

"When was that?"

"I told you. In the morning. Almost noon. I remember I told her she'd better have lunch before she went to the airport."

"You are sure she didn't say precisely when she was going to Washington?"

"Why should she? If she and Stu were to meet for lunch she might not have mentioned it. It wouldn't have been an intentional thing, trying to keep a meeting with Stu a secret. There was simply no reason for that."

"I'm sure you are right," Chan said thoughtfully. "As you say, I know Nadine. But it is not like her just to disappear this way. She must have seen the papers this morning or listened to a radio or—no, it isn't like Nadine. Well, now then, I am going to see this man calling himself

Wilkins. There's no use waiting for the police to answer my call.''

''*Oh!* But Chan—''

''It's undoubtedly a hoax and a cruel one, and I'll put a stop to it.'' He had risen. ''When the police return my phone call, tell them—him, whomever it is, that I've gone to meet this fellow who turned up.''

Lettie made a kind of warning gesture with her hands. ''If you think you must. But surely it would be better to wait for the police and let them see him?''

''Certainly, it would be better. But this is a big city. I wonder how many homicides . . . just tell them, when they call back, where I've gone and why. Now then, I know the general layout of this building. It's very simple. Lettie will tell you, Mady. Meanwhile don't either of you let anybody into the apartment. Bolt the back door. Make anyone at the front door have himself announced. Don't let anybody in you don't know. I mean it—''

He was out in the entrance hall by then, shrugging into his coat.

''But you—you don't think—I mean we can't be in—'' Mady cried.

''Danger?'' said Chan. ''I only mean take no chances.''

The elevator silently enfolded him and as silently departed.

''I wish he had waited,'' Lettie said slowly. ''The police—''

''It must be some crackpot. There are plenty of them around.''

''But what would he want?''

''What would he want?'' Mady stared at her. ''Money, of course. They always do.''

''Oh. I suppose you've had all sorts of demands.''

''Not demands exactly. Just requests for this or that— too many of them. I was always afraid Clarence would get hold of some particularly urgent appeal and send out money. So I learned to weed out the letters and turn them over to a girl in the Trust Department of the bank. I needn't tell you," Mady added rather dryly, "that the requests for money, for—oh, everything you could think of and many causes nobody in his right mind would ever consider—they all stopped. No encouragement, I suppose. You must have had the same experience."

"No," Lettie frowned. "That is, a few. But you see, I've been considered rich for only a short time. You grew up with it. But Stu tended to the begging letters, too."

Mady didn't like to think of Chan going to the St. Regis, asking for a Mr. Ernest Wilkins and finding him and—then what?

Danger, he had said. But there was no reason at all for danger to threaten her or Lettie. She said, however, "Chan said the arrangement of the apartment house is simple."

"What?" Lettie seemed to pull herself from some deep well of speculation, or more likely grief, for she said, "Mady, I don't know what I can do without Stu. He was everything to me."

"I know. That is, I can guess." With an instinctive effort to lead Lettie away from her quite justifiable shock and grief, she repeated, "The arrangement of the apartment house. Simple."

"Oh, yes." Lettie braced her small, black-clad figure. "It is simple. Twelve apartments, six on each side. It is considered small in contrast to these vast new buildings, but it has a special kind of dignity, big rooms, high ceilings, thick walls. The six apartments on this side are served by the same front elevator and the same back elevator, a service elevator. There are fire stairs, concrete, going down from the little hall behind the kitchen. No maid's room but we certainly don't need a maid's room. No live-in maids," said Lettie flatly.

"But the people who live on the other side—six apartments there, too?"

Lettie nodded. "But, Mady, none of the other residents would have the slightest reason to make his way into our apartment and steal a diamond bracelet and—and attack Stu.''

Mady took a quick look at her watch.

Lettie saw the gesture and rose. "I'm a bad hostess. There's some food in the kitchen. Gretchen left something and I think Chan sent out to a delicatessen—"

They went through the living room, now orderly and freshly aired, rid of its depressing party litter; the dining room shone with neatness; the great heart of red roses was gone; kitchen and pantry all glittered with cleanliness; there were packages from the delicatessen, as well as a double boiler of something on the stove.

For a while both women fell into a curiously domestic attitude and scene. Plates, cups, glasses, a pot of coffee.

"Not exactly luxury," said Lettie once.

"Nothing is now," Mady said. "Sometimes I think of the way things were when I was a child."

Lettie lifted suddenly very dark brown eyes. "I prefer not to think of my childhood at all. No money. No relatives—that is, nobody to care about me after my parents separated. I was entirely on my own. Not that I ever learned anything useful. And than I met Stu—" Tears came to her eyes.

"I can't say I ever learned anything useful either," Mady said, merely to say something. "Of course I did take that business course in the rather vague hope of becoming somebody's secretary. When Stu received that Cabinet appointment I thought perhaps he would take me on—as an assistant to Nadine, maybe. I hoped to see Stu at the Valentine party—" she stopped.

When the pantry telephone extension rang, both women sprang to answer it. Mady happened to get there first.

"McEvor, Homicide," said a voice she recognized too well. "Mrs. Channing?"

"No, I'm Mady Smith. But Mrs. Channing is here—"

"—yes, all right. I'll see to it—" That was spoken in an aside. Then McEvor's voice came back, directly in

Mady's ear. "Tell Mrs. Channing we got the message about this—this uncle of hers. Wilkins. There's no such man staying at the St. Regis. Sorry—but I'll have to go." Aside again he said, "Yes, yes, right away." The telephone clicked.

Mady put down the receiver. A big city, she thought dully. Homicides were far too frequent. She couldn't expect the whole police force to stand ready and able to concentrate on any one particular homicide.

"What did he say?" Lettie was standing beside her, napkin crumpled in her hand, face as white as the napkin.

"He got Chan's message. Somebody checked the St. Regis. There's no Ernest Wilkins staying there."

"Oh," said Lettie after a moment. "Then where is Chan?"

There was a sharp buzz from the bell beside the telephone. "It's the house phone." Lettie answered and called down the mouthpiece, "Yes! Send Mr. Channing up."

Full of their own news, Mady hurried for the entrance hall. Lettie followed. The elevator appeared and disgorged Chan who looked very tired. "He wasn't there. Are you sure he said the St. Regis, Lettie?"

"Yes, I'm sure. The policeman—I mean Captain McEvor just phoned. He had gotten your message and somebody asked at the St. Regis and—oh, I don't understand how anybody could be so cruel!"

Mady said practically, "Come on to the kitchen, Chan. You must eat. We were wishing we had learned to cook. Come on."

Lettie said with a sigh, "I was always so poor. I did learn to cook a little. But then I met dear Stu and then my uncle—" But her eyes flared widely. "Chan, this—this impostor—whatever he is, frightens me."

Eight

"Nonsense," said Chan, but not very firmly. "I also could do with a drink. I know, Mady, I had a good slug at your place but—Never mind, I'll make it myself."

Mady got out another plate. Lettie dished up some of the food. Chan came back from the pantry bar with a very dark mixture in a glass in his hand. "No need to be scared, Lettie. He is just what I said. Some crackpot. Told you the wrong place on purpose."

Mady, watching Chan, said slowly, "You mean more than that—don't you?"

"Not much. It's possible that he simply wanted to get you out of the house, Lettie. Maybe in the hope of another burglary. Anyway, don't think about it. If the news continues, a number of—" he hesitated, drank and said, "peculiar things may happen. Usually do, McEvor said. Widespread publicity. Valentine party. Home of distinguished ex-senator. The police are finished with his study, McEvor said. They also ransacked that new office on Larry's company's premises that Stu was about to move into. No—" he replied to Lettie's questioning eyes, "they found nothing of any special interest. Of course," he added as if merely an unimportant afterthought, "there's that little problem of no papers in his study here. Doesn't that machine make any noise, Lettie?"

Lettie hesitated. "I really don't think so, Chan. At least—yes, I think I've been vaguely aware of it."

"I can understand why he would want to leave nothing of his former correspondence or notes or anything that might be significant if it got in the wrong hands. Still—" Chan frowned and said after a moment, "that just isn't like Stu. Such a clean sweep. Should have left something, letters, checkbooks. However, we'll see what turns up in his safe-deposit box. Now I'll take the bed in Stu's office tonight."

Lettie straightened her slender back. "Oh, no, Chan! You've done so much. Mady will stay with me. She brought some night things. I'm not afraid. Not with Mady here. You really must go—perhaps not back to Ballantry tonight. But there's your club."

Mady said, "Yes, we'll be all right here. You need a night's sleep."

He gave her a glance in which she thought there was an element of gratitude. However, he resisted. "You two women! This character pretending to be your dead uncle. Shouldn't leave you—"

"But you must," said Lettie. She pressed her pretty hand down upon Chan's. "You've done so much for me. Please do this. Go to your club and we'll keep in touch. If anything should bother us—"

Frighten us, she means, Mady thought, but didn't say it.

"—we'll phone to you at once."

"I think the switchboard at the club goes off at—I don't know when. I think about three."

"Nothing," said Lettie, "is going to happen to us. We'll keep all the doors locked."

He himself tested the lock and then bolted the kitchen door. But as he was leaving, his overcoat half on, he said to Lettie, "Was Stu firmly decided about the Cabinet appointment?"

"Why, I—why, yes! I think so. It was a great honor."

"Nobody against it?"

"No! No, he'd have told me."

Chan got his other arm into his coat. "Was Nadine in favor of it?"

"Nadine!" Lettie's brown eyes widened. "She must

have been! She was very proud of Stu, you know, and she liked Washington.''

"She'd have gone with him?''

"Oh, yes! At least—oh, I'm sure of that. He would have wanted her. I wish—oh, I wish she would come back.''

"Come back?''

"It seems obvious to me, now that I'm beginning to think. She's simply gone with some friend out to Long Island, or the mountains to ski for a few days, or even south. She must have wanted a few days rest before launching into the Washington melee.''

Chan frowned. "I suppose that is possible. Of course there was yet to be the confirmation of his appointment by the Senate.''

"There couldn't have been any problem there. Stu may not have been the most distinguished man in the world, but he was certainly free of any—any—''

"Hocus-pocus?'' Chan said dryly. "Oh, yes. Everybody was sure of that. Here's the phone number for the club—'' He scribbled it on the tiny pad of paper, which Lettie, the nearly perfect and efficient housekeeper, kept beside each telephone.

Chan looked at Mady. "Now mind me. Don't open the door. Don't use the phone. Bolt this door after me—goodnight—''

She hadn't seen him press the elevator button. In its usual deft yet somehow stealthy manner the doors opened. They engulfed Chan, his thoughtful white face, and dark gray eyes looking at nothing.

Lettie sighed. "I suppose we may as well go to bed. I don't want to see the news.''

"Or listen to any more news!'' Mady said through her teeth.

"How right! This is the guest room. Oh, you know that. Chan used it last night. But I'm sure Gretchen changed the sheets and towels—''

Not that I would care, Mady thought when she turned

off the bedside light and sank into the comfort of the bed. It gave her an odd sort of warmth and pleasure to feel that her head lay where Chan's head had lain the night before. Dear me, she thought, I really have it bad.

Still, he did like her. Perhaps, just perhaps it was more than that.

They were perfectly safe. Bolts on the doors. Doorman on the alert. Possibly, just possibly, the policemen in a circling squad car somewhere near had been advised to keep and eye on the apartment house.

Unexpectedly sleep fell on her like a comforting blanket.

Something, sometime later, pulled her from the warm depths of sleep so she sat up, listening, her heart thudding and little waves of shock going through her. She didn't know what she had heard.

She didn't know what could have roused her so suddenly. It was as if her subconscious mind hadn't slept at all but had kept on the alert, aware.

So, she thought, bewildered, a fox or any wild animal might sleep—sleep but not sleep because it had to be aware at all times of any danger.

Danger! Oh, no!

But she reached out into the darkness, overcoming a feeling that something might be out there waiting to seize her. She jerked on the bedside lamp. Her watch was still on her wrist; she hadn't even had the strength to use the beautiful tub in the adjoining bathroom. It was only just after two o'clock. It felt much later.

Something was occurring in the apartment.

Well, then, she told herself, what?

There was no sound at all. Yet there had to have been something, some tinkle of a sound, some stir of movement. She could not have simply leaped out of very tired sleep for nothing.

She wouldn't be easy in her mind until she had at least looked out into the living rooms, called Lettie, discovered— oh, something, she thought vaguely, but with mandatory urgency. She had brought a dressing gown and she slid into it and bedroom slippers; she padded across to the door. Just before she opened it she was assailed with terror.

She couldn't breathe. She couldn't stop her heart's pounding. If I don't open that door now I never will, she thought wildly, and made herself turn the knob and open the door.

The corridor was lighted. Yes, they had left it like that.

But then there was nothing at all gliding along the corridor, sliding out of sight at the sound of the opening door, hiding somewhere, waiting. Just nothing.

She was letting fancy grasp her in its clutches.

She had sense enough to look down the corridor. She could see Stu's study door, which was closed. Lettie's door was closed, too.

Again she debated about awaking Lettie. But if she were to permit a wild impression to influence her to the extent of waking Lettie, asking her if she had heard anything— no, she wouldn't do that. Was there a movement in the library?

She'd have to look.

If she waited even for a moment she would lose what courage she had. She walked softly to the door of the library. No sound, no motion, no hands coming out to grab her, she thought with a grim sense of the absurdity of her own imagination. There was a switch for a light near the door; she remembered that and felt for it. The library sprang into being.

That room, too, was again in perfect order. The wooden Indian stared blankly at the sofa.

Her glance lingered for a moment on the telephone. But, no. How could she wake Chan and tell him—well, tell him what? That she had had (must have had) a nightmare, thinking there was some sound, or motion within the apartment. But still the notion of some movement, some presence in the apartment possessed her so firmly that at last, rather ashamed, she went back along the corridor and knocked lightly at Lettie's door.

"*What*—" Lettie sounded frightened. Her voice came up sharply. "*Mady! Is anything wrong?*"

"Not really. I only thought I heard someone—something—"

"Oh. I *am* sorry, Mady! I must have roused you. I couldn't sleep. So I went to the kitchen and got a glass of warm milk. I must have brushed against your door as I passed. I am sorry—"

"That's all right. I didn't know—"

There was a little pause; then Lettie called, "Want some milk? It does settle one down a little."

"No. No, thank you. Never mind. I'll go back to sleep."

So there was nothing at all to frighten anybody. But she left the bedside light turned on, which as a matter of fact made sleeping difficult, for whatever way she turned, the light seemed to shine into her eyes quite as if reminding her that murder had walked down that corridor into the room at the end of it.

The distant sound of a voice from a radio awakened her.

By the time she had crawled into her dressing gown and slippers and out to the kitchen, Lettie had turned off the radio on a kitchen shelf.

She turned a lovely yet pale face toward Mady. "They are making a real search for Nadine. They've got out a—I don't know what it is—something about all points—"

"That's for missing persons, isn't it?"

"It must be that. But Nadine—good heavens, Mady, she's only gone away for a sort of holiday. She never tells people just what she plans to do or when or—that is, she always let Stu know where he could get in touch with her if there was a press of work, but nobody else. When she left me here—" Her eyebrows drew together; she shook her head. "She only said she was going to Washington.

I'm not sure she actually said the Mayflower. Nothing more—''

"Was there anything else on the radio?"

"About Stu? Oh, yes. His youth, record in the Senate— so distinguished a record that actually he had been offered a Cabinet post. All that. It's true, his record was outstanding!"

Mady said wearily, "I'll make coffee."

"I already did—"

Chan and the newspapers arrived at the same time, for he brought the morning paper up with him after the doorman had announced him and the elevator deposited him at the door, which Mady obediently opened only after he had called to her.

He looked older and very tired. "Nothing to report," he said. "Have you girls anything to eat? I didn't take time for breakfast."

Back in the kitchen the whole scene became again domestic and quiet, totally removed from such bizarre events as murder. Eggs, bacon, fresh coffee, fresh orange juice, prepared clumsily by Mady, more deftly by Lettie, increased the sense of quiet domesticity. They didn't talk until Chan had sighed. "I didn't know I was so hungry. Now if we could only find Nadine. Don't you have *any* idea as to where she might be, Lettie?"

"I've told you! She could be anywhere!" Lettie pushed back her soft curls.

There were tired, blue shadows below her pansy brown eyes. "But, Chan, you mustn't, you really mustn't think she crept back in here and—and shot Stu. She didn't. She *couldn't* have."

"I don't know," Chan said. "I'm afraid it's what the police think."

"Is there anything new in the paper?" Mady asked.

"No. That is, of course it is still top news. Distin- guished former senator! I have a feeling that there could be some political implications I don't like. Neither would Stu."

"Political implications?" Lettie said. "I don't see—"

"Oh, bills some lobbyists were pushing. Good bills, however. Stu wouldn't have backed anything that wasn't sound. He pushed for more money for fusion development and—"

"For what?" Lettie said.

"Never mind. While Stu was in office, Congress and the Senate voted money for research in that field. Not as much as for the space program, but a step in the right direction."

"What does it mean?"

"In the end it means energy. If and when we can discover some practical means of employing it. That's what the problem is now."

"But—energy. I think—"

"I know. You think of atomic energy as fission. Most people do. But there may be also the other side of the coin."

"Fusion means putting together," Mady said, who knew in fact not much more about it than Lettie, but had heard more from Chan, most of which, she had to admit to herself, was completely incomprehensible to her. She had to make an attempt. "It has to do with the sun's energy—molecular and—and—"

A faint smile touched Chan's face, but he nodded at her. "Good old college try! The whole thing, Lettie, is if we are successful there'll be energy for everybody on this earth as long as—well, as long as the sun lasts. But don't expect it tomorrow or next year. The development of methods of use may take years. May never be accomplished, but I believe in it."

Lettie leaned her head on one hand, thinking. Finally she said, "And did Stu know about this?"

"He knew from me and many colleagues. He believed

in it, too. That's all. Nobody would have shot him to stop that.''

"Wasn't there—" Lettie stirred her coffee. "Wasn't there anything that just *might* have made an enemy for him?"

"Not that I know of. If so, of course Nadine might know. But I don't think it likely."

"But Chan, were you lobbying for this bill to appropriate more money for research?" Lettie asked.

"Why, I—" Utter astonishment was in Chan's face. Then he gave a short, but not amused, laugh. "I am not a lobbyist. You can be sure of that. A registered lobbyist can do very good and valuable work. But I'm not one."

"But you did—or would have tried to influence Stu?" said Lettie.

"Why, I—yes! Yes, I suppose so. In a sort of family way. I often talked about it. Look here, Lettie, physicists may not be able to accomplish a way of using this putative, but perhaps immeasurable, source of energy. But we're trying. Sometime, I believe it will be done."

Mady knew, she had heard, his next words. "And that," Chan said very quietly, "might actually lead to peace on earth."

Lettie held her spoon still in one small hand. "How?"

"Why are wars fought?" Chan said shortly. "Territory— seaports—coal—oil. Energy. Call me a dreamer if you want to but perhaps, in time—That's the doorman, isn't it?"

The house phone had begun to buzz. Chan was nearest it and took down the little mouthpiece. "Who—oh! Oh, yes, certainly. Send them up."

He replaced the mouthpiece. "You girls had better get dressed. It's McEvor and Swain again and they say they have found a dead man who may be your uncle, Lettie."

Nine

Lettie surged up, her shabby blue dressing gown falling from her shoulder. She clutched at it, her face as white as the cup on the table. "It *can't* be! *That man! It's all wrong*—"

"Get dressed," said Chan.

"He died years ago!"

"We have to see the police."

"Come on, Lettie." Mady took her elbow.

"Yes. All right—" Lettie went with her through the entrance hall just as the elevator gave a slight murmur.

The two detectives were waiting, slumped down in chairs, both of them, as if they had been up all night, when Lettie, with Mady a step or two behind her, returned to the library. It was beginning to feel like a courtroom, Mady thought with a sense of horror, the wooden Indian, the judge.

"Sorry about this," McEvor said, struggling to his feet.

Swain appeared about to speak but achieved only a lugubrious belch, which he tried to turn into a cough.

Chan said, "They want you to identify the victim, Lettie."

"Identify! But, Chan! I never saw him!"

This produced a silence on the part of both detectives. Finally Swain said, "But Mrs. Channing—"

McEvor said, "Do you mean to say that this—that is, you never even knew your uncle?"

Lettie nodded. She sat down, linking her hands. "No, I

barely knew of his existence until it developed that he had died and left all that money to me.''

There was another silence. Swain appeared to repress another rumbling belch. McEvor said at last. ''How did you hear about his death and the money?''

''I had a letter. From a legal firm. In Sydney.''

''Australia,'' Swain rumbled, apparently to himself.

''The letter told me that he had died and left me money and I was to identify myself and—and the money was mine. That's all.''

There was another silence. ''But then,'' McEvor said, ''of course you had further correspondence with this firm, lawyers, bankers, everyone connected with your uncle's estate.''

''Yes, of course. That is, I didn't myself. Stu—my husband was a lawyer, you know. He saw to everything. I just—'' A helpless, hopeless look came into her face. ''I just used the money. You see—'' She swallowed hard. ''I had very little most of my life. So I—perhaps I spent pretty—pretty lavishly.''

Swain said dourly. ''You can't mean there's nothing left?''

''Oh, no. I can't say just how much—''

Mady stared at her, all her Yankee ancestry rising in her blood. ''You mean you've been spending the principal, Lettie?''

''Why, I—yes! No reason not to. Stu always provided enough for us to live on.''

''But not the way you—'' Chan gave Mady a quick glance. Mady changed course. ''It's not important. Your own money—''

McEvor said dryly, ''Unless in fact he was still alive and wanted it back again.''

''But why on earth?'' Lettie said.

''Why would he want to find a place to conceal his money? Or person to claim it?'' McEvor said in a flat voice. ''Why, indeed! You'd be surprised if I told you some of the ways and reasons people try to hide money.''

''But I do not believe this—this man you say you found

this morning—I'll never believe he was my uncle. I think he was some crackpot, seeing all the news in the papers, thinking that I was very rich and—No! He couldn't have been my uncle!''

Chan said quietly to McEvor, ''Why do you think he is the man who came here yesterday, saying he was my sister-in-law's uncle and wanting her to come to talk to him?''

McEvor said wearily, ''He was found by a night clerk in a little hotel—Elderwood, in the Twenties. We were notified. The men who were sent there let me know that his clothes had been purchased in Australia. There *is* a chain of communications. One precinct to another. Homicide—''

''There was nothing else to identify him?''

Both detectives seemed to consider. Finally McEvor said, ''No passport. No letters. No addresses. No wallet. But he registered in your uncle's name. Ernest Wilkins. That's why we were informed.''

''But he couldn't have! *He's dead*—''

''The man we were called to investigate was certainly dead,'' said McEvor neatly.

There was a silence; Chan frowned at the rug. Lettie knotted her hands together. Mady just sat and Swain seemed to swallow another belch. ''Poor man,'' Mady thought. ''Explains why he is so morose.'' Having conquered his affliction for the moment, Swain said, ''That paper shredder in the senator's study shreds too well. We couldn't make out anything intelligible. Do you remember when he used it last, Mrs. Channing?''

Lettie gripped her hands together. ''I've told you. I don't know. The machine makes a kind of mutter, not much. These walls are thick and of course if he had used it during the—the party nobody would have heard anything. These walls—''

''I know,'' said Swain, ''thick. So thick that nobody heard the revolver shot that killed him.''

Chan stirred. ''How was this man killed last night?''

The two detectives exchanged looks. McEvor replied, "Shot. No gun found."

He rose and looked at Swain. "Might as well go. If you think of anything at all that might help identify this man, you'll let us know, Mrs. Channing."

Lettie stood. "He was not my uncle. I don't know why he used his name. But he couldn't have been my uncle."

"Since he used your uncle's name, we had to inquire." McEvor trudged out of the library, across the hall and pushed the elevator button.

In a moment the two detectives were gone. Chan turned to Lettie. "You're sure this—impostor told you the St. Regis?"

"Oh, yes. But you went there—"

"So did the police. No Ernest Wilkins. I can't see why—look here, Lettie, did Stu have any idea of returning to government? I mean before elections last fall?"

"I don't think so. If he had, he didn't talk of it. He talked only of the law firm. He seemed very happy about that."

"The Cabinet appointment, I believe that that was a surprise. What did you think?"

"I thought he was flattered. I think he wanted to take it. Who wouldn't? Of course he would have had to change his plans to go into the law firm. You know he had an agreement with Larry Todd and the other partners. But I was content either way. I like Washington, but I like New York, too. Whatever Stu decided was good with me."

Chan paced up and down the floor, pausing, as if at an idle impulse to touch the single scalplock on the Indian's head. "Ugly fellow, isn't he?" he said absently. "Lettie, now think hard. Was Stu at all concerned about his confirmation as a Cabinet member? You know—"

"Oh, I know. The Senate. No, I'm sure he wasn't. He had friends there. It's true, Chan, that he hadn't had a long time of service in Washington, only those twelve years.

But he had made himself an expert in the field of international trade.''

"Yes, I know. Stu was like that. Give him a problem he liked and nothing would stop him."

But something *had* stopped him, Mady thought sadly. Chan said, "I don't see how there can possibly be any political complication about his murder. Or any possible connection with this man using your uncle's name. Had Stu had any threats, any letters, any phone calls that upset him?"

Lettie was shaking her head. "No, I'd know."

"He might not have wanted to alarm you."

Lettie surveyed her hands as if she had never seen them before and lifted her candid gaze to her brother-in-law. "Honestly, Chan, I think I'd have guessed if anything bothered him. You mean death threats? Assassination?"

"No. That is, yes, I suppose I do mean that."

Lettie shook her head. "He was always just the same. There just was no enemy."

"Had to be an enemy," Chan said soberly. "You might just go with the police and see if you can recognize this man who was killed in the hotel—"

"'The police! No—"

"In the event he was somebody who knew Stu. Somebody you might remember—"

"No! You can't ask me to do that, Chan! Besides—I can't imagine anybody I know who knew about my uncle—that is, the man must have come from Australia but—oh, no, Chan. I couldn't possibly identify him. He must have been a perfect stranger to me. And I can't—don't make me go with the police and—and—please, don't make me, Chan."

"All right. I can see how painful it would be. But are you sure you can't say whether or not he was your uncle?"

"Perfectly sure."

"You don't have any family photographs. Snapshots—anything—"

"Nothing. Heavens, I'd remember. All that money—"

"Yes," Chan said heavily. "Yes—"

"You surely believe me. He simply was *not* my uncle. How could he be?"

"Yet the police do seem to consider that your real uncle—*perhaps* this man—may have been only pretending to be dead."

"Why?"

"Obvious, as they said. People, some people do try to hide money. Say he had got it all in some fraudulent way and suddenly needed to get it away from an investigation. He'd have to get some lawyer, a shyster (he would have to be a crook, too), to send you all the information and the money—then, when your uncle—*possibly* this man, Lettie—thought the coast was clear he came to get it back again."

Lettie took a long breath. "Oh, I don't know! I can't believe that, but how can I be sure! Stu understood all the information that was given him about the money and everything. I just didn't. I was overwhelmed by it. I didn't even ask Stu any details. I—" she said frankly, "didn't care! All that money. I just took it. And spent it!"

Chan paced the length of the room again and paused again at the Indian, who returned his gaze imperturbably. "I wonder," said Chan, "if by any chance all the documents concerning this inheritance from your uncle were among the papers Stu was shredding."

Lettie rubbed her eyes. "Oh, I don't know. I don't see why Stu would do that. He had no idea that there could have been anything fraudulent about it. Neither did I. But if there was the slightest tinge of—dishonesty, trickery about any of it, Stu would have seen it and stopped it and—Chan! You don't think that that is what could have happened?"

Chan resumed his pacing. After a moment, he said over his shoulder, "I don't know. Just now I can't see any connection—"

The telephone rang. Lettie took the receiver down but

then gave it a frightened look as if it might turn into a snake. "You take it," she said to Mady.

"All right. Don't be scared. Hello—oh! Why, yes, I'm Miss Smith. Oh, *no!*" She heard her own voice rising in shock. "No, I didn't know! I'll be right down."

Chan had rushed across to her as she dropped the telephone. "What is it? What's wrong—"

"Clarence—" She couldn't cry and she couldn't laugh and was perfectly sure that hysteria was threatening. "*Clarence—*"

"What's he done?" Chan gripped her arm.

"Been arrested."

"Why?" Lettie was standing, too, her hand on Mady's shoulder. "Don't let it upset you, Mady. It'll be all right."

"Oh, yes, I suppose so, but—" Laughter and tears choked her.

"Why was he arrested?" Chan held her harder as if to enforce decent control.

She choked again, nevertheless. "For being drunk and disorderly."

"Clarence!" Chan cried. "He can't have been!"

"He went to an auction this morning. I meant to get home in time to stop him—" She began to get some control over her shaken nerves. "But he bought something or other, some piece of statuary. Then he tried to get a cab to take him home with it and the cabby wouldn't and Clarence—somehow there was a ruckus and a policeman on the corner came up and Clarence—anyway, he's in jail. And he doesn't have money for bail. I suppose he'd spent all he had at the auction. I'll have to go."

Chan was touched slightly with hysteria, too; he gave an unsteady laugh. "Oh, no, you don't! I'll see to him."

"No. I've got to!"

Lettie said indignantly, "He's not your child, Mady. Honestly, you do act like it sometimes. I'd say, let him stew in his own juice for once."

Mady was already halfway to the entrance hall for her

coat. Chan was with her. "I'll go with you then," he said. "Where's your coat?"

"Drunk!" Lettie said. "At this time of day! I can't believe—"

"It's nearly noon." Mady slid her arms into her coat, wondering why on earth she always felt she must defend Clarence and at the same time knowing helplessly that she did have to defend him.

Chan said, "I'll be back, Lettie, but just now—"

"No—" Lettie said and seemed to stop herself. "Yes, I mean, yes, of course. I'll be quite all right here alone."

"We can't leave her like this," Mady said, at the sight of the dismal little figure. "It's all right, Chan. They told me where to go. I'll pay his bail—"

"Perhaps just a fine," Chan said. "Even so, I'd better go with you."

She had at some time pushed the elevator button, for the doors slid open beside her. "No, no, Chan. It's all right. I'll let you know when—" The doors closed, shutting off Chan and Lettie.

It wouldn't have been either kind or brotherly for Chan to leave Lettie alone just then, beset by—well, terror. That was the only word for it.

"I'll certainly give Clarence a piece of my mind," she thought with fury as the doors slid open again and a doorman signaled to her. "Taxi waiting, miss. Mr. Channing rang down—"

Actually, she didn't give Clarence a piece of her mind because the first thing she saw standing there when she entered the station house was a rather dilapidated, for one wing was gone, but unmistakable replica of the Winged Victory.

It added a nightmarish note to the otherwise rather bare and utilitarian room where Clarence called to her jubilantly from a bench. "I had a breatholater test! Never knew before just how it works! But I had one and they dismissed the drunken charge and—"

"But not the fine," said a policeman behind a desk.

Mady had luckily brought her handbag; she had a vague recollection of Lettie thrusting the handle over her wrist.

It was a richly deserved fine, she was sure. There followed a slight battle with Clarence who, insisting that he knew she had a cab waiting, wanted to take the statue with them. Mady, up in arms for once, kept stoutly refusing, until the policeman behind the desk said, "Okay, okay, leave it here. It'll give us a laugh until the garbage-disposal man comes around."

Clarence wailed. "But it's a perfect replica—"

"Not anymore," Mady said coldly. "One of its wings is gone—"

"What do you expect when a perfect stranger driving a cab takes a swing at you—"

"You're lucky he hit that—that thing instead," said the policeman, adding firmly, "Good morning."

"If it had been marble instead of whatever it is, plaster at a guess, that cabby would have known what he hit!" Clarence said valiantly.

The policeman at the desk eyed him with a certain interest. Probably, Mady thought, or at least she hoped, he had few customers, so to speak, with such peculiar and unusual activities. He said again however, dryly, "Good morning."

Clarence got into his overcoat, adjusted his scarf with nicety and allowed himself to be guided outside into the waiting taxi.

"Never find such another—" he began plaintively at last.

"Don't you try it," said Mady as fiercely as she could. "I will not have any more junk like that in the house—"

"Oh, well." Clarence settled himself resignedly in the seat.

"Was that man they found dead really Lettie's uncle?"

"How did you—"

"Newspapers," said Clarence loftily. "Radio. Think I'm not interested?"

"I think you're going to stay away from auctions for awhile," she said nastily.

Clarence unexpectedly agreed. "I can't say I fancied being taken in by the police. I didn't really like the breatholater either, to tell you the truth. Of course there are smaller things of interest in the art galleries if it is size that bothers you."

"That and all the money you spend."

"Oh, I don't worry about that. I mean, you are really very kind and patient with me, Mady. Also," said Clarence with conviction, "generous."

"No, I'm not. Money is money. It's not to be thrown away—"

"No," said Clarence dreamily. "But as investments there are ways—"

She eyed him suspiciously. "What are you planning now?"

"Oh, nothing much." Clarence was airy. "However, if you insist, there are, for example, Chinese snuff bottles. Of course, I have never taken snuff in my life, but as collectors value them—"

"Oh, Clarence!" It was almost a wail. "They cost like everything! Especially the good ones."

"I expect so. But one can always pick up some beauties. Also miniatures—"

At least there would be house room for small things and peace for Clarence. She said resignedly, "Just keep that silly wooden Indian out of the house."

"Oh, that. I imagine Lettie has grown quite attached to it by now. But you are quite right. It really doesn't go in our—your house. But I do regret my lovely Nike."

Mady was visited by a wild notion that her stepfather, having dithered on the edge for some time, had at last taken leave of his senses. "What on earth do you mean? Nightie?"

"My dear!" Clarence was lofty and reproachful as, Mady thought indignantly, he had no right to be after the recent incident. "My dear, have you forgotten your education? And a very expensive education it was, too, if I remember correctly."

"What has education—Oh!" Light broke upon her. "You mean—"

"Samothrace, of course. Nike of Samothrace. Called the Winged Victory, but—"

"But that was only a plaster replica—very damaged," she said crossly.

"I liked it when I saw it," Clarence said with an authority touched with regret. "But you are right. There's an exhibit of Chinese snuff boxes—" He broke off. "By the way, Nadine was at the house this morning."

"Nadine!" She whirled toward him. Clarence nodded affably. "We're stopping. Have you money for the taxi?"

"Did you see her? Did you talk to her?"

Clarence was bundling himself out of the taxi and holding up a courteous hand, still clad neatly in a lemon-colored glove, to assist her. She handed some money to the taxi driver, who seemed content with it and thanked her warmly, and Clarence, active as a squirrel, hustled her into the house and took a long breath. "Glad to be out of the clutches of the law," he said. "Dear me! What an odd experience."

"*Clarence! What about Nadine?*"

"Oh, yes. It was Nadine all right. No, I didn't talk to her. Mrs. Bayne wasn't here—not that she ever answers the door anyway. I heard the bell but by the time I got downstairs Nadine had gone."

"How do you know it was Nadine?"

"Saw her, of course. Through that window. I opened the door and called after her, but there was a snow shovel going down the street and she didn't hear me. But it was Nadine."

"You *saw* her—"

"Of course. She didn't see me, didn't turn around. Marched along, composed as ever. Very attractive woman, I must say."

Mady rallied all her forces of self-control. "If you didn't recognize her with the senator at the Four Seasons, how could you have recognized her this morning?"

"Oh, easily. She didn't have a hat on. Lovely hair. Real blue black and so smoothly arranged. I think she had on the same coat, some kind of fur, mink, I believe. Yes," Clarence said thoughtfully. "Of course. Mink. Your mother didn't really like mink, of course. Said it was the skins of little animals and—"

"Clarence! Listen to me! Where was she going?"

"Along the street toward Park."

"Why did she—" Mady broke off. A piece of white paper lay on the floor, under the bench. It had probably slid there when Clarence had opened the door and called after Nadine. Mady swooped upon it.

Clarence removed his gloves, folded them neatly, removed his scarf and watched her, his eyes bright. "It's a note from Nadine?"

Heavy, very definite black characters were written on a sheet from the kind of memorandum pad that anyone as efficient as Nadine would be sure to carry in her handbag.

Mady read it and read it again and then just stared at it, half aware of Clarence's prattling and then of his hands simply taking the paper from her. He read it aloud. "'Mady: Sorry you are not here, but I only want you to tell Chan that I'll come back when I can. Not now. I can't bear it. I can't go to the services for Stuart. I can't believe—I didn't mean—'" Clarence squinted, mumbled, "Some words scratched out here—" He got out the spectacles that out of vanity he hated to wear and squinted again. "For heaven's sake, it's a confession."

"*Let me see—*"

"Listen. She's crossed out 'to hurt him,' yes, I'm sure—look at it."

Mady looked at the heavy pen marks and could make out the words beneath them: " 'I didn't mean—to hurt him!'—Oh, Clarence, I think you are right."

"Go on—"

Mady read " 'Oh, Mady, ask Chan to tell the police to stop this missing persons nonsense. Nadine.' "

"Dear me," said Clarence. "So she did kill him."

Ten

"She doesn't say that. She doesn't confess—"

"Same thing. I said all along 'Cherchez la femme.' You'll have to give this to the police immediately."

"No. No—"

"But she confesses!"

"No. I don't think that—"

"You don't know what you think." Clarence spoke far too accurately. "I say give this to the police at once. Cherche—"

"Please, Clarence, if you say that again—No, there's something about this note. I can't say—I don't know—"

"I've told you. Perfectly obvious."

"It seems to me very sad. That's all. Just—"

"Heartbroken?" Clarence brightened, as if, terrierlike, he had sniffed an interesting bone. "That's possible, too! In love with the former senator. Adored him. Love not returned. Hell hath no fury—"

"Clarence," said Mady dangerously. "I've got to think about this."

Clarence shrugged and skipped upstairs in a huff, but

whistling as he went. The tune had a weird resemblance to "He was her man and he done her wrong."

" 'I can't bear it. I can't go to the services for Stuart. I can't believe—I didn't mean—to hurt him—' "

She read and reread the short note and found that she had only a devastating sense of pity. Nadine might be heartbroken; certainly the senator had thought of her as his right hand, but only that. Even though he had been older than Chan and Larry Todd and herself, Mady knew Stuart; well enough to believe in his utter honesty. Certainly she knew his love for Lettie. He had never, Mady felt sure, so much as looked at another woman. Surely he would not have involved himself and Nadine in a love affair that could bring nothing but sorrow to both of them.

Yet there was an element of something like guilt in Nadine's hurriedly scribbled lines. No word at all as to where she was going, where she had been, what were her plans. Only the request to call off the police's missing-persons inquiries.

Let Chan know, of course. She went to the telephone and Lettie answered. Chan was not there.

Lettie didn't know when he would return and what he had intended doing. She was all right, though, she said hastily. Mady needn't come back. Everything was all right, "—as all right as things can ever be again," Lettie added dismally.

"You *can't* stay there alone. It doesn't seem friendly or—" she hesitated for a moment and then risked it. "Nadine was here this morning! No, I didn't see her! She left a note—"

There was a long silence. Then Lettie said, breathlessly, "She's got to come here! I need her! Where is she?"

"She didn't say. She only wanted the police to call off the missing-persons inquiry."

There was another pause. Then Lettie cried, "But she's *got* to come back. I need her. Surely she realizes that. We've got to find her."

"I don't think she means to be found. Not just yet."

"There's the services tomorrow. She can't be so hard-hearted as to miss that."

"It doesn't sound like hard-heartedness," Mady said, floundering. "I don't understand it. But—well, that's all. Tell Chan—"

"But, Mady—"

Mady said good-by and softly put down the receiver.

Chan would telephone as soon as he went back to Lettie's apartment. Or, if he didn't, Mady would keep telephoning to him. Nothing else to do. She didn't think that giving the note to the police would be helpful to anybody, certainly not to Nadine.

Yet suppose Clarence was right. Suppose—no, no, she told herself. Nadine would never have killed the senator. So then who?

She trudged up to her room feeling as if the weight of the world had lodged itself upon her shoulders. She couldn't see why she felt so strong a sense of compassion for Nadine. Nadine was always a person to take care of herself and everyone else. She was a strong, firm character, and she would do what she had determined to do though the heavens fell.

Perhaps Mady herself was all wrong. She couldn't possibly gauge whatever feeling lay between the senator and Nadine. She only knew of Stu's devotion to Lettie.

When the telephone rang, she ran to pick up the second-floor phone, but Clarence had already answered on another extension and was talking. "—Yes, of course. It's utterly shocking. Nobody could have used your glove—oh, I see. Well, perhaps anybody *could* have used it, but certainly not you. Now listen, Rose—"

Crushing an intense, even practical, desire to keep on listening, Mady put down her own telephone and thought, amazed, Rose?

It seemed to her that there was a solicitous, almost a tender note in her stepfather's voice.

But no, surely not!

Rose Chavez was kind but firm and, Mady suspected, not precisely pleased about the fact that one of her gloves had been used around a gun for any reason, let alone murder.

Could a man have seized one of Rose's gloves and thrust his own hand into it? Rose's hands were large, in proportion with her figure; still, a man's hand would have to be rather small, as small as Clarence's, for instance.

Oh, what an ugly thought! Mady pulled herself back and, willynilly considered another aspect: that tender note in Clarence's voice. Did it have any special meaning? She went back over Clarence's recent activities. Besides his endless prowling of auction rooms there was nothing—she qualified that conclusion; he was always fastidious about his appearance; had he been lately just a little more fastidious, just a trifle more fidgety about the set of his ties, his carefully manicured hands and his neat and attractive haircuts? And just a suspicious trifle more devoted in speaking of her mother, as if he wished to convince Mady and even himself of that unaltered memory—before making a new marriage?

Unexpectedly, she wondered what relation Clarence's second wife would have to her. Would she be a step-stepmother? She was going too far to entertain such fantasies!

Clarence was always considerate to all his friends, let alone to Rose, who, in his bachelor days, must have frequently dined and wined him as a pleasant addition to other guests in the vast mausoleum that she inhabited during all her years of widowhood.

Chan didn't telephone. Mady still didn't know what to do with Nadine's letter. At last, about four o'clock, she decided to go to Lettie's apartment to see if Chan was there. She went downstairs and found Clarence in the so-called library, which in fact had become a rather shabby, comfortable all-purpose spot for lounging, having meals, reading, watching television. He was sitting in a deep chair, his eyes closed. He jumped up when he heard her and on an impulse she said, "Clarence, who were you having lunch with that day you saw Stu?"

Clarence touched his neat mustache and smiled. "Why, really I don't—"

"Of course you remember! At the Four Seasons."

"Oh, yes, of course." He paused. "My broker—" he said rather tentatively.

"But you don't have a—" she stopped. Perhaps he had quietly handed over some of his modest income to a broker. But she didn't believe it.

"You don't have business luncheons at the Four Seasons. You go to your club. Or down in the Wall Street district."

"Well, I really don't remember. Perhaps I was alone—" He saw immediately that that wouldn't satisfy her. Very few people take themselves alone to any of New York's fine restaurants. He said at last, "Rose Chavez. If you must know." He caressed his mustache, discovered a wandering speck of pomade, which made a slight smear on his hand, and got out a finely monogrammed handkerchief to deal with it.

He went on, "You wouldn't want me to take Rose to some hamburger joint, would you?"

Mady had to smile. Rose was one of the few people in the ever-changing scene of New York who still kept servants, obsolete though the word was becoming (in fact, she had inherited them from her husband's mother and scarcely one could be much under a hundred); she still had secretaries and so-called security men, and even two bodyguards, one who acted as chauffeur, and one who rode along with the chauffeur. Riding shotgun, Chan had once commented jokingly.

Clarence had recovered his usual poise. "My dear child, I am deeply indebted to Rose for her hospitality. Especially in the days when I was a bachelor. She is one of my oldest and very dearest friends. One of your mother's, too. Are you on your way out? What are you going to do about that note of Nadine's?"

"Clarence, did Rose see Nadine with Stu that day at lunch?"

"I don't think so. She'd have mentioned it. Now then, your coat?" He was always skillful at changing the subject. He skipped past her to the hall closet and drew out her red woolen coat, tut-tutted a little, said, "Dear me, it's still wet from the snow. You'll have to wear a fur coat. Now don't pretend you don't care for furs. I've seen your eyes glitter. There now, I'll whistle up a taxi. You can't say I'm not useful sometimes."

After that she couldn't say, "Just what is all this talk of warm friendship with Rose Chavez?" In the taxi, bundled in a fur coat, with her handbag containing Nadine's note in her lap, she had a vagrant flicker of a question: could Rose possibly have had any reason to kill Stu? The answer was no.

Nobody seemed to have such a motive. Yet Stu had been murdered.

Larry Todd let her into Lettie's apartment, once she had been suitably announced by an interested doorman. A flood of flowery scents greeted her even as Larry put out his hands, drew her warmly in and told her he was very thankful she had come.

Larry was what Clarence must have been in his younger days; perhaps Clarence's affection for Larry was a matter of deep calling to deep. Not that Mady had ever perceived much depth in either of them. Larry was of his own age, nonchalant, brief, charming—always charming. However, he had a quicksilver mind; he was far more intelligent than Clarence, although Mady knew Clarence had a strong sense of self-preservation, demonstrated by his wily way of seeing to his own interests.

Larry was a tall young man—not really young, he had to be in his middle thirties if not yet forty—but he seemed youthful in the same way Clarence had contrived to seem youthful even in his late sixties. Larry was adept at all courtesies to ladies or to anyone. He was not handsome or especially attractive, really, but invariably gave the appearance of delighted pleasure at seeing anyone, showing the pearly white teeth that were one of his best features. He was always immaculately dressed, unlike Chan, who could be caught anytime in old tweed trousers and a turtleneck sweater.

Both Larry and Clarence were what might once have been called dandies in their clothes and manners, Mady thought and was then ashamed, for Larry took her coat, took both her hands and said, "My dear, I am so very glad to see you. That is, I don't mean glad—only—only—" He shrugged. "Help me with Lettie."

"What's the matter with Lettie? I mean—"

"I know what you mean. She's had a rough time and it's getting worse by the minute. People keep phoning. Of course, now we simply don't answer the phone. But all these flowers—" One of his neat white hands, manicured with rosy nails, swept around, but there was no need to point out the masses of flowers all over the living room, dining room, everywhere. "There's even one from the White House," he said, showing both respect in the way he spoke and a kind of inappropriate pride. "From the Senate, too, naturally. Many of his former colleagues, many of his friends. I do wish they could have been sent directly to the church, though."

"Why weren't they?"

"My dear! Haven't you heard! The President is coming for the services. And that means—" He spread out rather stubby fingers. "Such a to-do! Secret service everywhere. Men in plain suits, like businessmen, but somehow different. They are at the church. Across the street. Examining rooftops, windows, everywhere. They'll have to inspect every single basket or wreath before they permit it inside. Good thing it's not St. Pat's. Now that would be a real problem!"

"Oh, dear," Mady said helplessly.

"Surely you realize what an honor—"

"I do, but—all those people. There'll be reporters and cameras and—Oh, dear!"

"Stu would have liked it that way," Larry said.

Mady sighed. "It is an honor. But—"

"Everything will work out perfectly. Some men are coming soon to remove the flowers to someplace where the secret-service men will see to them. At least those are the orders. After the services, the flowers are to go to the hospitals. But just now there isn't much we can do but put up with them. Smells—" His rather blunt nose lifted in distaste. "Smells like a florist shop."

"Where is Chan?"

"Oh, I don't know. Yes, I do know. He's making arrangements for tomorrow. I'm to be one of the honorary pallbearers. I hate it." Larry led the way to the library, where he dropped into a chair, leaped up again and drew a chair forward for Mady. "Lettie is supposed to be resting. I promised her I'd stay until Chan gets back."

Tell Larry about Nadine's note? It would be sensible. Larry was supposed to be a very good and, indeed, brilliant lawyer.

As she hesitated, Larry wiped his forehead and pushed back his cap of black thick hair, which always shone as if he had polished it. "This has been a real horror, you know. Letting in the florists' men with all these flowers. Trying to keep the cards straight. They are there in that cloisonné vase. Lettie will have to get Nadine to sort them out and reply." His narrow face sharpened. "Heard anything about Nadine?"

Why the question should decide her against telling him just what she had heard, Mady couldn't have said. Later it occurred to her that it was Larry's quick mind, his instantaneous grasp of any situation that determined her; like Clarence, he might consider Nadine's note a confession. She'd wait for Chan, she told herself. He was more considerate of other people's feelings. She felt that Larry scorned human emotions even though, as a lawyer, he would weigh them.

She didn't reply but, trying to steer him from the topic of Nadine's absence, said, "You were here, at the party, weren't you?"

"Yes. Not for long, however. I don't like these big cocktail parties. Can't hear what anybody says."

She rather felt that Larry could have heard what everybody said anywhere and stored it away for possible use later on. However, he was popular—as Clarence had been—and likely to be rather choosy about accepting invitations. As Clarence had been, she thought again. But an invitation from Rose Chavez had always been seized upon, she was sure, and would be now, too, especially since she and Clarence suddenly seemed to be so intimate.

She steered away from the fantastic conjecture almost as if Larry's bright green eyes could read the thought that had shot into her mind. "When will Chan be back?"

"Soon, I hope." Larry glanced at the elegant, very expensive watch on his wrist. "I really must go soon."

"Wait, Larry, about the cocktail party. I know it is a foolish question but—but was there anybody—anybody at all who—"

"Who could have shot Stu?" Larry examined the toe of one of his handmade loafers. "Hard to say, isn't it?"

"But you knew him so well. You've known him for years. Why, he was about to enter your firm as a partner—"

"A junior partner," said Larry delicately. "That is, of course, he had the brains and know-how to be a senior partner at once, but that is not our policy—I mean, a newcomer and—but no, my dear Mady, I simply know of nobody at all who would even consider shooting anybody."

She had to insist. "Stu never mentioned any—any cause for anybody's enmity—any—"

"Any motive for killing him? No."

"Who was here, when you left?"

He thought that over, swinging the handsomely shod foot. "I don't think I can answer that precisely. I had gotten caught in a corner with that girl of the Brights. Not up to her surname, I might say. But after all the Brights—"

"I know. Rich clients of yours?"

He flicked a bright, green glance at her. "Now, Mady. It's not like you to be a naughty little cat. But if you want to know, yes. Her father is one of our clients. Head of—"

"Oh, never mind! After you got out of her clutches, what did you do? I mean, who else was here?"

"Just about everybody, I suppose. I didn't even say good-by to Lettie. I just quietly made an exit, feeling rather stupid about it, but after all one does that kind of thing. I got the elevator down at once without being nailed by anybody. Went home."

After sneaking out, Mady thought unkindly.

"Listen, Mady." He became very serious, almost authoritative. "If I had any idea of whoever it was who shot one of my best friends, don't you think I'd say so?"

"I don't know, Larry," she said flatly. "If the murderer happened to be—"

"A client?" Larry's eyes could look rather dangerous. "Really, Mady, do you think I have no sense of justice? No conscience? For heaven's sake, I'm a lawyer!"

No, you definitely are not going to get Nadine's note, she decided.

He listened, heard a bell or some commotion, rose lithely and went out. The commotion became more clearly audible; men were taking away the flowers. Larry gave them directions. "Look out—those lilies! Tell the secret-service men that the wreath from the President must be put just below the altar. Prominent place, I mean—also from the Vice-President and his wife. And the Speaker of the House and—of course the mayor and the senators and—"

The note from Nadine stayed quietly in her handbag, but it was rather like a ticking bomb. Nadine would have made quick and efficient arrangements for everything.

Then she heard Chan's voice. "Okay, Larry. Thanks. I'll go to the church early tomorrow and see that the flowers are all in place. If the secret-service men permit me. But I really cannot read the eulogy. You'll have to read it, Larry."

"Me! No! Not me—"

"You were Stu's closest friend, at least you had been friends forever—"

"No! I really can't, Chan!"

"But you're a lawyer. You're used to public speaking—"

"I'm not that kind of lawyer. I don't think I have ever appeared in a court in my life. You know our business—"

Chan's voice, husky with weariness, broke in. "But you can read. You can talk—"

"Don't give me that. What about you and your three seminars a week of graduate students? You don't lecture with your hands, do you? No, Chan, I won't—" There was a pause, then Larry said, as if stunned, "For God's sake, who wrote this? Where did it come from?"

"Oh, somebody in the White House, I suppose. Anyway it was sent to me by special messenger. It does show how highly he was regarded and—" Chan stopped and then said dutifully, "It's got to be read, I suppose. But I won't do it."

"From the White House? Certainly, you must read it. I've got to go, Chan. See you tomorrow at the church."

There was a slight stir as the men removing the flowers seemed to depart out the back way and Larry, at the elevator, said, "Don't be so downhearted, Chan. I am sorry. We are all sorry—"

"Here's the elevator," said Chan.

He then walked slowly across toward the library. When he came into the doorway, he was putting a piece of quite official-looking paper in his pocket. He glanced at her. "Oh, Mady. Thank God you are here. It's all just too much. Stu wouldn't have liked all this furor. I can't see any sense in a lengthy eulogy. Everybody who knew Stu

well enough to come to the services tomorrow knew him
well enough not to need all that—'' He gave her a swift,
intent look. ''What's on your mind?''

''Nadine. Read this.'' She dug the note from her handbag and handed it to him.

He read it twice slowly, gave a low whistle and sank
down into a chair. ''Where did this come from?''

She told him as much as she knew. ''Clarence is sure it
was Nadine who left it at the door. It must have been. But
do you think it is a confession? Those words scratched
out—''

''I can see. She 'didn't mean to hurt him.' That could
mean a number of things besides taking a gun and shooting
him. No, I cannot take this as a confession.''

''The police will,'' Mady said glumly.

''And I can't tell them to stop looking for her. They'd
pay no attention. Then—oh, wait until—I don't know.
Nadine herself may come back and explain.'' He sighed.
''But perhaps not. I *cannot* believe she killed him. This
note sounds more heartbroken than anything. Of course,
she must have done something, said something that she
felt had hurt him—not physically but—shall I keep this
note until we can decide just what is fair and right to do?''

''Oh, yes. You do look so tired. Can't you rest?''

He stretched out his long legs. ''I believe I am tired,''
he said with a flicker of surprise. ''Tomorrow after the
services, Larry and the tax appraiser and I will open Stu's
safe-deposit box. There may be some kind of useful
information there. You see, Mady, all the papers having
been taken from Stu's study—all of them, mind you, tax
records, canceled checks, everything—does suggest that
whoever shot him was afraid of him—or something he
knew. Whoever shoveled all the papers in his desk into
that handy paper shredder must have been in a hurry,
couldn't take time to weed out the special information that
concerned the murderer. If there were such a thing! But we

may find something of that kind in the safe-deposit box—
oh, Lettie! Feeling better?''

Lettie smiled at Mady and sat down on the sofa. ''I
thought I heard you talking about Nadine.''

There was a short pause. Then Chan said, ''She's not
been found. I really expected her to turn up in time
for—well, in time.''

''For my darling's last—'' Lettie put her hands over her
face.

Chan said, ''There now. By this time tomorrow it'll be
over—'' He addressed Mady. ''We decided that the burial
would take place in the family plot in the little town
upstate where my mother and father were buried. Grandfather,
too. Next week. Very quiet—''

Mady nodded. Lettie lifted her head. ''Oh, it's all right
about food tomorrow. A kind of buffet luncheon afterward.
You must separate them—I mean invite the people Stu
would have wanted to come back here—''

Chan nodded. Nadine's note had disappeared, certainly
into one of his pockets.

But Lettie had not forgotten it. ''Did you tell Chan
about Nadine's coming to see you?'' she asked Mady.
''And about the note? Where is it, what did she say?''

Chan answered. ''She was sorry she can't be at the
services tomorrow. She didn't say where she is. It really
isn't much—''

''Give it to me.''

Chan, taken aback, calmly turned over the problem to
Mady. ''What did you do with the note, Mady?''

''I—'' She swallowed. ''Left it where I—I—''

Chan came to her rescue. ''Where you found it, I
suppose. It is really not very important, Lettie.''

''Of course it's important if Nadine wrote it! I can't see
where she would go and why she would stay away—''

''We'll settle all that when she returns.'' He quickly
changed the subject. ''Lettie, have you ever used Stu's
safe-deposit box?''

"Why, no! I didn't even know he had one. That is, I suppose I didn't think of it. There are probably insurance policies and other papers."

"Probably. Larry, the tax appraiser and one of the detectives and I will open it tomorrow afternoon."

"Oh," said Lettie.

"We'll let you know the contents, of course. Now then, I'll be going. Mady, you will stay here with Lettie tonight, won't you?"

"Oh, no," Lettie cried. "That is, I do thank you, Mady. You stayed in this place last night and I am so very grateful but—but, Chan, it is not—I'll be so much easier in my mind if you'll stay again. I can't help it, but I do have a kind of sense of—danger, I suppose. That man who was shot after claiming to be my uncle and—and please stay with me, Chan."

Eleven

So Chan stayed and Mady went home.

"I'd back Lettie," Clarence had said, "about getting a man."

Mady then accused herself of all kinds of shocking frailties, such as jealousy, selfishness and distrust of Lettie, and reached home to find that Clarence wasn't there but had left a short note. "Concert and dining with Rose Chavez. Home early."

She had heard Mrs. Bayne—or Mrs. Bayne's friend—vigorously vacuuming at intervals during the day. Nobody was in the house now and it was so still that she had a twinge of sympathy for Lettie; at least there had been no shocking and tragic murder in Mady's home. On an impulse she went to the liquor cabinet. Never drink alone; whoever laid down that rule had probably never been alone and—all right—afraid, yet afraid of nothing in the house.

She was sipping with no stab of conscience whatever when Larry Todd arrived. She was actually glad to see him and said so. "The house is getting on my nerves. That or just the silence. Leave your coat there. I'm having a drink."

His bright eyes twinkled. "I didn't know you had taken to solitary drinking."

"I haven't." She ignored the blatant evidence of a glass on a table near her chair. "But honestly, Larry, I can see why Lettie hates staying alone in that apartment. It's so—"

"Scary," said Larry rather sarcastically.

"Big," said Mady repressively. "There's the cabinet. Pour your own, will you?"

He did so; he was as graceful and certainly as dapper as Clarence. His glass, however, had a cautiously light color, but then Larry was not one to indulge himself in drinking. He said, smiling, "I knew I'd find you here. I came to take you out to dinner. You can't sit around here alone. That is, I take it Clarence is not here."

For no reason at all, again, she didn't want to give Larry the slightest hint of her own pleasant suspicion of Clarence's interest in Rose Chavez. As Larry swirled around his almost nonexistent Scotch, she wondered briefly about Rose's reaction to Clarence's hobbies. Would she—if Mady's fantastic conjecture proved to be a fact—would Rose control Clarence's hobbies? (Or his being arrested as drunk and disorderly?) Or would she merely smile indulgently and kindly?

That was the likeliest response on Rose's part; she was vastly tolerant and generous; and since all those attendants she had retained (probably because they refused to leave) were in fact such very ancient retainers, Rose must look upon Clarence as a handsome young fellow. And indeed a very good and pleasant companion. It would be, Mady thought swiftly, a welcome marriage for her, relieving her of trying to keep strings of a sort upon Clarence. But that was really going too far. Marriage, for heaven's sake!

Larry said, "What are you smiling about?"

"Nothing. That is, I only happened to think of Clarence's latest escapade. Drunk and disorderly."

That did get through Larry's firm skin. He sat up. "Drunk and disorderly! Clarence!"

She told him briefly of the plaster Winged Victory episode. He sat back and actually took a long swallow of his drink. "Can't you get rid of him?"

"Oh, no! My mother asked me to see to him. He has a life tenancy to this house. And besides, I like him!" She finished rather defiantly, for Larry was not one who invited sentimentality.

He sighed. "Your problem. However, get a wrap and come out to dinner with me. Better than sitting here alone."

Indeed, it was better. She thanked him sincerely. "Give me time to change."

"You look lovely as you are," Larry smiled.

"I'm not sure where you are taking me, but wherever it is I am sure that a tweed skirt and sweater won't be correct." She rose and Larry gave a short laugh.

"All right. No hurry. It's early—"

She slid into the very simple, very chic and very expensive dress she had permitted herself to buy that winter, after a short struggle between what she considered her own good sense and her own feminine vanity. The dress was a bluish mauve and exactly right for an amethyst-and-diamond pin at the throat, one of the few jewels that had belonged to her mother that she had not left at the bank. It was inconspicuous but lovely, and she brushed her blond hair so it shone and used some lipstick and began to feel a little like herself, certainly more like herself than she had felt since the Valentine party.

His car was waiting, he said nonchalantly, and the sidewalks were cleared so she needn't bother with boots;

he eyed her black suede pumps with approval. Larry, admittedly, liked a fashionable appearance for anybody, especially, she suspected, any lady he invited to dinner.

"A handsome car." She settled herself into an extremely luxurious, leather-upholstered seat.

He got in behind the wheel. "I'm about to be made a senior partner. So I thought I could splurge a little. Wish it could have been a Rolls, though."

"Really? I think this is splendid enough. But then, of course, your father always had fine cars."

"Yes." He negotiated a traffic light and corner. "There have been times when I wished he hadn't liked the good things of life quite so well."

She remembered the Todd family clearly enough to remember also that they—at least his father—had indeed liked the good things of life. There was some tragedy about his father's death that she couldn't recall. She said, not liking the edge in Larry's voice, "I expect you are glad now that your father did enjoy life."

"I'm glad I had finished an education and had a job when he had the bad taste to fall down an entire flight of stairs. Drinking," said Larry and checked the car smoothly for another traffic light.

"Oh! I'm sorry. I didn't remember—"

"Why should you? However, I've managed to get along without any fine inheritance. Nothing to inherit, which you may not understand. Since you have all that money—"

"Oh, Larry! Don't—"

"I'm not going to. Here we are—" It was the Four Seasons.

They took the long flight of steps upward. Larry was evidently a frequent and respected client, for he was greeted impressively, chairs were pushed out, the wine steward came, huge menus arrived and smiles shone all around. Larry muttered something to the wine steward ending with "and a twist—" which was all Mady heard, and asked her for her choice of wines. She would leave that to him, she said.

After another brief conference with the wine steward, Larry said, "Let's forget our little bickering. I expect I'm overly sensitive about money. You have so much—"

"Not that much. Not like—well, like Rose Chavez."

Larry laughed. "Nobody's like Rose. At least very few people. Dear Rose. Loves everybody and yet, do you know I don't think anybody has ever imposed upon her. She's got very good practical sense."

"Is she one of your clients?"

He gave her a sharp look, as if to make sure she was not speaking with sarcasm, saw that she was not, and replied, "No. I wish she were. I should have chosen a different place for dinner. I forgot that Stu is supposed to have been here with a woman the day he was shot. Didn't Clarence see him here?"

"So he says. But he didn't recognize the woman."

"He must have seen her."

"Oh, yes, he knew it was a woman. He didn't see her face."

"I suppose," Larry said thoughtfully, "it was Nadine."

Nothing now would induce her to tell him of Nadine's note. Chan would have to decide what, if any, course they should take, but not Larry.

"He couldn't be sure."

A waiter brought her a martini. She hadn't heard Larry give the order. His own looked like Perrier water, bubbles and a twist of lemon peel. He lifted his glass to her and said, "Vodka. Did you ever try it?"

She replied politely, "Oh, yes, of course," and glanced around the big room, half afraid that Rose and Clarence would be dining there again.

If they were she didn't see them and Larry, making circles on the tablecloth with his glass, said flatly, "No use brooding over Chan, you know. Moping is another word for it."

"*Moping!*"

"Oh, don't pretend. Anybody can see it. Anybody but Chan. You'll never get him, you know, Mady."

"But you—why, I—you mustn't—Really, Larry!" She was sputtering indignantly, but could feel the color rushing into her face.

Larry laughed and put one small, rather stubby hand over her own on the table. "There, now. I'm only Larry. One of your friends. Remember, I danced with you at your debut party."

"But I—really, did you?"

He nodded. "You see? You had eyes only for Chan even then."

Her memory of that dance was a rosy one, flowers and white dress and young men and music—and, yes he was right, Chan. "But weren't you—"

Larry nodded. "A little old for that kind of party? My dear, reasonably polite, reasonably presentable but unattached young males are always in rather short supply. Oh, yes, I was there and danced with you and you looked straight over my shoulder every time Chan danced past with somebody else."

"All right. Why not?"

"I told you. You'll never get him."

She was suddenly angry and Larry knew it. "Now don't ruffle your feathers. It's your money, of course."

"My—but Chan—"

"Chan, too, has his own ideas about money. He's fully settled in as a teacher now and it is—really, Mady—it is his life. To put it bluntly, he can't support you in the manner to which you are accustomed and he's got much too good sense to leave his own profession and branch into something that might pay him more. Like his brother, actually."

"Stu was going to leave politics—but then—"

"Oh, yes." His face sobered. "Poor old Stu! I wish he'd never been proposed for a Cabinet post."

She looked up quickly. "Do you mean that appointment had something to do with the murder?"

"Oh, no, I didn't say that."

"You implied it."

"If I did—well, I have to admit, everything was going along well until the appointment was announced. Stu was going to enter our firm and seemed content. Lettie, too. It's true that at first he wouldn't have had a very fine income. But they could have struggled along—" Larry grinned briefly, "on Lettie's money. For a while, anyway. Stu would have been earning a very good income, was my guess, in a short time. But then the appointment—No," he said very soberly, "I don't say it had anything to do with his murder. But it was, in a sense, coincidental. That's all. Finish your drink. And stop brooding over Chan. I won't send you a bill for my advice, but that's it."

She really couldn't have given herself away to everybody! Larry merely had very sharp eyes. And Chan! She was sure that Chan liked her. Larry seemed to follow her reasoning in a disconcerting way. "You are determined about Chan. But I know him. He seems very quiet. He makes up his mind with care. His whole training, I suppose, has been to make the most exact decisions and analyses. I understand that and so must you. But what I think you don't understand is Chan's dislike for being supported by a woman—"

"I wouldn't think of—"

"Oh, yes, you would. Couldn't help it. Just suppose there was something you wanted, a house or a car or a dress like that one," he said astutely. "Or anything Chan couldn't give you. Do you think he'd be happy, standing by and almost literally forbidding you to use your own money? You ought to know Chan better than that."

"I never heard that money—not money like Rose's but, yes, some money, was a—a deterrent to a woman's happiness in life!"

"You've heard now," Larry said good-naturedly and leaned back as a most dextrous waiter began to serve them.

"And, also," Larry resumed as delicious fragrances

arose from the table, "Chan can be extremely forceful. When he wants to be. I saw him knock out a fellow once—he needed it, yes, but most of us would have simply let the thing go. I can't even remember what it was, some nasty remark about somebody—anyway Chan simply walked quietly up to the man and knocked him ass over—I should say—" Larry corrected himself, the social and tactful young lawyer, "base over apex. Nobody said a word. Chan just brushed his hands together and walked away. Still waters really do run deep with Chan. So, darling, don't make up your feminine mind to get the best of him because you can't, and I don't want you to get a dent in your charming little heart. The waiter wants to know what kind of dressing for your salad."

Mady got her breath, replied, and became aware of an odd little quiver of uneasiness. Larry did seem to be questioning in a roundabout way, probing very delicately, and she didn't know why or what he wanted to know. Larry said, "Now if Chan gave up his job in that two-bit college—"

"Ballantry College is nothing of the kind!"

"No money," Larry said, but watched her, she suddenly felt, rather slyly.

She said firmly and truthfully, "It's nothing of the kind. It ranks with the top—"

Larry lifted scant eyebrows. "With M.I.T.? With the Plasmas Physics Laboratory in Princeton? With—"

"With all of them," Mady flashed hotly. She sobered, though, thinking of Chan's explanation for the emergence of a small, little-known college into one with the undeniable prestige Ballantry College had acquired. An eminent and highly regarded physicist, tired of the inevitable, internecine feuds and factions which do often emerge in the academic world, had gone to Ballantry, thinking to find a small college with opportunities for his own research. As a result, Ballantry College was now a recognized force. And Chan was part of it, she thought proudly.

Larry munched on some endive and said, "No money—"

"Oh, yes. It is now very liberally endowed."

"That doesn't mean that Chan is liberally endowed." But he looked at her sharply over his salad and she thought again, what does Larry want to know? Why?

No answer, unless she accepted the fact as she knew it: Larry was simply that kind of person, incurably inquisitive, not always with generous intentions.

Yet she couldn't help suspecting he was probing for some particular nugget of information even though she couldn't discover what it was at the moment. Presently she said, "You needn't worry about me, Larry. We have enough, too much to think of now."

"You mean Stu."

"Yes. Did anyone object to his taking the Cabinet post?"

"Why, I—" Larry did look just faintly surprised at her change of subject, but she didn't intend to sit there and talk about the futility of any thoughts she might have adopted about Chan.

Larry chewed, swallowed and said slowly, "I see what you mean. The answer is no. Certainly not to the drastic extent of shooting him. Of course, the senior partners in my firm were disappointed. The papers had been drawn up and, I believe, signed. But it was all very agreeable. Stu said that he was sorry to be obliged to break his agreement with us. So he must have made up his mind to accept the appointment. But—no, there was no special grudge about it, for heaven's sake."

"Lettie says she didn't care. Anything Stu decided was good with her."

He nodded. "Same with Nadine. At least—" It seemed to her that the sharp, observing look came back into his eyes. "I don't know of anything to the contrary. She'd have been pleased, I should think, to go back to Washington, as she certainly would with Stu. He depended upon her. And she liked Washington. I am sure of that. Also she would have been top secretary to a Cabinet member. That's something in the Washington hierarchy. As a matter of fact, I rather think that Nadine could have acquitted herself very well indeed as a Cabinet member herself. She never could have been appointed, of course. She didn't—I mean hasn't the experienced and informed background, but she's unbelievably efficient. That is why," he said a little too slowly, "I can't believe that she crept in and shot Stu. It was an inefficient kind of thing to do, if you understand me."

"So inefficient," Mady said sharply, "that nobody knows who did it. Do you really call that inefficiency, Larry?"

"No," Larry replied equably. "No, I can't say that I do. But all the same there were some risks. Eat your dessert—"

She was rather surprised to discover that she had eaten a very large meal; she looked at the dessert with pleasure. I must have been half-starved, she thought, and tackled the enticing Strawberries Romanoff before her.

Coffee came. Larry had lapsed into a rather enigmatic silence. People were arriving. People were leaving. Gratuities were being slipped into palms. Charges were being signed. Larry signed his neatly after first, very exactly, totting up the items.

Mady tried not to look at the total, but couldn't help it. "Oh, Larry!"

He laughed. "Merely average. But Clarence must be in the chips if he can take a lady friend here to lunch."

"How do you know—"

"Had to be a lady friend. I might take a customer here or a lady, nobody else. Ready to go?"

A man in uniform presented Larry's car. The night was dark, but clear. Headlights shone upon heaps of soot-dotted snow along the sides of the streets.

Clarence was at home. Larry deposited her in the hall, said hello to Clarence, noted, Mady was sure, Clarence's elegant dinner jacket, accepted Mady's thanks for the lavish dinner and departed all in the most pleasant manner.

But suppose, she thought dismally as the door closed after him, just suppose he was right about Chan.

"Larry took you to dinner. Good. I like Larry." Clarence bolted the door.

"I don't," Mady said crossly.

Clarence lifted surprised, jet-black eyebrows. "Why on earth not? He's a brilliant, very successful young lawyer. You'd do much better to set your cap for him than for—"

It was contrary to polite custom to slap a stepfather. So Mady only snapped, or more accurately yelled, "Mind your own business," and fled upstairs.

She would never be able to sleep, she told herself angrily, ashamed of having let her feelings for Chan become so evident. Probably Chan himself knew it and was carefully sidestepping her advances. Advances? she thought, horrified. Perhaps not really advances, but if Larry had noticed and also Clarence and—no, Chan would show no knowledge whatever. Still waters do run deep. They ran just too deep in Chan for Mady herself to attempt to—well, what, wade out into them? She had had too much dinner and far more wine than was usual with her, so when she fell into bed, refusing to think of the dismal prospects of the day ahead and all the questions surrounding her and Chan and Lettie and—and everybody, she quickly fell into sleep.

Nadine arrived early the next morning.

Twelve

Again, however, it was only to leave a brief note. And a flower.

Mrs. Baynes, in view of the sad event of the day, had arrived earlier than usual to see to their breakfast. Mady was drinking coffee, Clarence was munching his way happily through a fresh brioche when Mrs. Baynes came in again. She did not condescend ever to place a message of any kind upon the small silver waiter which was kept in the hall for that purpose. She smiled tightly at Clarence and shoved the note at Mady. "For you. And there's a rose."

Mady read the note. "Dear Mady. Please put this flower near him. Nadine."

Mrs. Baynes also produced a large red rose wrapped lightly in cellophane. There was no card with it.

"Where is Miss Hallowell?" Mady hurriedly jumped up from her chair.

"The lady who brought that? Oh, she went away. Just handed me that and left." Mrs. Baynes gave a sniff at such *outré* behavior, but her eyes gleamed with curiosity. Mady sat down again. Clarence took the rose and said appreciatively, "A lovely one! How like dear Nadine!"

"Dear Nadine is going to have something to explain," Mady said crossly.

"My, my!" Clarence eyed her worriedly. "What on earth did you have to drink last night? Larry ply you with champagne?"

"No. Wine."

"Shows where his heart is," Clarence said blithely. "I'm going now. I'll see you at the church."

He skipped up the stairs. Mady was still drinking coffee, and looking at the rose Nadine had sent, when Clarence came down again, in correct morning coat. "I talked to Chan last night. I'm to be one of the honorary pallbearers. Larry, too. The President is expected. If his wife comes, she should be seated with you and Lettie—"

"Me!"

"Oh, yes. Lettie wants you and Rose to sit with her and Chan. Quite proper." He adjusted a glove over one small hand and said, almost with an untimely giggle, "Think of it! The President! And there'll be all those bigwigs from Washington. Friends and former colleagues of Stu's—and the governor and the mayor—dear me! Do I look all right?"

Mady nodded. Clarence said, "There's Rose's car. She's sending it for me. Me and two bodyguards! Dear me!" said Clarence again and at the door called back, "It's very cold this morning, Mady. Not snowing but a raw wind. Don't wear that red coat. Not suitable. Furs—"

The door closed smartly.

Mrs. Baynes came in. "Now don't cry, Miss Mady. It's all very sad, but—"

"I'm not crying, but thank you." Mady took Nadine's rose upstairs with her. Somehow the rose and Nadine's short note would have convinced her, if nothing else could have, that Nadine truly was in great grief and indeed had almost certainly been in love with Stu.

The point would be, that day, not to ignore the manner of Stu's death (that could not be done), but not to talk of it.

She did wear a fur coat and a hat. Chan met her at the church door; for once in his life, he, too, was correctly attired in formal morning coat, and looked so drawn and white that Mady put out both her hands. "Oh, Chan, I'm so sorry—"

"Yes, I know. Mady, Lettie wants you to sit with us. You and Rose Chavez and the President's wife if she—oh, there they are—"

Mady knew that at every vantage point there were secret-service men. She surmised their inconspicuous but alert presence all through the church. Just then the presidential escorts, running at a sober pace around the big car, came into view through the open church door. There were motorcycle policemen, blue-helmeted, everywhere. Other cars followed in sedate (perhaps watchful) procession. Mysteriously, word of the arrivals had spread; already there were people crowding the sidewalks. The President got out, turned to give his hand to his wife, who had her own quiet but charming dignity, and did not even try to avoid the flashes from cameras along the short walk to the church steps. Chan went to meet them as they came inside.

Apparently the President asked for Lettie, and he was shown to the room at the side where Lettie, Mady and Rose Chavez waited. He spoke to Lettie, and she lifted her heavy black veil to respond to his expression of sympathy. She shook hands with him and his wife. Rather to Mady's surprise, both knew Rose and again shook hands. But then Rose knew everyone.

The other dignitaries and their wives almost overflowed the small church where Chan and Stu had been christened and had always kept up their memberships. An usher at last touched Mady's arm and, with Lettie and Rose and the President's wife, led them with Chan down the aisle to the flower-bedecked altar. (So each basket and each wreath had been carefully examined by secret-service men.) But nobody questioned the rose Mady carried in her hand. Their pew was directly below the altar, so she did have a chance to put the flower beside Stu's coffin, the best she could do, because the casket was closed. Nadine would not have to know that. She thought that Rose saw her quiet and quick motion.

The service was short and solemn, ending with a psalm and a prayer; Stu would have liked it.

He wouldn't have been human, Mady thought, if the attendance had not pleased him. The President, it was true, had to hasten back to his airplane and several others joined him. Nevertheless, it was a very distinguished group that gathered, at Chan's quiet words of invitation, in Lettie's apartment for the buffet luncheon, decorously and efficiently served, but with plenty of liquid refreshment on the long serving table for all who chose to refresh themselves. Almost everyone did.

Larry made himself useful; he was here, there and

everywhere and seemed to know everybody. He was indefatigable, properly subdued, always polite. Clarence devoted himself mainly to Rose, and as people began to leave, he escorted her down to her car and did not return. Mady, left almost alone except for the grave-mannered caterers, discovered that Chan, too, had disappeared, and Larry with him. They must have gone to the bank; probably the bank had obligingly kept its vault open for the inspection of Stu's safe-deposit box. It could have waited at least another day, Mady thought, and then it occurred to her that one of the faces crowding the dining room had certainly been vaguely but disturbingly familiar. It took her a moment to run down that feeling of unpleasant recognition before she realized that the man was Captain McEvor, dressed carefully in a well-tailored suit, but with extremely watchful eyes.

Well, he was gone, too.

Lettie had disappeared sometime, quite soon, she thought, after their return from the church. She went into the library where Clarence's Indian offered neither counsel nor solace and then to Lettie's room where the door was open. Lettie was not there. She was, it developed, nowhere in the apartment.

Perhaps she had gone with Chan and Larry; it seemed proper for Stu's wife—widow—to be present when his safe-deposit box was opened.

Mady was suddenly very tired; the events of the past days seemed to surge around her in kaleidoscopic fashion, giving her flaring glimpses of this face and that and whirling on. She wondered vaguely how many people she had spoken to that day, how she had remembered their names, if she had; Senator this, Congressman that—Cabinet member so and so; there were two generals and at least one admiral. The admiral was in dress blues and thus she recognized him as an admiral; unluckily, she had felt at the time, she also recognized a tiny yellow ribbon among the miniatures that decorated his chest and, making conversation, asked him how he had gotten the Congressional Medal of Honor. Instantly, she was embarrassed; surely only a brash civilian would have dared ask such a question. But the admiral's blue eyes twinkled. "Well, my dear, it's simple. Something must happen. You must be there when it happens. And somebody must see you there when it happens." She didn't know what she had replied, but whatever it was the admiral had nodded at her, smiling kindly.

So now it was over, but the very grim fact remained; someone had shot Stu Channing.

Whoever it was, it was not Nadine. The rose was Nadine's sad tribute not only to Stu's death but to her love for him. Mady was now sure of that if she had ever doubted it, as she hadn't really, after receiving Nadine's first note.

She longed to see her. Nadine had a very analytical mind and she might have a suggestion about Stu's affairs which might—just might—lead to his murderer.

There was no use in trying to find Nadine. The police, she thought dismally, might as well give up their search for her. If Nadine chose to remain hidden, nobody in the world would find her.

Sometime, she must emerge. But not until she herself decided upon that course.

On the other hand, Mady reflected, staring absently at the Indian who kept an enigmatic silence (he couldn't really help that, she thought rather wildly), on the other hand if Nadine actually had a good idea as to Stu's murderer she was almost sure that Nadine would eventually come forward with that knowledge.

It was close to five o'clock and darkening when Chan and Larry returned, and they had found one unusual thing in the safe-deposit box. Chan asked for Lettie at once.

"She's not here. I thought she had gone with you. Did you find anything that—anything?"

Larry dropped his topcoat and then dropped himself

neatly in a chair. Chan said, "Yes. That is—oh, the usual, birth certificate, marriage certificate, university diploma, law degree—all that, a copy of the will—or I believe this was the original, wasn't it, Larry?"

Larry nodded.

"A passport—"

Larry spoke then softly, "He must have been planning a trip to Europe and Africa. It was visaed and ready."

"A vacation, before he got down to work again?" Mady hazarded.

Chan's face was very still. Larry nodded, but his eyes were bright. "May have been intending that. Lettie should know. However—"

"I don't understand where Lettie has gone," Chan said. "She must have just walked out."

"I suppose she felt she had to get away until all the guests were gone."

"It's been rather a long time. We'll have to ask her what she knows about this—" Chan turned to Larry, whose face had assumed its ferrety look.

"Oh, we'll ask her," he said. "Also, we'll have to talk to Rose Chavez."

"Rose!" Mady cried. "What on earth has Rose to do with anything in the safe-deposit box?"

Larry said, "Did Lettie have access to the safe-deposit box?"

Chan said soberly, "You know she didn't, Larry. She told me that. I told you. Besides, the man at the desk showed us the cards. All Stu's signatures. Lettie knew nothing of the box."

Larry said thoughtfully, "She must have known that Stu carried all that insurance for her."

Chan nodded. "When Lettie gets back we'll talk to her."

"And ask her when—and why Stu was planning a trip abroad," Larry said softly. "But why would Rose give a check to Stu?"

"Rose!" Mady cried again.

"For fifty thousand dollars," said Larry, watching her. "Fifty—"

"A check made out to Stu," Chan said. "Obviously not cashed."

"Dated in January," said Larry. "I know who Rose's business manager is. But there's no use trying to get any information out of him. Much as his place is worth."

Chan gave him an annoyed look. "We don't have to talk to him or anybody but Rose. She'll tell us why she gave this to Stu—"

"And why he accepted it?" Larry asked very softly.

For no perceptible reason color came into Chan's face and anger in his eyes. "He didn't cash it. Whatever she was paying for—"

"Rose," Mady said blankly. "I don't understand."

"Rose will explain it," said Chan and went to the telephone. After speaking in a normal voice and then shouting, he put it down. "That old butler must be well over a hundred. Can hardly hear. But can still say the proper things. Rose is not in. She'll get in touch when she returns."

"This check," Larry eyed Mady, "is in Rose's handwriting, her signature, of course, and the entire check. Nothing that came from the Chavez Industries offices. Any one of them."

"Any one—" Mady said blankly.

Larry made an impatient gesture. "My dear child! A person with Rose's money needs—at any rate, prefers a certain diversification of interests. This may have been old Walldon's idea, he's the top man for Chavez Industries. Rose was certainly guided by his business judgment. So I can't see why she should pay Stu such a sum for, say, unofficial lobbying, since he was out of office. Still, he would have some influence, a great deal probably. But what Rose would want to lobby about—" He lifted his handsomely tailored shoulders.

Chan shoved his hands in his pockets, walked to a window and back again. "What gave you that idea, Larry? Rose wouldn't have tried to get Stu to influence any sort of vote. Besides, in January he was entirely out of office. Just put that out of your head."

Larry shrugged again. "The most sober, dignified people can do the oddest things, you know. Or would know if you were a lawyer."

"May I see the check?" Mady asked, hoping rather wildly that it was not, in fact, written by Rose Chavez.

Chan shook his head. "We had to leave it there in the box. The appraiser wasn't sure whether it was an asset or not, at least he seemed uncertain. Maybe he had never encountered an uncancelled check for any sizable amount. Or perhaps Rose Chavez's name—oh, no matter. The check is still there. For the moment. Don't get upset, Mady. Rose will explain it."

Larry eyed his polished shoe. "Seems odd Lettie's not back yet. It really is dark and New York streets at night, a woman as expensively dressed as Lettie always is—"

Chan looked at his watch, glanced at the darkened window, jerked on another lamp. "She's not been mugged," he said, as definitely as if he were assuring himself. "The police would let us know."

Mady was momentarily diverted. "One of them was here for that buffet luncheon. McEvor. I didn't see Swain."

Chan thought it over. "I didn't see either one."

"Maybe they've got some different men on the case," Larry suggested.

"Larry, they are both good men. Doing this job as well as they can—"

"Oh, I'm sure of that, Chan," Larry broke in. "New York's finest."

"I mean it. We've got to help all we can. Stu *was* murdered."

"I'm not saying we shouldn't help," Larry was perfectly pleasant. "I'm just saying that it's possible this—this tragic affair is more prominent in people's eyes than most homicides. Newspapers. Television. The President today. Half the Senate—or at least many dignitaries. Not to mention the mayor and the governor."

"I know. The police certainly feel that Stu was so much in the public eye that they will be obliged to put some of their best men on the job. And keep them there. Of course the sheer manpower of the police is not unlimited. But McEvor and Swain both—"

The telephone rang. Mady was nearest so she took it as Chan leapt for it. It was not Rose.

"Mady?" Lettie said in a faraway, unsteady voice.

"It's Lettie," Mady told them over her shoulder. "Yes, where are you? We've been worrying about you."

"I'm coming home. Is everything all right?"

"Why, yes. That is, Chan and Larry had to go to the bank and I thought you had gone with them."

"No, I—did they find anything of interest?"

"No. That is, yes, insurance for you—" She glanced questioningly over her shoulder at Chan, who said, "Very generous. Tell her not to worry—"

"Chan says a very generous policy and not to worry, but, Lettie, where have you been?" She had an instant's fantastic surmise that Lettie had tracked down Nadine or had been approached by Nadine.

"Oh, just walking and walking," Lettie said, her voice very faint.

"But where are you now?"

"Pay phone. Near the Metropolitan. I couldn't stay at home, Mady. I couldn't stand it another moment. All those people. So I—I just left."

"Get a cab and come home, will you?"

"Oh, yes." The telephone clicked.

"No weather to walk in," Larry said after Mady had repeated the brief conversation. He rose. "I think I'll go now. Let me know—"

His ferrety look was in his face; his voice was as smooth as butter.

"He's up to something," Chan said as the elevator took Larry out of sight.

"I know. He's got some notion about that check of Rose's. Chan, I didn't tell you. I didn't have a chance. Nadine came to our place this morning. She left a rose—"

He listened to that, biting his lip. "Poor old Nadine! That is, she's not so old. But she—oh, I may be wrong, Mady. But I think—"

"So do I," Mady said. "I'm sure of it. I did put the rose as near—as near Stu as I could."

Chan's face warmed. "Dear Mady. That was right. I'm glad."

"Nadine is so brave, so strong and—I do wish she'd come forward and—and—"

"Tell everything she knows even if she doesn't know anything that would help the police. Mady, I'm not a bit sure that we are right not to report Nadine's notes. They've really got some fine officers on the job, experienced and damn smart. But they have just so many men available. Yet the case will continue to be a sensation until they get results." He broke off. "I wish Rose would let us hear from her."

"Rose is having dinner with Clarence."

"*What!*"

Mady nodded. "I'm sure of it. At least—yes, I think so."

A faraway twinkle shone for a second in Chan's eyes. "Do you mean there's a thing going there?"

"I think so. I really do think so."

Chan thought for a moment. "Good for Clarence. Good for Rose. She's been a widow for—I can't remember—ten years or so. Lonely, I should say, in spite of all her interests and do-gooding and parties and—"

"Servants. Ancient or not she's got them." Mady heard the tinge of bitterness in her own voice and laughed. "Never mind me, Chan. I'm only a woman, and a housekeeper—''

"A marriage like that for Clarence—that would be a good thing for you, too."

She sighed. "Yes. I suppose so. I'm accustomed to Clarence, you know. He exasperates me, but—"

"But you like him. I told you so." Chan really smiled warmly and at least affectionately.

But there was a click across the living room and Chan sprang to the door. Lettie came in.

"Hello." She sank down into the sofa beside Mady, who said uneasily, "Why in the world did you go for such a long walk in those pumps?"

"Darling, don't scold. I sat on a bench in the park for a long time. I couldn't, I simply couldn't stick it out here. Everybody saying things to me and shaking my hand and I couldn't stand it. I had to leave."

Chan said, rather slowly, "You'd better get into dry things. That is—"

"Oh, it's not snowing. Just unpleasant. What about the safe-deposit box, Chan?"

He repeated its contents to her briskly. "And also," he finished, "an uncashed check from Rose Chavez."

Lettie sat up. "From Rose! What on earth—"

"Nobody knows. We hoped you would."

"But I don't. I haven't an idea. I can't imagine! Wait a minute. I'll get into something warmer—"

"At any rate she didn't get her shoes wet," Mady said as Lettie vanished along the corridor. "She couldn't have walked as far as she thought she had. She doesn't know about Rose's check. I know Lettie. She's too—too open and frank to hide anything."

"She's too secretive to tell us where she's been all this time. My guess is," Chan said coolly, "she's been with Nadine. Doesn't want to tell us. Probably Nadine made her promise not to tell where she is."

"Oh," Mady considered it and finally nodded. "I thought of it, but—"

"We are all wrong to keep this Nadine business from the police. This decides me. How about you?"

"I don't know. Nadine's note. And that single flower. Really, I do believe that if Nadine knew anything at all to help the police she'd come forward."

They fell into a thoughtful silence, debating, both of them probably. It is not always easy to tell right from wrong; Mady realized she was getting into old and tried, but always deep, waters.

Chan said, "It isn't easy, is it?"

Lettie came back. She had slid into a long, warm housecoat, soft brown velvet with a daffodil yellow scarf at her throat. She had brushed her hair; the lovely curls were glowing.

"Rose must have asked Stu to accomplish something for her. I can't guess what. But that was to be his pay. Don't you agree?"

"I don't know," Chan replied after a moment.

Lettie sat down with a tired sigh. "Nadine would know. I do wish she would come to see me or—or something. Nadine always knew Stu's business affairs. By the way, an odd thing. Did the police take my gun?"

Chan said blankly, "*Your what?*"

"My gun, of course. I got out this scarf and I always keep my gun in the drawer with it. Under some other scarves, you know. It's not there."

Thirteen

Chan looked as if somebody had struck him. "I didn't know you had a gun."

"Why, of course. Stu got it for me. When we were

living in Washington. Seems to me, cities have changed so much. No woman likes to be out at night or alone at night for that matter. So Stu got a gun for me.''

"Now, see here, Lettie—'' Chan moistened his lips. "Tell me about this gun. How long have you had it?''

"I told you. That is, I don't remember just when Stu got it for me. But—oh, it must be two or three years ago.''

"Did he have it registered?'' Mady thought that Chan's face showed just a shadow of relief.

If so, it was short-lived. "I don't know,'' Lettie said. "I suppose so. If that is the law.''

"It is the law,'' he said shortly. "Now, Lettie, try to remember. When did you last see it?''

Lettie ruffled up her shining auburn curls, blinked and said slowly, "Chan, I just don't remember. I never used it, you know. I—no, I *can't* remember. I just supposed it was there.''

"Loaded?''

"I don't know that either—well, yes. I expect Stu would have loaded it for me. I think I've heard him say that there's not much use having a gun around unless it is loaded. Oh, dear, if only your gun hadn't been here, Chan. And loaded and—there, Chan, I wouldn't hurt you for anything!'' There were tears in her eyes.

"I know, I know. But this gun—your gun! Did the police search your room?''

"Yes, no—oh, I'm not sure; there were so many of them all over the place. The gun was in the drawer for scarves and things like that, just below the drawer for jewels.''

"But did they question you about it?''

Lettie shook her head. "No. Not a word. But they must have taken it. Who else would even search my room?''

Mady thought suddenly of Clarence's unnerving comments upon the average hard-working policeman's reaction to the display of lavish jewels like Lettie's. She said abruptly, "Are all your jewels still here? Safe, I mean?''

"Oh, yes, I think so. I feel sure my emerald necklace is somewhere around. I had it just before we found Stu. But not my diamond bracelet. Stu had that."

"That hasn't turned up?" Chan asked.

Lettie shook her head. "I didn't have it insured. Stu always said, what's the use of carrying insurance? It costs so much and as a rule is not necessary." She smiled sadly. "He used to say, go ahead and wear the jewelry."

It sounded like Stu, always indulgent to his Lettie.

"I'm sure the police will make the round of pawnshops and well-known fences. This Ernest Wilkins! Have the police questioned you again about your uncle—"

"No! He wasn't my uncle! I don't care what he or anybody said."

"Of course not. But the police—I don't think they are sure of that."

"But why not? Wouldn't I know?" Lettie cried.

"Not if you never saw him before," Mady said rather crossly. Sheer weariness and a kind of emotional fatigue were making her irritable. She also felt in her bones that Chan would feel it his duty to stay with Lettie at least for that night. Possibly even until Lettie had made some permanent living arrangements. She said, "Are you going to keep this apartment, Lettie?"

"Why, I haven't had time to think of anything like that," Lettie said desolately.

"There's no hurry." Chan was, quite naturally, Mady told herself, sorry for Lettie. He said, "I don't think you listened about Stu's life insurance. It's quite a sum—"

"Oh, yes, I heard that. I didn't know he was carrying so much insurance. But it was like him, you know, Chan. So like him—"

"Good night," Mady said and didn't wait for Chan to accompany her. However, he did follow her to the entrance hall where she rummaged for her coat.

"I'm going to talk to Rose as soon as I can—"

"I'll ask Clarence where she is as soon as he comes

home!" It came out with rather a snap. She called back to Lettie, "Good night."

She thought Lettie answered as she pushed the elevator button. Chan stood beside her, looking very serious.

"Are you upset about something, Mady?"

"Oh, no! That is, yes, certainly. But I'm tired—this morning and all those people."

"I've got to stay with Lettie tonight."

"Naturally." Why was the usually prompt elevator so slow? "I'm glad the President came. And all those notables and—the doorman will get me a taxi—"

"I'll ring down—" Chan began as the doors silently opened and Mady moved inside the elegant cage.

She went out to a waiting taxi, escorted by a solicitous doorman who said, disappointedly, "We all thought that the President would come here, too—"

"He didn't. Thank you."

She was so terse that the doorman moved back, startled.

Very soon, surely, Lettie would decide upon some way of living that did not require Chan's constant attendance.

When she reached home, Rose and Clarence were sitting comfortably in the library watching television.

She wouldn't wait for Larry or Chan to inquire about that check; it might be none of Mady's business, but on the other hand—

She put down her coat and saw the very last of a picture of the President and his party leaving the church. Clarence said, "That was a nice picture of you, Rose. Not as lovely as you but a nice picture."

"Hello," said Mady.

She wasn't sure; they were sitting together on the sofa, but she felt that Clarence's small hand was gripping Rose's hand. If so, they drew apart not guiltily, not even embarrassed, merely politely, as Clarence stood. "My dear! We thought you were never coming home! Where have you been?"

"Lettie's, of course." Strike while the iron is hot, she

thought. "Rose, dear, they opened Stu's safe-deposit box at the bank this afternoon."

"Oh," said Rose. "Naturally. Although it does seem a little premature, doesn't it? Still, under the circumstances of Stu's death and the police inquiry—did they find anything of interest?"

"Stu's life-insurance policies, marriage certificate, all that. And also—" she did gulp a little here, "also a check written by you, Rose, for a large sum of money."

"What?" Clarence cried, "for heaven's sake—"

Rose seemed unmoved. "Oh, they found that, did they? Poor Stu! He didn't cash it then."

Clarence blinked rapidly. "But my dear, Rose. Don't you look at your bank statements?"

Rose was completely unperturbed; she smiled at Clarence. "Oh, my personal checkbook and bank statements, of course. Just domestic things! Groceries, servants, purchases. Anything else goes through the Chavez Industries. I mean stock purchases or sales or anything of the kind."

Clarence turned to Mady. "A large check—"

Rose, however, replied, still placidly, "Fifty thousand, as I recall."

"Fifty—but that is a very large sum of money!"

Rose apparently decided to say nothing to that. Yet somehow Mady had a notion that behind her placid face a very good brain was going full tilt. Clarence only stared at Rose.

Mady said, "It was dated, I believe, sometime in January—"

"Yes. I believe so." Rose was still completely undisturbed. "Dear Stu! I daresay Chan and Lettie—or, of course, the appraisers will return it to me. I really must go home, Clarence. It has been a very tiring day. I saw you put that rose near Stu, Mady. It was a dear and loving little gesture. I wish Stu could have known. Perhaps he did," she added gently. "Is my car at the door, Clarence?"

"I think—I don't—I'll see—" Clarence, his white hair looking rather ruffled, shot toward the door.

Rose said, "Don't worry about that check, Mady. It was only for something I wanted Stu to do for me. But then his invitation to become a Cabinet member came along. Of course, he couldn't have any conflict of interest, so he didn't cash it. I expect he simply put it in the safe-deposit box when I first gave it to him and then—yes, Clarence. Thank you. No, you needn't take me home. Good night. Thank you for dinner. I'll see you soon." She kissed Mady lightly. "Try to rest, child. This has been a—a very trying time." She allowed herself to be folded into a sable coat.

She only hoped that Rose felt as affectionate toward Clarence as he, obviously, felt toward her. He came back from seeing her into her car and shut the door with a bang. "Really, Mady! It wasn't nice of you to question Rose like that. But *why*! That is a large sum of money! What did Rose expect Stu to do for her? A bit of informal lobbying, maybe?" said Clarence reflectively. "He could have done a very good job of it if he chose to. Knew all the right people, all the angles, all the strings to pull—"

"Good night," said Mady.

"Not even a nightcap?" All at once Clarence was wistful and appealing.

"No!" But as she reached the top of the stairs she relented and called "Good night—" over the banister.

She shouldn't have questioned Rose about the check. Clarence was right. Far better to have left that to Chan.

Surely Larry had a particularly inquisitive look on his narrow face when he talked of the check. She was sure that he intended to do a little, or a great deal, of exploring for himself.

Stu wouldn't have leaned toward lobbying as a profession; after all, he had promised to enter the law firm in which Larry was a partner.

She was ready for what she felt would be an entirely sleepless night when she realized that part of her low spirits were simply due to hunger. She must have nibbled at this or that during the luncheon at Lettie's apartment after the service, but, in fact, she had eaten almost nothing all day and nothing at all for dinner. She got into her warm dressing gown and slippers and tiptoed down the stairs.

"Needn't creep around like that," Clarence said from the dining room. "I heard you. I can't sleep either."

He was sitting at the table, his curly white head had apparently just risen from his arms, still crossed disconsolately upon the table. A glass of milk stood beside him. "I'm upset, Mady. So very—you see that *was* Rose's glove."

"Rose's—why, yes. But she didn't have anything to do with shooting Stu."

She went on to the kitchen and began to hunt through the refrigerator. She had a sandwich and a glass of milk for herself when she returned to the dining room where Clarence still sat, immobile and gloomy. "But she might have," he said dismally.

"Shot Stu? For heavens sake, Clarence, pull yourself together!"

"She's worried. I can tell. She didn't like talking about that check."

Mady sat down. "Nobody in the world could blame Rose for a dreadful thing like that."

"I don't know," Clarence said miserably. "I just don't know. Rose is—is very determined—in her way. Mady, do you realize that I met your dear mother at a party Rose gave?"

"Why—no, I don't think I remembered that. If I ever knew it."

Clarence eyed her thoughtfully. "Sometimes you really do resemble your dear mother," he muttered. "Her blue eyes. Her lovely blond hair. Her—I can't describe it—but something of that mischievous kind of laugh in her eyes. You are taller than she was, though."

"Ten feet at least," Mady said shortly.

"Now, Mady. I know your height. Five feet five. I know

because I'm only a few inches taller than you. But you're not a cuddly little thing. That's right. Not like Lettie," he added, rather unfortunately from Mady's point of view.

She munched on her sandwich, swallowed and said irritably, "Isn't there something in Leviticus about not marrying your brother's widow—"

Clarence's troubled eyes brightened. "Why, of course! That's what all old King Henry's troubles were supposed to be about. Wanted to get rid of his first wife because she had been married to his brother. But many years after his own marriage he wanted to marry Anne Boleyn so—"

Mady rudely interrupted. "Dear Clarence, I do remember that much of English history. I'm sure I can't think why that occurred to me."

"I'm not a fool, I can guess why," Clarence said succinctly. "Lettie really is in a very difficult situation right now. I think the least Chan can do is to rally around." The common sense in his words was rather diminished when he added, "Of course Lettie is a very charming woman. Appealing." He nodded his white head as if recovering from his gloom and stroked his mustache in a knowing man-of-the-world way. "Yes, she is a most attractive woman. Now she," he said warmly, "is the cuddly type."

"And I'm not!" Mady spoke so sharply that she bit her tongue.

"No, but you are a very—dear me, don't you ever look in the mirror? Very lovely. Very desirable. Very. But if Lettie has got her eyes set on Chan as her next husband, I'd advise you to get to work on Chan." Clarence assumed a judicial air. "I really think you must not let your pride interfere. Show Chan how you feel about him. Or, of course, there's Larry. Now he'd be a much better match for you—"

"*Clarence!*"

"Now, Mady. Do you know that when you get mad your eyes turn very dark blue and flash like lightning and—now your mother never let herself show anger. She was always a lady.''

"So, I'm not a lady either!"

Clarence was all contrition. "I didn't say that. I didn't—" His face became thoughtful. "I suppose it's your father coming out in you. He was said to be a quite ruthless businessman. And his father before him, Amyas Smith, Senior. Runs in the family—"

"Clarence," Mady began dangerously.

"There now. I've apologized—I—the fact is I want to ask you something."

"Go ahead," Mady said shortly, wishing by no means for the first time that slapping a stepfather was merely a polite gesture of disapproval.

But Clarence's next words did not prove to be quite the thunderbolt he evidently expected them to be. "Do you think sixty-five is too old for marriage?"

"Sixty—"

"I should have said sixty—" he hesitated and, without any visible remorse, added a couple of years. "Sixty-seven, perhaps. What do you think?"

"If it's Rose, I think it's great. Go right ahead. Have you asked her yet?"

"Oh!" He was deflated and meek. "I didn't realize that you saw so much."

"How can anybody help it! Dancing attendance, taking her to dinner, going around in her car. With the bodyguards," she added mischievously, in spite of herself. "Now, Clarence, whatever your age is, you'll never be old."

His face brightened. "You really mean that?"

"Yes," said Mady with conviction. Her stepfather simply was not a person to grow old. Possibly, it occurred to her, that was because he had had so few encounters with the harsh realities of life. As a rule, all Clarence had ever had to do was be himself and people rallied to him. However, Detectives McEvor and Swain had not seemed overcome by Clarence's pleasant, if rather feckless, character.

Wooden Indians! Winged Victory in plaster! Drunk and disorderly! But he had not been drunk; he had only wanted the cab driver to do something the cab driver did not want to do—oh, stop it, she thought, and took another bite of sandwich.

"If you eat so fast you'll make yourself sick." Clarence spoke with a kind but detached interest. In any event, he had drifted away from his unwelcome talk of Chan and Larry.

"But the point is," he fidgeted with his mustache again. "Is this the time to bring up the subject to Rose? I mean matrimony and—"

"Any time, I should think."

"Yes, but—if that glove—if she shouldn't be able to explain that check so as to satisfy those detectives—or anybody—I mean," Clarence wriggled but went on, "just suppose they say there was her glove showing gunpowder stains. There is that check. If she shot Stu, as someone certainly did, he couldn't have cashed the check, and fifty thousand dollars—"

Mady didn't quite choke on the last crumb of sandwich. Indeed, she felt infinitely better after she had also finished the milk.

"Nobody in the world would suspect Rose Chavez of killing a man—someone she had known probably all his life—for fifty thousand dollars. With all her money!"

Clarence brightened for a second, but then sobered again. "No. I'm sure nobody could seriously believe that she could have shot Stu just for that. But listen, Mady. Will she think I'm after some—just some of her money? Doesn't cost much to keep me—that is, what do you think?"

She rose and on a ridiculous impulse stooped to kiss the top of his head, which was at least a change from wanting to slap him. "I think she'll take you and you'll both be very happy. Good night—"

She left him smiling, pleased, yet still, she thought, a trifle solemn.

But she might have helped two people on the path of true love, she thought wryly, crawling back into bed again.

She hadn't done much to help herself. Clarence was right about that. But how can a young woman of any—any spirit, she thought defiantly, turn herself into a cuddly little creature.

"Can't be done," she said aloud.

Clarence was right about the kind of day it had been, tiring not only physically, but emotionally exhausting.

Morning was better in one way, for nothing at all happened except that the newspapers were filled with accounts of all the prominent persons who had paid their respects to Stu. She read the news almost phlegmatically, still feeling rather drained and still stubbornly haunted by a remembrance of Chan's loyalty to Lettie. It did him credit, she told herself; it was like Chan. That reflection was no help.

Lettie certainly was an appealing little woman. Clarence had had to say just that! It made Mady feel enormous, tall, strong, capable of anything but certainly not cuddly.

Mrs. Baynes, probably feeling that she had overexerted herself by giving so much time to Clarence and Mady the previous day, did not turn up at all. There was not even the comforting hum of a vacuum going, or the fragrance of cooking from the kitchen. The telephone obstinately did not ring.

Clarence was nowhere to be seen or heard, and she noted with a qualm that a page from the newspaper, showing art galleries and their auctions for the day, lay at his end of the table.

The day was contrarily sunny and mild. Gray sulkiness would have been more in tune with her feelings. The morning went on, the grandfather's clock in the hall kept ticking loudly. Mady wondered idly if that particular grandfather had been, as Clarence had suggested, a little more ruthless in his business dealings than had been strictly necessary. Probably not; all the Smiths had stayed well within the limits of the law, which they had been too prudent, she was sure, to overstep. She considered vaguely Rose's really great wealth; she knew almost nothing of Rose's one-time husband, Jacob Chavez, now gone for ten or twelve years. But nothing about him mattered and Rose was almost certainly going to be her stepmother! She tried to find that amusing, but failed.

During the bright afternoon she tore herself away from the telephone and the silence of the house and went for a walk. Her comfortable red coat was not in the hall closet. Probably the previous day Mrs. Baynes had noted that it was still damp and sent it to the cleaners; it would be like her, for she often made rather dictatorial, if helpful, decisions about household affairs. Mady yanked out the fur coat she had worn the previous day and started out for what developed into a long walk—until it was suddenly an early, clear, spring dusk and she hurried for home, firmly convinced all at once that Chan had been trying to telephone her—or even, just perhaps, trying to find her at the house.

She was wrong. Larry Todd's beautiful car stood at the curb and he got out as she came along. "I saw you on Park Avenue and I've been waiting."

He was, as always, elegant, very spruce, and surely there was a kind of triumphant shine in his green eyes. "Aren't you going to ask me in? I do have some news."

"Of course." She dug her house key from her handbag.

He took the key from her hand with all the automatic courtesy, she thought unkindly, of a practically professional man-about-town. He unlocked the door, held it for her, followed her into the still-silent house and said, "I have a little news. Not much. But I think you'll find it interesting. It concerns Chan."

Fourteen

"*Chan!* What? They haven't—they couldn't have accused him!"

"No. Don't look like that, Mady. He's all right. If you'll be kind enough to offer me a drink—I'll mix it; I know where to find things."

"Of course, go ahead."

When he returned, he brought two martinis on a silver tray. "I hope I got it just right. Only a whiff of vermouth and—"

"Tell me."

"That's why I came," He settled himself comfortably in a lounge chair. "I thought you'd be interested."

"Why does whatever it is concern Chan?"

"Can't get your mind off him, can you?" But he said it agreeably. "It doesn't concern him directly, at least I don't think so. But—all right, don't jump at me. That fifty-thousand-dollar check of Rose's—"

"She said it was payment for Stu to do something for her."

"Oh, you asked her."

"Yes. I saw her last night—that is, she was here—"

The ferrety gleam came into Larry's eyes. "With Clarence?"

She was conscious of an absurd wish to protect Clarence and Rose, not from anything in particular, unless it was the sharp look on Larry's face. "They were talking. We all talked a bit. I asked her about the check. She went home."

158

"She didn't say what she wanted Stu to do for her?"

"Why should she?"

"It's rather interesting. Although I don't see precisely—"

"What is it about?"

"It's rather complicated. But if you'll listen carefully—"

"Oh, Larry, don't act like the cat that swallowed the—"

"I didn't swallow it, really, at least not all of it. All right. Here it is. One of Rose's interests, a company calling itself Chavez et Cie, is suspected of working privately and secretly on some facet of nuclear energy. Possibly one of several special fields. Possibly fusion."

"Fusion—Oh!"

"The research that Chan is deeply involved in—"

"He always says he is the smallest spark in the galaxy."

"I expect he is. But still—"

"Oh, do go on. How could Rose—I think I begin to see!"

He gave her a rather complimentary look. "I thought you would." He twirled his martini glass and to Mady's surprise took quite a sip from it. "Chavez et Cie, which actually belongs to Chavez Industries—as a diversification of interests, I gather—is in South Africa, and the company has been importing physicists, trying to raid universities for scientists, buying laboratory equipment, all that. I don't pretend to understand the scientific processes. Actually I don't know precisely what the aims of Chavez et Cie are, I'm only surmising."

"But this check of Rose's—"

"Oh, yes, it does concern Chan as you'll see. If Stu went about it the proper way he could have done some very efficacious lobbying to get more money appropriated for—oh, any kind of nuclear research."

"But he didn't! He didn't even cash the check! He was going to become one of your partners."

"I'm not sure that that would have prevented his doing a little lobbying on the side."

"But—"

"No, he didn't even cash the check. I think it likely that

he intended to return it to Rose with an explanation to the effect that he was going to be asked to accept a Cabinet appointment and thus would have to disclose all business connections—you know, Senate confirmation would have required a disclosure of anything that might be called a conflict of interest—''

"How could any project of Rose's create a conflict of interest? How could Rose's concerns involve Chan?''

"I'm not sure,'' Larry for the first time looked indecisive, but thoughtful. "I'm only guessing, but I think it could be like this—'' He stopped to watch his own glossily manicured fingernails tapping the arm of his chair. "You know Chan's favorite subject—''

"Oh, yes. Fusion. But he always says he's not important, only one of many in the whole research program.''

"I think that is true. Besides other universities of our own there is always Germany—'' He lifted one finger. "Russia—'' He lifted another finger. "Japan. From all the information we've been able to get—some of it speculative, that's true but still—those countries may have been more active than we have been. There's one appropriation that did get through Congress, but it's not big enough. So say the people I have been able to talk to. Mind you, all this is hearsay. But, yes, a Senate confirmation committee just might consider Stu's relationship to Chan, or a check from Rose—''

"Why Rose? Really, Larry—''

He eyed her for a moment. "But I told you. If one of the various outfits operating under the name Chavez Industries *is* secretly working on any kind of nuclear research without the customary authority—without I should say, monitors—it would certainly be an occasion for investigation. As I say, I am only guessing, but I do know that this is a very sensitive area to our own government and others. Yes—'' he said thoughtfully. "I'm guessing. Informed guessing, in a way, but guessing.''

"But Stu would have had nothing to do with any of this—this guessing.''

"Mady!" He shook his head. "Don't you realize that such a regulatory agency would fall under Stu's sphere of—not direct control perhaps, but certainly influence?"

She shook her head. "I don't know much about anything that Stu was interested in."

"I'm sure there are many government departments which the average person knows little about. But if this explanation of Rose's check is a fact—combined with his brother's specialty—yes, if all that were known, I rather think Senate confirmation would have been difficult."

She eyed him steadily for a long moment or two. "Larry, where did you get all this information? If it *is* accurate information."

His eyes sparkled for an instant. Then he smiled. "My dear, I am thankful to say, a rising young man needs to keep his ear to the ground."

"You didn't get this out of the ground. Who told you?"

"Nobody *told* me, but I don't mind admitting that I have various—let's call them sources of general information."

"And for this—"

"Mady, you do like to get down to brass tacks, don't you? All right. A girl in the offices of Rose's top executive, John Walldon. I've known her in a merely friendly way for some time. So," he shrugged lightly. "I invited her to lunch."

"At the Four Seasons, I'm sure."

"As a matter of fact, no. We went to La Côte Basque. That needn't concern you. She's a very nice girl, make no mistake about that. And she's a bit of a talker. Not that she had any notion of what I wanted to get a slant on, I'm sure. But she did let out a few points without realizing, however, that they were of any particular interest. I learned that this Chavez et Cie does exist and something about their activities. The rest I'm guessing, but I think I'm guessing accurately."

"Chan would be furious—"

Larry shook his head with its shining, plastered cap of dark hair. "Not at all. I told him about it this afternoon. I came from Lettie's after that to see you. I thought just perhaps, knowing of your friendship with Rose, you might know something of—oh, anything. The check, for instance.''

"What did Chan say?"

Larry's face became very impersonal and noncommittal. "Nothing much. Being Chan, he didn't say anything. He can be a clam when he wants to be, as you know.''

That was true. After a moment she rose. "I think you are making too much of this check of Rose's and of Chan's influence over Stu. Really, I can't see either of them having the slightest effect on anything Stu decided.''

"So—" Larry said with a casual air, but watching her closely, "you really know nothing at all of lobbying on the part of—oh, anybody?''

"No!"

Larry sat back in his chair, frowning. He put his short hands together, joining the fingertips and studying them. Finally, he said, "As a matter of fact, this idea does seem a rather far-fetched notion on my part. Yet it would explain Rose's check in a way. I wonder what she'll tell the police when they question her about it.''

"Police! How would they know about the check?''

He shook his head again. "Dear Mady! Surely Chan told you that a very astute policeman—in plain clothes, as a matter of fact, but I found later that he is a very high-ranking member of the force—was present when we looked into Stu's safe-deposit box? If Rose has not yet been interviewed by the police, she soon will be.''

"Then she'll tell the whole truth. Larry, I'm perfectly certain that Chan would never have tried to influence Stu—''

"That's not the point. Someone may have felt that Chan might try to influence Stu and that Stu might agree—''

"But—who? You are trying to say that something about all this indicates—''

"*Might* indicate," Larry said. "No, I'm not saying that anything about this odd notion of mine would point to

Stu's murderer.'' He paused, adjusted a spotless cuff and said, ''No, I'm not saying that—''

''I don't know what you are saying, except it all seems nonsense to me!''

''Where is Nadine?'' Larry asked abruptly.

He was trying to catch her off-base, Mady thought swiftly, as if she were a reluctant witness.

''I don't know!

''Have you talked to her?''

''You have no right to question me like that. But, no—I have not talked to her.'' That was true; she could stick to the absolute truth. He needn't know that she had heard from Nadine twice. She wasn't afraid of Larry; she did feel an odd kind of uneasiness about his relentless prying. If a friend were caught in a trap, she had the ugly suspicion that he wouldn't lift a stubby finger to release the jaws of the trap. Unless, of course, such a release would react favorably upon Larry.

At that moment Clarence returned, pausing in the doorway to greet them. ''Larry! Glad to see you. Where have you been all day. Mady? Having drinks, I see. Well, it's that time—'' He was clearly in good spirits. Either he had asked Rose to marry him or he had found something at an auction which warmed his being.

It proved to be the latter, for he ducked back into the hall and returned with a parcel, which he unwrapped eagerly. ''There you are, Mady. Lovely, isn't it?''

''Yes,'' she agreed, meaning it, for it was a charming miniature, its colors as fresh as if they had been painted yesterday, framed in an oval of gold set with tiny garnets.

''You should say lovely, indeed!'' Clarence was elated. ''It's a Füger. Came, I think likely, from the Morgan Collection. Of course the lady in it is rather dish-faced. Not pretty-pretty as in many miniatures. Adds to its authenticity, really.''

''Oh,'' Mady tried to be properly impressed, but she

didn't deceive Clarence, who chuckled in the best of humor. "I'll tell you—"

"Will you excuse me just now?" Larry rose. "I've got to go. By the way, Clarence, this check of Rose's made out to Stu—"

"I wouldn't pay the slightest attention to that," said Clarence cheerfully. The doorbell rang and he spun around to go into the hall.

It was, at last, Chan. But not Chan alone, for a man accompanied him, a rather slight gray man, with a thin face, intelligent eyes, not much hair and an air of objective detachment; Larry caught a quick breath. So Larry must recognize him, Mady thought.

Chan introduced him. She heard only, "Lowell—Inspector, Homicide. He would like to talk to you about—about everything," said Chan.

Larry hesitated; clearly he felt he ought to leave and just as clearly wanted to stay. Clarence decided for him. "Too bad you were just leaving, Larry. Well, see you—"

There were times when Clarence could be very quick. He ushered Larry out almost before Larry knew what he was about.

Chan said, "It's nothing special, Mady. Just what we know of this uncle of Lettie's. The inspector very kindly came here rather than ask you to go to his office. He has talked to Lettie already. He only wants to know if you happen to know anything that Lettie doesn't remember."

In short, Mady knew, he wanted to confirm whatever Lettie had said. That would be easy. Clarence had quietly produced chairs for them all. The inspector said to Mady, "I know that you have met Captain McEvor—"

"Oh, yes."

"—and Lieutenant Swain. And young Joseph Ball—"

"I don't—"

Chan said, half smiling, "He was at the phone, bald head—"

"Oh. Yes."

Surely there was a kind of twinkle in the inspector's pale gray eyes. His face was pale, too, with neatly arranged features. His manner was friendly but impersonal. "Good men," he said, "McEvor and Swain, both came up from the ranks. As I did," he added, but Mady could not imagine a man of such dignity and quiet self-possession pounding a beat. However, he must know. She sat back.

"Now, then, I'm sure you realize that a crime of such prominence has stirred up considerable inquiry on all sides. Rather pressing inquiry, as a matter of fact. Naturally every murder that occurs in the city is of major importance to the whole police force. But—" he lifted scant gray eyebrows slightly, "when such a distinguished man is killed—you've seen the papers, I'm sure—in short we have to do our best. Not that we don't always try to do our best but in this—well, there! I only want to ask you a few questions. Now, Mrs. Channing's maiden name was Skeffington?"

"Surely she told you—"

"Oh, yes. As a matter of fact I was shown her marriage certificate. Wilkins was her mother's maiden name. Her mother, I understand, was widowed and has remarried."

Chan intervened. "Lettie's father died several years ago. Stu knew this and mentioned it to me merely by chance. Lettie told me that her mother had married again."

"The mother lives now, I believe, in Switzerland. We'll get in touch with her. Merely to check on her brother, Ernest Wilkins. Evidently her new name is Mrs. Sarim Hadah. Possibly an Arab name or—in any event, Mrs. Channing seems to believe that the new husband, Sarim Hadah, is very wealthy. However, she says she hasn't been in close touch with her mother for some time."

"That's right. Lettie was left with barely enough money for her education. But she met the senator. I mean, he was a senator then, and they were married. And then of course her uncle died and left her all that money."

"Now that is interesting. Like a fairy tale. Unexpected fortune."

Chan shifted in his chair. Was Inspector Lowell suggesting that it was a fairy tale?

He was.

"As soon as this murdered man was discovered we got in touch with Interpol. Interpol, by way of Sydney, Melbourne, Perth, Port Adelaide, has been most cooperative. However, only a little information has so far come to us about Ernest Wilkins. Certainly no Ernest Wilkins had recently left Australia by air or sea, as a matter of fact. Up to day before yesterday," he added precisely.

"So then this man—" Mady began.

"We can't be sure of that, really. The murdered man's passport—at one time he must have had one, that or an obliging friend or relative who sent him Australian-made clothes, a suitcase and an airlines bag—"

"Airlines!" Clarence said. "H'm."

"Yes, a quite new bag, as a matter of fact. But no Ernest Wilkins had been discovered so far on the passenger list of any plane coming from Australia. None of the contents of his luggage, which I assure you have been studied very carefully, so far has given any hint as to this man's identity. There is only the fact that someone tried to talk to Mrs. Channing, saying he was her uncle. The Australian police did find an Ernest Wilkins, who has lived for many years in what they call the back country, the owner of a sheep ranch. He does not seem to have ever been a man of tremendous riches. Certainly no criminal record."

"But then," Clarence said, leaning forward, his mustache bristling with interest. "That proves it. Whoever it was who tried to talk to Lettie was an impostor."

Chan said, "He could have seen the newspapers, Clarence. He could have thought that somehow he could get money out of Lettie."

The inspector said gravely, "Ernest Wilkins was the

name under which the murdered man was registered at the hotel. It is quite possible that the man calling at Mrs. Channing's apartment, whoever he was, had seen the news of the murder and somehow discovered that she was reported to be the heiress of Ernest Wilkins, and thus approached her. Simply called himself Ernest Wilkins—clearly with a view to convincing Mrs. Channing that he was her uncle.''

Clarence never stayed quiet very long. ''But there is no proof that this murdered Australian is the same man and in fact had anything to do with Lettie.''

The inspector agreed pleasantly. ''None. But, you see, somebody *did* apparently try to approach her. He sent word—no,'' he glanced at Chan as if restoring his memory, which, Mady felt, required no restoring. ''No, he talked directly to Mrs. Channing and asked her to see him at the St. Regis. There is no Ernest Wilkins registered at the St. Regis. As to the little hotel where the murdered man was found—the fact is,'' he sighed faintly, ''it has been on our list for—shall I say, quiet observation for some time. No, no.'' Clarence had made some motion, for the inspector addressed him. ''Not for anything, precisely, just for being possibly not quite within the law. However, the hotel is cheap. All the dead man's money along with his papers of identification was gone. But the name of Wilkins was almost certainly assumed. In addition, we're following up a report about a well-dressed woman in a long purple coat who was seen by a hotel employee.''

Clarence leaned forward. ''But sir, I don't understand why you apparently feel that the death of this—this Australian has anything to do with Stu's murder.''

''Probably nothing,'' the inspector replied. ''We are interested only because a man turned up at the Channing apartment house, desiring to speak to Mrs. Channing and because he did speak to her over the phone and asked her to come to meet him. It is, of course, barely possible that the Ernest Wilkins Interpol knows to exist did have, at one time, a great deal of money, which for one reason or another he wished to conceal by sending it to Mrs. Channing, intending to retrieve it when it suited him. He may have sent this man to pose as himself. Although to me, that does not seem likely."

"It would be very difficult," Chan said slowly.

The inspector nodded. Chan went on. "There would have to have been legal forms, a will, something that would convince anyone that this money was a perfectly legal inheritance."

"There are shyster lawyers," the inspector said.

Chan's chin took on its very firm line. "My brother was not a shyster. He was a lawyer and a very good one. He'd have had nothing to do with anything questionable."

The inspector only nodded, but did so rather sympathetically.

Clarence said, "But it was Stu who saw to the whole thing about Lettie's inheritance." He paused and said, "Where did her money come from if not from that uncle?"

The inspector said, "We'd be interested in the answer to that question, too." He rose. "Thank you very much. I have trespassed upon your time. Miss Smith, you will let me know, won't you, if you remember anything that your friend Mrs. Channing may have mentioned and does not herself recall? I mean about her uncle."

"But I—why, yes. Yes, certainly—"

He bowed politely to her and to Clarence, who responded by popping out of his chair and going with the inspector and Chan into the hall.

Surely Chan wasn't leaving again. No, he was back, along with Clarence, who stroked his mustache and said, "Dear me!"

Chan sat down as if exhausted and stretched out his legs. "That man really did us a great favor, coming here—and going to see Lettie, too. He asked me to come to his office, so of course I did, and I never saw such an imposing city office. At least not many, but then I haven't visited many—Utrillo prints, good rugs, handsome desk—I gathered that he rarely does anyone the honor of going to their home—''

"Wanted to get background," said Clarence with his worldly wise air. "A man of great perception."

"I'm sure I hope so." Chan looked at nothing, but seemed to be thinking hard.

Clarence said dreamily, "I always said *cherchez la femme.*"

"What on earth do you mean by that?" Chan didn't snarl, but almost.

"Why, it's obvious, isn't it? This impostor tried to see Lettie—but he wasn't an impostor. He was the real uncle. So she made a date with him and shot him. She couldn't have liked giving up all the money she thought he'd left her. Besides, she has certainly spent a great deal. Couldn't return it to him."

"Mady," Chan said. "Is there a chance of shutting up your stepfather? I'd suggest a padded cell, but I don't like to hurt his feelings."

Mady shook her head, but laughed. Chan groaned. "Then give me a drink, will you? It's been a long day. The inspector was altogether right when he said they were really cracking down on this."

Clarence had trotted away and was already returning with a brimming glass in his hand. The ice tinkled and Clarence's voice couldn't have been more melodious. "Hope I didn't drown it."

Mady said with real curiosity, "Clarence, why did you get rid of Larry when the inspector arrived?"

"Larry's ears were sticking out." Clarence sat down again with an air of complacence.

"But you like Larry," she insisted.

He gave her an odd, disapproving glance. "I should think you could guess. I was afraid the inspector intended to question us about Rose. I didn't want anybody as nosy as Larry to hear it.''

"He already knows, or at least surmises the reason Rose gave Stu that check. A possible reason, that is,'' Chan said slowly.

"Rose has some perfectly good explanation. I don't know what, but I trust Rose. I don't trust Nadine. Can't. She could have shot Stu. And even this Australian fellow if she'd wanted to.''

"Why Nadine?'' Chan was so startled that he sat up, splashing whiskey and soda.

"*Cherchez la femme*,'' said Clarence, risking peril from Mady, but pleased with himself. "Where is Nadine? If she's got nothing on her mind, why doesn't she turn up? Or why doesn't somebody find her? You're not hiding her yourself, I suppose. If you are, I'm sure it's for a good reason, but I do wish you'd let me know.''

Fifteen

"I am not hiding Nadine! I do not know where she is! And I wish you'd keep your views to yourself. Really, Clarence—''

"My dear boy, I only say what occurs to me and, of course, I don't mean any of my suppositions are necessarily true. Merely fancies. Notions. What was Larry doing here anyway, Mady?''

Chan replied. "He probably wanted to quiz you about Rose's check. Larry does like to inquire—''

"Snoop," Clarence suggested and added, "And I admire him for that inquiring mind."

"You said snoop," Mady said.

Chan sighed. "Rose will tell us in her own good time just why she gave that check to Stu."

"Certainly she will," Clarence declared, puffing himself up like a very natty little Bantam rooster.

"And why he didn't cash it?" Mady asked.

"Yes. Larry suggested his idea to me; he may be half right—or entirely wrong. He asked if I wouldn't have tried to persuade Stu to promote a large appropriation for nuclear research. I suppose I might have, but I don't for a moment believe that Stu would have paid any attention to me. In fact, if I had tried to put pressure on him—if anybody ever tried to pressure him into doing anything, it would only have made Stu very careful, very wary and rather likely to oppose whatever it was."

"Like a mule," Clarence said from the bar, to which he had again retreated.

Chan gave him a thoroughly weary glance. "No. No, Clarence, not at all like a mule. You knew Stu. He was always fair—"

"Yes, I think so," Clarence said with a judicious air. "Fair enough to bend backward perhaps. But you see, Chan, I can't think—at least I can't see how this peculiar Australian can possibly have anything to do with Stu's murder. Even if he did in fact have some connection with Lettie's uncle, or even with Lettie, he couldn't have shot Stu. Oh, wait." His young-looking face was suddenly furiously concentrated. "Anybody could have gone into the apartment in spite of caterers and guests. Nobody would have noticed him. He went along the corridor, knocked at Stu's door. Stu let him in. He got hold of Stu's gun—"

"How?" said Chan flatly.

"Oh, I don't know."

"And Rose's glove?"

"Oh—oh, all sorts of ways. Anyway, he shot Stu and then mingled with the guests and escaped the same way he came in."

"Couldn't have," Chan said. "Besides, the police have questioned the caterers and all the guests. I do wish, Clarence, you would keep your thoughts to yourself."

"One can't prevent one's thoughts," Clarence said with great dignity. "Why didn't you give Nadine's note to the police? I'm sure you didn't. They'd have—" he paused for a moment and continued with a pleased air of having found just the right words. "They'd have spread a dragnet for her. And found her by now."

Chan swished around the drink in his glass, frowning. Finally he said, "Honestly, Clarence, I just can't believe that Nadine shot Stu. It's all contrary to her character."

Clarence lifted his shining black eyebrows. "I'm sure I don't know much about her character. You must be far better acquainted with Nadine than I am."

This, Mady suspected, was supposed to be a neat dart. Chan only shook his head. Clarence went on, "Nobody can tell what a woman scorned will do. You can't deny that."

"I can deny that Nadine killed Stu. So forget it. And by the way, I want to talk to Mady—"

"Alone?" said Clarence. "Dear me—oh, well, I have things to do." He tripped off and up the stairs.

"He's going to phone Rose," Mady said.

Chan thought that over. "Somebody's got to get her to explain that damned check. The police will eventually, but it would be better if one of us did it. However—oh, Mady, I've never been so tired in my life. Stu was my brother and I was and am still very proud of him. So there's that to be thankful for. But oh, Mady, I shall miss him—"

She went to him because she had to; she put her hand on his shoulder, and he looked up at her, his eyes deep gray and sober.

"Dear Mady."

"Don't grieve, Chan. You can't change the fact that Stu is gone. When all this is over and you can get back to work, you'll feel better—"

"No, I'll never forget Stu. You know, Mady, how it was with us. He was older but so—so great and—"

She moved closer to him and held his head against her. "Don't, Chan. Don't—"

He put down his drink and put both arms around her. "Dear Mady," he said again, and Clarence came skipping down the stairs.

Mady drew away. Clarence said, "Can't get Rose. That ancient-of-days butler of hers is so old I think he's held together with string and glue—anyway, he doesn't know where she is. Or says he doesn't. Probably she's doing good works somewhere. Shall we go to dinner at my club, Mady? You come along, Chan. Do you good. Club is near, as you know. I don't feel like cooking tonight—"

This surprised Chan. "You cook?"

"Why, certainly. Whenever necessary. I'm not a bad cook, am I, Mady? You see, Chan, if a man has a rich, pampered wife and there's a shortage of cooks, he'd jolly well better learn to do the cooking himself. Come on now. Get yourself pretty, Mady."

"She's always pretty," Chan said, but stared at Clarence, and added thoughtfully, "I'd never be able to cook."

"Well," Clarence reminded him cheerfully, "you haven't got a rich wife."

"I meant only, if I had one—" Chan looked quizically at Mady, who suddenly felt like a child, shy and self-conscious and awkward. So she didn't say, "You can have a rich wife—or at least a sort of rich wife, not like Rose, but you can have her any time you want her."

Instead, turning suddenly chilly and stiff she said, "The food at the club is good. Do come along, Chan."

He sobered instantly; she felt rather as if she had slapped him. Yet surely he hadn't meant—but perhaps he had meant it and she had been too stupid, too utterly without savoir-faire to say anything at all except "the food at the club is good." She went upstairs, wishing she had had more enterprise.

She heard Chan below. "Thank you, Clarence, no, I can't. I've got to get back to Lettie. She does need someone with her, you know. That big apartment—"

"Ought to go to a hotel," Clarence's voice came from the hall; presumably he was getting into his coat; he called up the stairs, "Hurry up, Mady. I phoned for reservations."

"Tell Mady good night for me. See you—" The door opened and closed. Oh, yes, Mady thought, back to Lettie! How soon would Lettie make some permanent arrangements about how she was going to live—where and with whom?

Not with Chan; not if Mady could help it; but if she went on acting like a stupid schoolgirl, there was no telling what would happen. Chan's sympathy for Lettie and his grief for Stu would count very strongly in his relationship with Lettie. How nice it would be if people still held with old Leviticus, she thought irreverently, made her hair neat and went to the club with Clarence, who was in a exuberant mood.

Over the soup he told her one reason why. "That Larry, he's a sharp one. Nosy, yes. But he's got what it takes, Mady, and he likes you. I can see that. Much better take him than moon around after Chan."

"I don't moon."

Clarence considered it. "You are not exactly forthcoming, though," he said at last. "When you had a chance to say that no matter what the circumstances, a rich wife wouldn't expect the cooking to be done by her husband, you didn't say a word. Not even an encouraging look. You should have said something, you know. Delicate. Seductive, I mean."

"I wouldn't—"

Clarence eyed the filet mignon that was being served

him, and then nodded. "Just right. Eat, Mady. Good for you."

She swallowed so hard that tears came to her eyes. No sense in being just a plain fool! Throwing Chan into Lettie's arms. But then—a tiny spark of comfort came into her mind; Lettie might desire Chan's company and protection just now; that was reasonable. But she'd never consider marrying a man with no money to speak of. Mady didn't know what Chan's salary was, but teachers were not always paid very well and Chan himself had often said that he was only a very small spark in the entire research galaxy of scientists, many of whom were real stars in the wide-ranging field of physics.

No, Lettie wouldn't actually want to marry him.

Just perhaps, too, he didn't want to marry Lettie.

Good heavens, she told herself angrily; Stu was buried only yesterday and already I'm accusing his widow of making a foray on a man whom she really has a right to rely on now. She was conjuring up goblins to frighten herself with, she decided firmly, and the decision lasted a good ten seconds.

She and Clarence walked home through a rather mild night, which gave some promise of spring, and found Rose's long car, complete with the two bodyguards, standing at the curb. Rose leaned out. "I phoned as soon as I got home from that committee meeting, but you weren't at home—"

Clarence sprang to assist her, actually brushing aside the stalwart young man who had quickly gotten out of the front seat and opened the car door for Rose. Clarence took her arm. "Dear Rose, I tried to reach you. Do come in—"

The car evidently had standing directions to wait until Rose sent it away. Clarence had his house key out as swiftly as a magician. "Really, Rose, we ought to give you a latch key. We can't have you sitting in the middle of the street when you are kind enough to come."

He bustled happily around, seeing to liqueurs, asking

Rose if she would like coffee, making himself thoroughly agreeable and showing himself radiantly happy. Rose seemed glowing, too, in a way, and happy when Clarence showed her the miniature he had bought that day.

"Lovely," she said, "oh, lovely!"

"A find! A bit costly, but you can see—"

"You always have such wonderful taste," Rose said admiringly. Her silvery hair was smooth, done by a hairdresser, Mady was sure, not one of her ancient maids. Her pink and white complexion was like a girl's, her large blue-green eyes with their sweeping eyelashes were full of respect—and perhaps something else—as she looked at Clarence. Mady had no idea how old Rose was and it didn't matter; she was Rose, full of kindness, energy, generosity and not just the vestiges of beauty, but beauty itself.

She put out a white hand, laden with diamonds, and gave the miniature back to Clarence. Mady wondered fleetingly if she would approve of Clarence's taste about the wooden Indian; thankfully he seemed to have forgotten it.

"I had some callers this evening," Rose said. "I thought I'd better tell you about it. Police."

"Ah," said Clarence. "A very gentlemanly inspector?"

"Yes, and a Captain McEvor."

"The inspector is very important," Clarence said. "I suppose he asked you about that check to Stu."

"Oh, yes. And, of course, I explained it. You see—oh, it's very simple. Mr. Walldon—he is the chairman of Chavez Industries (it's become a conglomerate you know, for diversification). Mr. Walldon is getting on, a bit of an old dodo in fact, but he does keep a tight rein, an acute watching brief, as he calls it, upon every facet of the entire business proceedings. He began to get suspicious about something calling itself Chavez et Cie operating in Africa. He got a look at its various cash sheets, yet he began to suspect that they were secretly experimenting with the development of nuclear energy. Now as everyone knows, this has its dangerous possibilities. So I decided to get Stu to look into these proceedings. Not officially for me, naturally, but merely as an interested citizen. He was then at rather a loose end after his Senate seat was gone, and he hadn't yet decided to join that law firm. So I gave him a check just to cover his expenses on a trip to look over the office and anything else he might have to—" a tiny pink flush came into Rose's cheeks, "just perhaps he'd have to—well, the only word for it is bribe some employee to tell him precisely what they were doing. All so hush-hush, you see. Nothing properly monitored. Yes, I'm afraid very suspicious. Of course, Chavez et Cie involves many interests, I'm sure. I gave Stu the check ahead of time. Then he had an offer from the law firm Larry is a partner in, and he had almost decided to take that. He had certainly intended to return my check. That's all," said Rose, sighing.

Clarence said promptly, "That's what I surmised. That is, not exactly, but the general trend. Isn't it, Mady?"

"Yes, I—yes." In a *very* general way, she added in her mind. Mainly whatever Clarence thought or said now proclaimed his faith in Rose. Only the night before he had sat brooding over the fact that Rose's glove had been found with gunpowder stains on it.

Clarence was always a weather cock, Mady reminded herself. But a charming weather cock when he chose to be. He was charming now. "How very dear of you, Rose, to tell us all this! And very, very perspicacious of you to suspect something of the kind going on. You were right to try to find out and put a stop to anything that could be questionable. Your money, money from America, financing this foreign research affair, yes, yes, you were right. Now we can simply forget all this—"

"My glove," said Rose. Suddenly her placid, really lovely face was quite determined. Mady had never before noted the firm line of her jaw or the deep flash in her blue-green eyes. When she was younger, as Mady remembered her, she had been a really gorgeous blond, always a little larger than other women, always a little sturdy in her bearing; but particularly as she grew older, the sturdiness became dignified composure, the blond hair had softened to its shining silver, done in a neat French roll that showed her pink ears, which were usually adorned with simple yet, Mady suspected, very costly earrings.

She had been so much a part of the close-knit circle Mady grew up with that she couldn't then remember when she had first been aware of Rose as a person; she did remember her calm beauty and her great and unstudied kindness. But she knew as if from some intuitive reasoning that when Rose looked just like that it meant she was going to get to the heart of the matter, as she had proposed to do when she got the first hint of questionable business done in her name. Also, which would wound Rose more deeply, in her husband's name, for Jacob Chavez had been both a very, very rich man and a completely respected and trusted man among his peers.

"My glove!" Rose said again, her chin very firm.

Clarence wouldn't look at Mady; he would never, Mady knew, admit for an instant that he had grieved and fretted about that glove.

"Somebody," Clarence looked steadfastly away from Mady, "simply got into the coatroom and took it and used it."

"And whoever that was killed poor Stu during the party after I had arrived. Obvious. I can't believe that anybody would deliberately try to involve me in murder, but I intend to find out who it was," Rose said, almost too quietly.

Clarence nodded. "Yes, dear, yes. Perhaps——" He was evidently casting about for aid of some kind. He did then just glance at Mady. "Perhaps—that is, I wonder—I happened to think of Larry. He's got a very inquiring mind and—he does take a great interest in all this. Praiseworthy. Trying to help."

"Larry Todd!" A flush came up into Rose's cheeks. "Not that young man! He's looking after himself and nobody else—"

"Oh, now, Rose." Clarence waved his small hands. "Larry is a fine young fellow—"

"He is a nosy, get-ahead-no-matter-what kind of fellow. No, I wouldn't think of asking Larry, for instance, to do what I asked Stu to do for me."

"I didn't mean that. I was only thinking he is a lawyer and—"

"Has he been hanging around Mady?" Rose asked astutely.

Clarence, averting his eyes from Mady again, replied. "Now, Rose, he admires Mady—"

Rose turned to Mady. "Don't believe anything Larry tells you—"

Mady didn't care that much for Larry, but felt she had to be fair. "But, Rose, he really has had such a hard time. You can't blame him for trying to make a place for himself any way he can. After that dreadful thing about his father—"

"What about his father?" Rose's eyes were as bright and sharp as Larry's. "What's he been telling you?"

"I don't think he meant to speak of it. It just came out. His father, losing all the Todd money and then falling downstairs when he was drunk and—"

"My God," said Rose who never, never used any kind of what might be called profanity. This time it came from sheer astonishment. "Did Larry tell you that? Not a word of it is true. I knew the Todd family well. His mother died—oh, years ago. It's true his father rather gambled about investments, bought the wrong things, all that. Certainly his father enjoyed life and I realize that he couldn't have left much in the way of inheritance for Larry. But if Larry told you—why did he do that? Look here, Mady. He's after something. I suppose—" Rose leaned back serenely, even smiling a little. "I suppose it is you. And your money." A flash of worldly and rather cynical wisdom came into Rose's fine eyes. "Now see here, Mady. I know your trustees, both of them. I can guess something of how your capital is invested. Pay no attention to anything Larry tells you. If he's careful how much he drinks when he is with you, it is because he wants to keep his head clear. Especially don't let him take over the management of your money."

"I—no—I wouldn't think of it," Mady said, but feebly.

Clarence agitatedly twitched his mustache. "But Rose, Larry is sure to get ahead."

"Oh, I'm sure of that." Rose became placid and serene again, but added, "What a liar that boy is!" She sighed, adjusted the soft folds of pink chiffon at the throat of her simple (probably hideously expensive) gray dress. "Of course when you reach my age, everybody seems young."

Clarence instantly rallied. "You simply can't be old, Rose. You look so young and lovely—"

"Thank you, Clarence. But I know the facts. However, I do rather think sometimes that I have, so to speak, worn well."

"Lovely," said Clarence again, rather at a loss, Mady was sure.

"But my glove—" She looked all at once tired, shocked and suddenly pale. "Stu was a fine man. Not many like him. I can't see why anybody would do such a terrible thing."

The telephone rang.

"I'll answer it," Mady cried, getting ahead of Clarence by a hair's-breadth.

It was Chan.

"Mady, can you come? Lettie is very upset."

"Why, I—yes!—What's wrong?"

"It's nothing wrong exactly, but something has come up and I don't know what to make of it. Larry's here, too, and he doesn't understand either."

"Chan, what is wrong?"

"I told you. Not exactly wrong, but Lettie's uncle has turned up."

"He couldn't have. He's dead—"

Clarence was at her elbow, ear pressed close to Mady's. Rose was not far behind him.

"He's here," Chan said simply. "Passport, all sorts of identification. Lettie really needs you. Can you come?"

"Yes!"

"I'll send a taxi. Have Clarence come with you. I don't want you on the street alone. No—wait, Larry says he'll come for you—"

Clarence had contrived to hear what Chan had said and certainly Chan's voice was very clear. He removed his ear and rubbed it.

"—says Lettie's real uncle has turned up, Rose. Lettie's upset—Chan wants Mady to come—he'll send Larry—"

"Nonsense," Rose said firmly and loudly. "I'll send her in my car. It's out there waiting, Mady. You'd better take night things. Lettie may want you to stay—"

"No. I'll be back—"

Chan had clicked down the receiver.

Clarence was getting out Mady's fur coat.

Rose opened the door and beckoned; one of the body-guards sprang to attention and came racing toward the steps.

"But it can't be her uncle," Mady said. "He's dead. It just can't be—"

Sixteen

But the tall, attractive man who rose as Mady entered the library was (or at least was certainly accepted to be by Chan and Larry) Lettie's uncle. He said cheerfully that he wasn't dead at all and shook hands pleasantly with Mady as Chan introduced them.

Lettie sat like a doll, not moving, in a corner of the sofa. She hadn't been crying, but her pretty hands folded and unfolded while she stared with huge, brown eyes at the newcomer as if she were in a state of stunned disbelief.

Ernest Wilkins settled himself again; he seemed perfectly good-natured and cool, although certainly he must have been extremely, not to say violently, interested in the events which Chan (and of course, Larry, who wouldn't have missed such an opportunity for explaining) had related to him. Mady doubted whether Lettie had managed to say a word.

"He just arrived tonight," Chan began, but Mr. Wilkins intervened with an apologetic glance at Chan and spoke to Mady. "It was really by chance that I heard of the former senator's tragic death. I actually live in what Australians call the outback, the back country. I run sheep, some cattle. I had gone to Melbourne to arrange for the shipping of some wool. Happened into the club and picked up a newspaper and saw a brief paragraph about the former senator's death. So I felt that my niece needed me.

182

Haven't seen her," he said regretfully, "since she was a baby. You look very like your mother, Lettie child."

Lettie lowered eyelashes over her pansy brown eyes.

He was an extremely good-looking man, Mady added to her first impression; he was well built, with a tanned and weather-lined face and a sprinkling of gray in his crop of thick curly hair. There was a family likeness in the curls, although not in his rather craggy features; his eyes were brown, but had a depth and deep sparkle beneath gray eyebrows, which just now were drawn together in a rather puzzled way. On a tangent and surprising herself a little, Mady sent forth a silent wish that Rose would not see him and, possibly, reconsider Clarence. But then Rose was not one to change her mind quickly.

"—so I dropped everything and came on here. Thought I'd take my niece back to Australia with me, give her a home. If she needed one. Least I could do. Of course my place is quite a long way from a city—"

"You certainly arrived here in a short time," Larry said, a little too casually.

Ernest Wilkins gave him a rather sharp glance, but said pleasantly, "You've heard of airplanes, Mr. Todd. Why—" he smiled, "we even have a small plane on the ranch. Two motor. Need it—"

"So you haven't seen the police at all?" Larry persisted.

"Certainly not. Didn't know anything of all this you have told me. But—" He turned politely to address Mady again. "I've just told these—these young men and my niece that I think I can guess, in fact I'm reasonably sure I know who this man was who turned up here claiming to be me. George Shelton," he said. "That's his name. He worked for me." He was still addressing Mady, but Chan and Larry were both listening intently as if they might discover some discrepancy in his previous statements. Mady believed every word he spoke.

"He was a kind of secretary, clerk, saw to some of my business details. Not a bad man, by any means, although I never quite trusted him. Can't say why. In any event, some weeks ago he simply left. Now George was silly, but by no means stupid. He had had plenty of opportunities to look into my—oh, letters, business records, anything like that. I'm sure he knew that my niece was the wife of a retired senator. So—'' he lifted his broad, tweed-clad shoulders, ''so the way I see it, once George saw a notice of the late senator's death, or perhaps heard a news flash, he saw, he thought, a way to get money out of Lettie.''

''He didn't ask for money,'' said Lettie. ''He only asked to see me. If that is, if it was the same man—''

''But you believed he had money on his mind?'' This time he addressed Chan.

''Yes, sir. No other reason for approaching Lettie just then. And since she had never seen you—''

''My loss,'' said Ernest Wilkins with grave courtesy. ''My sister and I have not seen one another since—dear me, child, since before she and your father separated and she went off to—to—I had a letter or two from her. I believe she settled for awhile in Mentone—''

''She has married again,'' Lettie said in a stifled voice, almost a whisper.

''Ah, yes. I understand. How long has it been since you have seen your mother, niece?''

''Since I was in school. Somehow she got money from my father for my education, but that's all.''

The stranger's eyes warmed. ''Poor girl,'' he said gently. ''You've had a bad time. I am sorry that I didn't send you all that money.''

So Chan or Larry had told him about the fortune Lettie had supposed she had inherited from him. Chan, however, said to Mady, ''Mr. Wilkins knows nothing of the money Lettie received.''

Ernest Wilkins, again politely, broke in. ''I wish, Lettie, you could remember the name of the law firm in—Sydney, didn't you say?''

Lettie nodded, ''I think so—''

"You see, if you could only remember the name—"

"But I can't," Lettie looked as if she might begin to cry. "I told you. My husband saw to everything. He even kept my checkbooks for me, he did everything—" She put her hands over her face as her voice wavered. Mady went quickly to sit beside her.

"I can't help it," Lettie sobbed. "Stu was so wonderful to me. Saw to everything. I shall miss him. I do miss him—"

"There, there, child," said Ernest Wilkins kindly. "The truth is even if I had died, I wouldn't have had a fortune to send you. Something perhaps, from the sale of my sheep run, a few odds and ends. Yes, they'd have come to you as my next of kin. If there should be anything left. I'm in rather good health," he said almost apologetically.

Chan said quickly, "Yes, sir. And it's really great that you came on to help Lettie as soon as you read what had happened."

"It was only a brief paragraph under United States news. Having been born in America, I always read any items from home that I can. I regret that I didn't arrive in time for the services for your husband, niece. Now then—" He turned to Chan. "I believe you have told me all that you know of this troublesome situation. I suggest that you and perhaps your lawyer friend here—"

Larry, sitting in a straight chair, his face a careful blank, nodded. "Certainly, sir."

"I expect the thing to do is for all three of us to go to the police and try to explain, at least, this particular aspect. Then I may be able to see this man who purported to be me. If it was George, I can certainly identify him. Now I must say goodnight. I find I'm rather fatigued—It's a long flight from Australia. Pleasant, but long."

Lettie rose. "You must stay here. Uncle," she added the word firmly.

He shook his head. "No, no. I can't impose upon your hospitality like this with no warning, no preparation. I stopped on my way here to check in at a hotel. On Fifty-fifth Street. It is called—''

"Oh, don't!" Lettie cried. "That's where he said he was registered. Only he wasn't."

Mr. Wilkins grasped her meaning at once. "I'll see you tomorrow, Lettie. Now then, I expect I ought to get a cab—''

Larry sprang up, all attention. "I'll go down with you, sir."

Mr. Wilkins bowed to Lettie, he bowed to Mady; he almost bowed to the wooden Indian before he checked himself and gave it a rather blank look, which the Indian returned. Suddenly he and Larry were gone.

Chan said, "But Lettie, *where* did all that money come from?"

Lettie began to cry. "I don't know! I just don't know!"

"Don't cry," Chan said helplessly. "Think about it. How did the money get to you?"

"I told you," Lettie sobbed. "I told you, over and over. I told Stu. He saw to everything, Chan, you know that—''

"But now, Lettie dear, please listen. This money you spent. You must have had a bank account so you could write checks. You must have been at least interested in the man or whoever it was who sent you that money."

"I only believed it and let Stu see to everything. If I needed money, I asked him, and he would just laugh and say it was mine and give me anything I wanted to spend and—oh, Chan, it's all so dreadful."

"It isn't very dreadful for your real uncle to come all this way to try to help you."

"No, no, I didn't mean that! I'm just so upset and—'' She lifted tearful eyes. "Are you perfectly certain he *is* my uncle. I mean this man tonight?"

"Yes. Both Larry and I saw identification galore. The police can and probably will confirm it, but yes, I believe him."

"I believe him," Mady said boldly. "You ought to be glad, Lettie."

"Oh, yes, I am. Of course I am. But it's so—so—Chan, *who* sent me all that money?"

"That, Lettie, is what I asked you."

"But I thought—and now I don't know. I just don't know—"

"Can't you even make a guess."

"A guess?" Her eyes were wide and astonished.

"I mean—oh, some disappointed suitor of yours. You must have had one or two before you met Stu."

"No!" She shook her curls. "No! Not anybody who would do that. Oh, of course, there were boys I used to dance with. Go out with sometimes—but not after I met Stu. No!"

"Then perhaps somebody close to your mother. Maybe somebody in love with her and—"

"Chan, I am not an illegitimate child, if that's what you mean!"

"I didn't mean that. Although—" Chan paused for a moment. "Your father! I mean your mother's first husband. Perhaps he sent it to you."

"Oh, I don't think so. I don't remember him at all, you see. I was so small when they separated and my mother went to Italy and—" Lettie said dolefully. "I never knew where my father went. I did have a letter from my mother saying he died. And when later she married again."

"We'll soon find out the facts." Chan was far more cheerful than Mady felt he had a right to be. But he might say anything, she guessed, to stop Lettie's sobbing, which had broken out anew, her pretty head on Chan's shoulder, so he had to look down at her curls. He glanced hopefully over them at last, at Mady, who said as briskly as she could, "All right, Lettie. No use doing all that crying now. Tomorrow—"

"Yes," Chan said. "Go to bed now, Lettie. Tomorrow we'll try to straighten this out."

He was still in the library pacing up and down, when Mady returned after seeing Lettie into bed, light turned off but door left open.

"She all right?"

"I think so. But it has been quite a shock. Coming after Stu's murder and everything."

"Lettie's mother seems to be a rather unreliable kind of woman," said Chan with sudden sharpness. "Did you know her?"

"I never saw her. I know nothing about her. Except that she has paid almost no attention to Lettie. So naturally I don't like her. That is, the idea of her."

"Did you ever see a picture of her?"

"No. Wait a minute—yes, I think I did. Years ago. She looked—" Mady added rather reluctantly, "very much like Lettie. Rather, Lettie looks like her mother. When her mother must have been younger and—but that doesn't mean anything—"

"It doesn't tell us who killed Stu. Or why," Chan said wearily and flung himself into a deep chair. "I like that man, Wilkins."

"I like him, too. I like his coming here at once because he thought Lettie might need him. And a home."

"Will she accept it, do you think?"

"No idea. But he is very attractive."

Chan gave her a quick look. "He's rather old, isn't he?"

Was there just a flicker of latent jealousy in that? No, Mady decided gloomily. "Not so very old surely. Doesn't look it. Rose's car is waiting. I must go home—"

This time there was no question about Chan's staying with Lettie, but he accompanied Mady to the street where the doorman inadvertently gave them some shocking news.

He was the same man who had been on duty the night of Stu's murder. In at the death, Mady thought, and was appalled at the familiar phrase. It was a fleeting reflection, for the doorman, all solicitousness, all politeness (probably also impressed by Rose's car; Mady was again rather shocked at her own cynical idea) insisted on talking. "Ah, Miss Smith. Going home? Your car is waiting. Too bad you just missed Miss Hallowell."

"*Miss*—" Mady began.

Chan said, "*Miss Hallowell! Was she here? When?*"

"Not to say here—that is, she was here, yes, but she asked if Mrs. Channing was alone and of course I know Miss Hallowell, so I told her no, Mrs. Channing had her brother-in-law and Miss Smith and Mr. Todd and Mrs. Channing's uncle with her."

Chan actually took him by the shoulder. Mady wasn't sure he spoke between his teeth, but it sounded that way. "Where did she go? Why didn't she come in?"

The doorman shook his uniformed shoulder rather indignantly from Chan's grasp. "Really, Mr. Channing, how could I know? You see, Mr. Todd and the other gentleman—I mean, Mrs. Channing's uncle came down just then, and I got them a taxi. I held the door, naturally." He had hastily reassembled his dignity. "I heard Mr. Todd tell the taxi driver to go to the St. Regis. They left and when I turned around Miss Hallowell had gone. No," he said as Chan's hand came out toward him and he backed away precipitately. "No, I don't know where she went. Not even the direction. That's all."

He had an air of grievance; he had clearly behaved according to the best rules of his occupation.

"Oh! Yes. Sorry I clutched at you. I was only—never mind. Here's Rose's car, Mady."

Here it was, indeed, and one of the burly young men was holding a sturdy uniformed arm for Mady. She said good night to Chan and got into the limousine.

So, Nadine was still in the city. Nadine was trying to see Lettie.

That was all. If they had been seconds sooner, if Larry had only noticed Nadine and stopped her!

Lettie still felt she needed Chan's support. Perhaps her uncle would offer that support and give Chan a break.

It was possible that Chan didn't want a break. Yet she couldn't see him as a noble knight, cavorting around on a white horse, rescuing a maiden—no, a widow—in distress.

She was rather cheered by that idea and sat back in the luxury of Rose's automobile, vaguely thinking of her mother and her mother's cars and chauffeurs. Rose was clearly able to keep up such state, but very few people did now, certainly not Mady. She smiled a little thinking of Rose's warning about Larry. Larry would not be likely to propose any permanent bond such as marriage until he was absolutely sure of the financial standing of his prospective bride.

Rose was ready to go home when the car drew up at the curb with stately ease. Clarence, his coat collar turned up, came down the steps with Rose and again brushed aside one of the two young men in order to see Rose into her car himself. Both of them looked rather smug and certainly happy. So perhaps Clarence's wooing was going well.

Clarence could scarcely wait until they got into the house to question her. "Was it really Lettie's uncle?"

"Yes, I'm sure of it. Of course there'll be inquiries tomorrow. But I feel sure that he is the uncle."

"Then how did Lettie get all that money?"

"I don't know. She says she doesn't know—"

"Lettie doesn't know! Now, really!"

"Oh, you know Lettie. It seems that Stuart took care of the whole thing. She simply accepted the fact that it came from a dead uncle and let it go at that. I can't say I blame her."

"H'm." Clarence caressed his mustache, his eyes calculative. "Still it is an odd set-up."

"Yes—"

"This man who claimed to be her uncle—"

"Her real uncle thinks the murdered man was a former

employee—'' She told him the facts Ernest Wilkins had
outlined.

"So he'll identify him. George Shelton, did you say?"

"If he can. I suppose the police—''   ·

"Oh, yes. I believe they keep an unclaimed victim for
some time in the hope of identification. Now if he identifies
him, fine, but that still does not explain Stu's murder.
Seems to have nothing whatever to do with it.''

"How did you get along with Rose? You both looked
very happy.''

"I *think* it's going to be all right. I really think so.''

"You mean nothing is settled yet?''

"Not yet. But there are signals—''

"Well, keep her away from Lettie's uncle.''

"*What!*''

"He is a real charmer. I liked him enormously.''

As Chan had done, Clarence said, "Isn't he rather
old?''

"Not for Rose,'' Mady said wickedly. "Not even for
me. He doesn't look as if he could possibly age.''

Clarence took this as a personal compliment, and indeed
it was deserved. "Some men just don't age.''

"I suppose everybody ages at their own speed. Oh, by
the way, Nadine was there tonight!''

"Nadine! Did you talk to her? Where has she been?''

"Nobody had a chance to talk to her. She arrived just as
the uncle and Larry Todd were leaving, and then she
disappeared again.''

Clarence nodded, sagely. "I told you. *Cherchez la
femme*—''

"Clarence, if you say that again—''

"Don't look like that, Mady. You'll get old and sour
before your time,'' said Clarence airily and not very
comfortingly.

Mady could think of no crushing reply. She said good
night and went upstairs.

It was remarkable, indeed highly unlikely, but she slept

exhaustedly without dreaming until she awoke to the fragrance of Clarence's coffee.

Morning brought one expected and one unexpected development.

The first was that Ernest Wilkins had been accepted, by his credentials and probably by some communication with the Australian police, as Lettie's uncle. He had identified the murdered man as George Shelton, and the police accepted that too. Chan telephoned to report to Mady while Clarence nonchalantly, but rather swiftly, skipped to an upstairs extension.

The second development came an hour later, also from Chan.

"It's Lettie's mother. She's on her way to New York. She'll arrive today. With her husband."

Seventeen

"Lettie wants you to come," Chan went on. "They'll get here this afternoon. Lettie had a cable. They tried to reach her by phone, but couldn't."

There was a gentle click of the extension in Clarence's room as it was lifted.

"That isn't all," Chan continued wearily. "I talked to Lettie's uncle and he has a date with Nadine for lunch."

"Chan! I don't believe you!"

"Neither do I." But Chan added a faint chuckle. "Seems true though. I asked him how it happened and he said a young woman by the name of Nadine Hallowell had phoned him and said she was Stu's secretary and wanted to see him. So—lunch."

"Where?"

"Oh, I don't know. He has a magnificent room at the St. Regis."

"But he said, that is he implied, that he didn't have much money."

"I think he was underplaying the state of his finances. Out of politeness, I suppose. Or just habit. Some people—you know Rose never likes her money to be talked of."

"Could he possibly be in the same—same—"

"League with Rose? I shouldn't think so. But he's no pauper."

"I suppose you couldn't have—"

"Invited myself to lunch with them? No."

"But Nadine! I can't understand—"

"I think I can. Remember last night when you were leaving. That gabby doorman told us how he had got a cab for Mr. Wilkins and Larry, and Larry had told the cabbie the St. Regis. When the doorman turned around Nadine had gone, but she could have heard that. Anyway, Uncle Ernest said she phoned him—"

After a moment, Mady said thoughtfully that she didn't see what they could do about it, since they didn't want to betray Nadine to the police.

"Nothing." Chan was almost cheerful. "But it does show that she is still in the land of the living."

"Living! I never once thought—"

"I did. After the things that have happened—yes, I was afraid. Nadine could have known more than Stu's murderer wanted her to know. Obviously, she's ready to talk to somebody. We'll just have to wait. She must have heard that the police are eager to question her. Now Lettie thinks the plane from Italy will get in about five o'clock. It'll take some time to get here from Kennedy. I'm to meet her mother and stepfather. But you will come to be with Lettie?"

"Yes! Oh, yes!" She didn't say, "I wouldn't miss it," but Chan must have guessed, for he gave the soft little chuckle, which with other men would have meant a hearty laugh.

"See you."

Chan was feeling better, at least; the shocked and somber attitude of the past few days seemed to have lightened a little.

Clarence came skipping down the stairs. He made no bones ever about listening to her conversations and didn't then. "So Nadine has come out from hiding! Now what has she got to say? Why does she want to talk to Uncle Ernest?"

"He may tell Lettie—or Chan."

"H'm." Clarence shook his head mysteriously, picked up a newspaper and folded it open at the art galleries page.

"Dear me, I really must get that wooden thing out of Lettie's apartment. But do you know I've lost all my admiration for it! Can't see why. I wish she would shove it out with the trash."

"Perhaps she has by now."

"I'll be off. See you at Lettie's—"

And *you* wouldn't miss this for anything either, she decided. Birds of a feather.

She wondered vaguely if somehow Larry Todd wouldn't insinuate himself most charmingly into the meeting between Lettie and her mother—and her mother's husband. But then Larry couldn't know everything.

Mrs. Baynes appeared to have taken another holiday. So again the house seemed altogether too quiet. When the doorbell rang about two o'clock, it had the air of something portentous, indeed something rather ominous.

Nadine, tall, slim, her black hair smooth, her jetty eyebrows drawn together, her handsome face neatly and charmingly made up, stood at the door. She swept her long black mink coat around her and said calmly, "I want to talk to you, Mady."

Mady all but clutched Nadine's arm. "Oh, Nadine. We've been needing you—come in—"

Nadine shrugged out of her coat as she entered and dropped it over the bench. Her face was rather stiff and pale, but her blue-gray eyes were steely between long black eyelashes. "I thought you might need me," she said. "But I couldn't come until I had thought—had come to some sort of decision."

"What did you decide?"

"Wait, Mady. I've got to know more than I do now."

Mady said after a moment, "You saw Lettie's uncle."

"Yes. He is her uncle, I'm sure. The police are sure, too. Only Lettie, I understand, seems a little uncertain. However, tell me everything, Mady. Mr. Wilkins didn't know much—that is, he knew the main facts, but not the entire thing."

"Where have you been?"

"In a little apartment on Seventy-ninth Street. I took it last November. A six-month sublet so my name is not in the phone book. It's been a good place to hide. I couldn't—" Nadine sat down and that seemed to steady her. "I had to have some time."

"You were in love with Stu," Mady said gently.

Nadine's fine eyes swept up. "Of course. For years. There was no affair. He saw me as his right arm, he always said. But not—not *in* his arms," said Nadine with a desolate throb in her voice.

Again Mady waited a moment. Finally, she said, "Did you go to Washington that day—the day Stu—"

"No. I was troubled about something. I was in my apartment when I heard the news on the radio. Now, Mady, that dreadful day is over. I try not to think of it. As if trying ever meant forgetting!"

"Nadine, I'm sorry."

"I'd had lunch with Stu, you see."

"Clarence saw you at the Four Seasons. He didn't recognize you. He said the woman with Stu wore a hat. I never saw you wear a hat."

Nadine didn't smile. "I did that day because—I suppose

I wanted to hide as much of my face as I could. You see, I hurt Stu very much. So,'' her fine throat moved as if she swallowed very hard, but she looked straight into Mady's eyes. "So he went home and wanted to kill himself."

"No, no. He didn't! He couldn't have. He was shot in the back."

"Oh, I know. I found that out later when I read all the newspapers. I didn't know what to do. Today Ernest Wilkins told me some of the facts as he knew them. As he knew them," she repeated softly and took a long breath.

Mady could only wait. Nadine was wearing an exquisitely simple dark-blue dress, so well designed that it could have been worn anywhere—could have been worn in Stu's office without exciting comment. There was a touch of white at her long throat and at her wrists. Her hands were strong and beautiful with no jewels.

At last she said, "Mady, did you put the rose—"

"Yes."

"Weakness on my part. I only wanted—I don't know what I wanted. To try to show him, to try to make up for what I had done—"

"You said you didn't mean to hurt him."

"I scratched out that part of my note to you. But of course you worked at it until you could read it."

"Clarence did. I helped."

"Who has it now?"

"Chan. We couldn't give it to the police, Nadine. I was sure that you wouldn't have wanted that. I was sure you hadn't murdered Stu."

"I might as well have murdered him," Nadine said somberly. "I didn't pull the trigger, but I'm to blame."

"Why, Nadine, *why*?"

Nadine fingered a fold of her skirt and eyed it. Finally, she shook her head. "No. What are the police really doing? I know only what I see in the papers or hear—"

"I don't know. That is, yes, I do, in a way. Since Stu

was so prominent, the police feel they've got to make an arrest as quickly as possible.''

Nadine broke in astutely, ''But they can't yet? Naturally they have to have what is called jury evidence. Yes, I understand that.''

''Nadine, why did you hide like that? Surely now you'll go to the police and tell them whatever it was you did that could have hurt Stu so terribly that you felt as if you had killed him?''

Nadine gave her a fleeting smile. ''So you have a brain back of that pretty face. I always knew it. Where is Chan? Staying with Lettie?''

''Yes. She needs him—''

''I'll stay with her now,'' Nadine said flatly. ''That is, if she'll have me.''

''She has asked constantly for you. She does need you.''

An oddly wavering look crossed Nadine's face. ''But I'll stay whether she wants me or not. Now, Mady, there's something I want from you. Simple, really. Just tell me everything—everything that has happened. I know it is hard for you, but you must try. Every word, every—oh, everything. Don't leave out anything.''

''That's a tall order,'' Mady said soberly, thinking of the hurry-scurry past few days. But she began.

She began at what was for her the beginning, the meeting with Chan at 21. She had a not at all obscure desire to prove Chan's alibi for his brother's murder. Nadine merely nodded. Then the trip through the snow, late and getting later so the Valentine party was over before they arrived at the door and met Lettie, the grocery bag in her arms. And later finding that Lettie had swiftly transferred her jewels to the brown grocery bag, below cans of soups and frozen packages of food; the jewels and her house key were there but the diamond bracelet was gone.

Nadine said, ''Then what?''

Then the long inquiries, they seemed to have taken days; the position of the key in Stu's study, the position of the gun and the possession of the gun.

Nadine broke in again. "Chan couldn't have killed his brother! Go on."

Mady went on; it was a very familiar course of travel, too familiar for it had haunted her days and nights.

Nadine listened intently, her long black eyelashes sweeping her cheeks. Her gaze plunged up to meet Mady's, however, when Mady told her of the study, stripped of every used paper. "Now, why—" Nadine began and stopped. Her eyes narrowed, their steely glint like two sharp knives. After a moment she said, "That was not in the news. What do the police make of it?"

"I don't know really, but I believe they're considering the possibility that Stu had some kind of information in his study—desk, wherever, that might injure somebody—"

"And that somebody may have shot him because of it." Nadine sighed and lowered her eyes again. "Stu was very exact in all his arrangements. Filing, business correspondence, of course, I did most of that. No—or at least few personal letters. Go on, Mady."

Mady finished. "Lettie's mother and new stepfather are on their way here now. They expect to arrive late today. Chan will meet them, and I promised to be with Lettie."

Nadine still looked down. Finally, she said, "I'll go with you."

"Oh, Nadine! Will you?"

Nadine nodded only once, but decisively. "The police will question me, I'm sure. I can tell them only that I met Stu for luncheon the day he was killed."

"They'll ask you why he was killed and if you have any idea who did it."

Nadine nodded slowly.

Mady said, "You were not surprised about Rose's check."

Nadine lifted her steely eyes again. "Of course not. I knew all about it. Her explanation is perfectly true. I was going with Stu. My passport was ready. Oh—'' A fleeting look of half amusement, half desolation, touched Nadine's face. ''It was not to be a romantic trip, if that's what you are thinking—''

''No, I wasn't thinking that. I knew it would not be like that.''

''So did I,'' Nadine said wearily. ''I always knew just where I was in Stu's life. Important in a way. I liked that. But not as Lettie was important. I don't think,'' she added softly, ''really, I don't think that Stu so much as guessed my own feelings about him. No, I'm sure of it. Well, then, when are you to go to Lettie's?''

Mady glanced at her watch. ''Now, I think. Or soon—''

Nadine rose, took up her handsome coat and slung it around her shoulders; even that careless gesture, because Nadine made it, seemed graceful and dignified. ''I'll try to whistle up a cab—''

''No need. I have one waiting,'' said Clarence bouncing in the door. ''I heard that Lettie's mother has arrived already. Sorry. I came home awhile ago and I simply had to stop and listen. I'm very, very glad to see you, Nadine, my dear. You ought to be a great help. Have you any notion of an enemy of Stu's? Anybody who might have shot him?''

Nadine merely looked at him.

Clarence persisted. ''You know the police want to question you about that. They think you might know or at least have a suggestion—''

''Did you say you have a cab? Then perhaps—''

''Yes,'' said Mady.

So the three of them, Mady in the middle this time, took the route to Lettie's apartment; Mady felt as if she had been traveling these particular streets for a hundred years and never getting anywhere; it was like a nightmarish dream of unending paths, arriving nowhere.

They did, however, arrive at Lettie's apartment.

They were in the elevator when Clarence exploded his bomb. "Oh, by the way, that diamond bracelet of Lettie's—"

Both women turned swiftly toward him. Clarence adjusted one lemon-colored glove. "I saw it. It's on sale. That is, at an auction."

Mady got her breath. "It can't be—"

"Oh, yes. I recognized it."

"Do you mean the thief, murderer simply took it there to be auctioned off?" Mady asked sharply. Nadine was silent.

Clarence said, "Naturally, I asked who had left it there for sale. They wouldn't tell me. Their policy. If somebody puts up something for auction, it is the principle of the gallery to conceal the name. Unless the name—permitted, of course, by the seller—would add to the price of the object, you understand."

The elevator opened. Clarence frisked out because he happened to be standing beside the doors. Nadine and Mady followed him. He was about to ring the doorbell when Mady seized him by the arm. "Wait, Clarence! You must have more knowledge of this thing. Are you sure it was Lettie's bracelet?"

"Of course I'm sure. I've seen her wear it a million times." He jerked away from Mady's grip, adjusted his coat and pressed the bell.

Mady turned to Nadine. "Would a murderer simply walk into a gallery, one presumably with a reputation for honesty, and leave a bracelet he had stolen to be auctioned off?"

"I don't know."

"I'm sure Clarence would recognize it. He has a very sharp eye for such things."

Just then Chan opened the door. When he saw Nadine, his face lighted. "*Nadine!* Thank God—come in!"

Immediately they were aware of a murmur of mixed voices coming from the library. Once they got inside this was explained by the five other people in the room. Lettie was there; Larry was there; Ernest Wilkins was there; a woman who resembled Lettie and a thin, swarthy man were there, also.

Chan explained. "It's Lettie's mother and—and her husband. They arrived early."

Lettie sprang up, her lovely face warm and happy. "Nadine! I have so much wanted you to come!" She ran to fling herself upon Nadine, who submitted to the embrace stoically. Sentiment of that kind was not in Nadine's nature, Mady thought, and Chan said, "Chairs—we'd better adjourn to the living room, Lettie. More chairs. Oh, and drinks—of course—"

Lettie's mother looked wistful; she was an older version of Lettie, plump and pretty but rather nervous, Mady thought, for she watched everybody with quiet, yet very observant, brown eyes. As she hesitated, her husband, the dark gentleman, put his hand on her shoulder and she said, very promptly, "No, thank you. I—we—do not drink alcoholic beverages."

"However," her husband, Sarim Hadah, large dark eyes almost moist-looking with friendliness, said carefully, "orange juice, perhaps. If not too much trouble."

His English was easy, but had a slight accent, quite untraceable. Lettie's mother nodded, her fleshy chin going up and down above a handsome jewel-set necklace. But she still looked rather wistful.

Mady said, "I'll see to things, Lettie."

What was her mother's name? Mady couldn't remember until she heard Uncle Ernest say, "It is very good to see you again, Letitia. Even in such tragic circumstances."

Letitia, of course; Lettie's full name was Letitia, but she had been called Lettie all the time Mady had known her.

Chan was beside her. Larry, swiftly as a well-tailored and polished eel, had taken Mady's arm. Both men went with her to the pantry. Larry, obviously knowing his way around, began to assemble drinks and glasses efficiently.

"Tell me about Nadine," Chan said. "Where did she come from?"

"And why?" Larry asked over his shoulder.

"I honestly don't know." Mady sat down on a high stool near a table. "She's been staying in a little apartment in the city. She came to my house, and I think that she felt too sad, too grieved to talk to anyone before this. But she has kept up with the news and she had lunch with Uncle Ernest and—I believe," Mady said slowly, trying to reason it out satisfactorily, "she felt that Lettie needed her. But also I get the feeling that she may have some idea about Stu's murder. No—wait—" Larry had splashed whiskey onto a table top and the pungent reek crept over the shining, modern pantry. "I don't think she knows for certain who did it."

"But she has a pretty accurate idea," Chan said soberly.

"No, I'm not even sure of that. Actually, all I'm sure of is that she came to me and asked me to tell her everything, details that were not in the news. Then Clarence arrived and he knew Lettie's mother had gotten here—"

"Oh, yes," Larry said quickly. "I told him that. Met him in front of some art gallery. Chan had phoned to me about their early arrival. He thought I might be of some help—I don't know how, but help. I saw Clarence going into the gallery he frequents and stopped him and told him. Thought he'd be interested."

"Larry, did you see Lettie's bracelet there? In the gallery, I mean?"

Chan stared. "The bracelet? The diamond bracelet?"

"Clarence says so. He says he recognized it. But he couldn't get them to tell him who left it there for sale. They said it was not their policy—"

"I wonder," Larry said, getting ice from the refrigerator. "I do wonder if—why, Clarence himself might not have left it there! He always seems to need money—"

Mady leaped off the stool. "How can you say that? That's a lie! That's libel—"

"Slander," said Larry, smiling. The ice clattered into a crystal bucket, which was outlined in silver filigree. "Not printed. I don't really think Clarence stole the bracelet. I only said that, just a stray thought."

Chan said, "Let's not have that kind of stray thought."

Larry looked up, so startled at something in Chan's voice that his eyes flickered like those of a nervous horse, showing whites. Mady had a swift recollection of Larry's description of Chan's reaction when angered. And indeed, Chan did look rather dangerous just then. She put her hand on his arm. "We'd better take the drinks back. I suppose Mr. Whatever-his-name-is, is a Muslim or something. Certainly he sticks to whatever faith he has."

"Makes his wife stick to it, too," Chan said, still looking angry. Larry obligingly took a tray and filled it with glasses and ice. "Bring the liquor will you, Chan? I'll see if there's some orange juice."

She went with Chan, steadying a decanter as it wobbled on the tray. At the door of the living room he looked down at her. "Thank you, Mady. I was about to take a poke at Larry. He's so damn nosy. I've often wanted to," he added with a half smile, but instantly sobered. "Did Nadine explain those words about hurting Stu that she'd crossed off in her note?"

"No, she said she might as well have taken the gun herself."

Eighteen

Lettie was sitting in a fragile armchair, its pale blue covering setting off her slight figure, in black, of course, and her quiet pale face. Nadine stood beside the piano, not leaning against it, but as if she needed some kind of bulwark. Lettie's mother sat beside her husband on a small sofa. She was dressed almost certainly by some famous dressmaker; her suit was very conservative, yet there was style in every fold of it, a jacket short enough to disguise the bulk of her hips, a neatly tailored black skirt and a white blouse the price of which alone probably could have dressed most women, Mady thought swiftly, for a year. Even her feet, small and rather pudgy below plump ankles, were shod in pumps obviously from some equally famous house. Her hair's reddish tones were undoubtedly her hairdresser's secret and had been most adroitly applied. Her face was fleshy but skillfully preserved. She didn't look happy, but she did look rather smug, for they were speaking of hotels and where Letitia and her husband were to stay. It seemed, Mady realized as she helped Chan and Larry with drinks, that the husband had a small interest in a newly opened, very elegant hotel. Chan muttered in Mady's ear, "Interest of probably only thirty or forty million. I'd like to dash some vodka in this orange juice. I don't think he'd know it until too late."

Uncle Ernest stood beside Nadine as if he sensed something embattled and troubled about her, needing his protection. His gaze at his sister was fascinated, but rather puzzled.

Lettie shoved away her glass. Chan said softly to Nadine, "Mind if we get away for a minute and—"

"I know. You want to question me. No."

"But Nadine, if you really know, that is guess—"

"No," said Nadine firmly again.

Mady was near them, she felt that none of the others heard the few words between them, although she wasn't sure about Uncle Ernest, who, she suspected, had ears in the back of his good-looking head.

Letitia had reached out her hand toward Lettie, seated near her; Lettie accepted it, but not warmly, for which Mady could not blame her.

Letitia, too, seemed to be feeling some kind of strain in their reunion. "We phoned your apartment, you know. Just to tell you that we were coming right away. My husband insisted on it, of course. He wanted me to be with you in your bereavement. But nobody answered in your apartment, nobody at all. I must have had the wrong address. At the airport we looked in the phone book. You must have moved—"

Her husband's dark hand pressed lightly on Letitia's plump knee. She gave him a swift glance and said, "But this one is so beautiful—"

This one, Mady thought, perplexed. There is only this one. Except, of course, the place they had had in Washington.

"Oh, yes," said Mr. Hadah, too quickly, it seemed to Mady, but very agreeably for his moist-looking, very dark eyes were traveling the room—assessing the quality of rugs and draperies, Mady thought shortly.

Uncle Ernest, for no reason, drew closer to Nadine so he almost touched her arm. Clarence came prancing from the library holding up a hand from which dangled a glitter of green and flashing diamonds. "Look what I found!"

Everybody looked, no question of that. Lettie sprang to her feet. "But that—"

"Of course," Clarence said. "Your emerald-and-diamond necklace. Didn't you even miss it?"

"Why, I—where on earth was it—"

Sarim Hadah went lightly to meet Clarence. "I'll see to it," he said pleasantly, ignoring Clarence's astonished stare and his still-outstretched, but suddenly emptied, hand.

"Oh, thank you," Lettie said. "I *had* forgotten it. All this—I wore it sometime recently."

"You were wearing it at the Valentine party," Chan said, swirling his whiskey and soda absently. "Frankly, I remember thinking you were not very wise to wear such valuable jewelry out in the street—"

"I don't know what I did with it," Lettie was watching

not her necklace, but her stepfather's face. "I certainly didn't mean to lose it—''

Clarence was triumphant. "My wooden Indian! It was inside the head. Somebody has been tinkering with it. I told you it was supposed to come to pieces. That girl who works for you must have found it, Lettie!" Clarence's affection for analysis crept into his expression; he squinted his eyes upward. "I see now. That girl of yours took it and intended to make away with it. Probably intended to put it up for auction as she did your diamond bracelet."

Sarim Hadah smiled. "Do go on, Mr.—Fotheringay, is it? What about Lettie's diamond bracelet? I didn't know she had lost it."

"You must have known," Chan said pleasantly. "At least—no, perhaps our talk has not been entirely complete, I mean all the circumstances of my brother's murder. You see, he had taken Lettie's diamond bracelet for repair. It disappeared the day he was—was shot."

Sarim Hadah shook his glossy black head. "How very sad! Yet perhaps the murderer—''

Uncle Ernest said abruptly. "This is no time for family talk. The police have this in hand. You will want to see the police, Letitia—'' He very obviously did not address Mr. Hadah. "I'll take you to see them if you like."

"Oh!" Letitia seemed to shrink into herself; she gave her husband a darting glance and said, "Really, I don't— that is, what could I—dear me, Ernest, it is a tragic, tragic thing, but I can't—''

"I'll see the police," her husband said pleasantly. "Anytime you say, Mr.—I mean brother Ernest."

Nadine stirred. "I'm going home. I'll be back later, Lettie."

Larry said swiftly, "I'll go with you, Nadine—'' His ears were practically sticking out; naturally he wanted a chance to question her.

"A car is waiting for us," said Sarim Hadah pleasantly, but there was a steely something in his voice and in his manner that suggested a certain command over money and over people, too, Mady thought.

Clarence was reproachful. "But Lettie, aren't you glad I happened to find your necklace? You really must do something about that maid of yours—"

"Yes," Lettie said. "Yes—"

Her stepfather said, "I'll just take care of this for you, Lettie," and quietly slid the necklace he had adroitly taken from Clarence into an inside pocket. "Come, my dear," he smiled down at his wife. "You really must get some rest. You've had a very long trip. Thank you, Lettie, my dear. What a delightful surprise to find a lovely daughter— and so like her mother."

"Not to be wondered at," Chan muttered again in Mady's ear. Decidedly, Chan was not at his best just then—but perhaps he was beginning to recover his usual self-possession, even a glint of humor, even, Mady thought, just perhaps his affection for her. She wouldn't use, even in her mind, a stronger term. Decidedly, it was rather as if Chan had had an illness and was barely beginning to find himself again. Larry seemed spurred by Mr. Hadah to even more than his usual air of polite attendance. Smelled money, no doubt. Anybody in Mr. Hadah's vicinity must be aware of that not unpleasant aroma. He also looked very healthy and sure of himself; it was Letitia who was overly plump and overly desirous of pleasing. Lettie said to her mother, "I'll let you go now then. Of course, you must rest."

Mr. Hadah looked at Chan and smiled. "May I speak to you, Dr. Channing?"

There was the slightest emphasis upon the word doctor. Mady saw Chan's face change, becoming, in the flicker of a second, quite cold and blank. "Why, yes. Certainly, sir. Here—"

"Oh, no," Mr. Hadah glanced around, still smiling. "I'd like rather more privacy, don't you think? At my hotel, perhaps?"

Chan's eyes were very dark and intent. "Why not here?"

Mr. Hadah seemed agreeable, yet Mady wondered fleetingly if that was always true; something about the way he had put a hand on Letitia's shoulder suggested hidden, indeed rather unpleasant, force.

Chan still eyed Mr. Hadah intently. "Why not here, Mr. Hadah?" Before Mr. Hadah could refuse, Chan lounged off into the library. Mr. Hadah appeared to hesitate for a second. But then as he turned to follow Chan, Chan called back, "Mady, will you look at this—"

Mr. Hadah glanced once at Mady: she was perfectly certain he did not wish her company, but she followed into the library. Mr. Hadah did not stop her, but he closed the door and stood against it, still smiling, his teeth flashing in his swarthy face. As if he might bite, Mady thought unexpectedly, and then saw what Chan was looking at, which was the wooden Indian's head.

It lay on the carpet. She gave a half cry and Chan said, "Never mind. Clarence said it was hollow. Someone found it a good hiding place. Well, now, Mr. Hadah, my answer, sir, is no."

Mr. Hadah put a smooth-skinned hand on the back of a chair; he wore a ring that glimmered red in the light and looked old and elaborate and valuable. He said softly, "But I haven't asked you anything yet, Dr. Channing."

"It's no use," Chan said.

"But you don't know—"

"Oh, I think I know."

Mr. Hadah was silent for a second or two. Then he said, "But I can triple whatever salary you are getting now. Indeed, I can give you almost anything you like. Perhaps the beautiful young lady here ought to give her opinion."

Chan laughed. "No, Mr. Hadah. She doesn't even know what you are talking about."

"Are you sure that *you* know?" Did Mr. Hadah ever stop smiling? Mady thought.

She also began to get a notion of the offer he was making Chan. She cried, "No! He intends to stay where he is."

Chan now looked just faintly amused. "She's beautiful, yes. But also brighter than she looks," he said to Mr. Hadah. Then he sobered, "You see, sir, there are firm international agreements concerning at least one of your undertakings." He paused and then said flatly, "How much does Mrs. Chavez know of this involvement?"

The smile vanished from Mr. Hadah's thin face. "What do you mean?"

"Oh, I'm sure you know." Chan picked up the hollowed head of the wooden Indian and tried to refit it in its base. "Mrs. Chavez wants her money out of your concern and intends to have it. As for me, no, thank you." The wooden head clicked back into place. "I like it where I am."

"That unimportant, poor little university! When you could have millions at your disposal!" Surely Mr. Hadah's mouth could never have smiled; it was now a thin, cruel slash.

"But you see," Chan said pleasantly. "I happen to like that university. Oh, I'll grant you it has no big laboratory. Not like the Princeton Plasmas Physics Lab. Or M.I.T. or—"

"But you *are* working on nuclear research. I can help. I can supply all the money—"

"Not from Mrs. Chavez," said Chan unexpectedly.

This seemed to startle Mr. Hadah, but he covered the sudden flicker of his eyelids swiftly. "You know nothing of the money that is back of my laboratory."

"Back of Chavez et Cie," Chan said. "Mrs. Chavez is so concerned about it that she asked my brother to investigate with a view to getting her money out of Chavez et Cie. It would never have been invested there in the first place if she had been informed—indeed if any of her business representatives had been suitably informed of its possible aims."

Mr. Hadah's eyes narrowed. "What should anyone have to know! The accounts are in order."

"I'm sure of that. But you see, Mrs. Chavez concurs with our belief here that all nuclear research should be suitably monitored."

"Nonsense!" Mr. Hadah snapped.

"It is for the general good, you know that. Mr. Hadah, you do seem to want reliable physics researchers—"

"You should be flattered!" Mr. Hadah had recovered his aplomb.

"No," Chan said seriously. "I'm not flattered. I don't like what I suspect are your intentions."

Mr. Hadah showed white teeth in a smile. "But you'd be very much richer—"

"Get out," said Chan pleasantly.

"*What*—" Bright lights of astonishment leaped into Mr. Hadah's eyes.

"*Now*," said Chan, taking a step toward him.

Mr. Hadah backed toward the door, slid through it like a snake and Chan gave a low laugh. "Didn't like me. I wonder what I'd have done with him."

"Chan! He wanted you to give up your post and enter this—this Chavez et Cie at some fabulous salary, because you *are* a brilliant scientist, that's why. And it only made you good and mad—"

"Oh, no." Chan laughed softly. "But I don't like him or—never mind. That's that. Come on—"

She went with him back to the living room, where curiously the entire atmosphere had changed; it had become like a carefully directed scene in a play; Mady's swift glance around was involuntary. But she heard Mr. Hadah speak to Larry. "Will you accompany us, please." It was not a question. He walked serenely toward the hall. Lettie's face suddenly turned pink; she reached one hand toward her mother and her mother quite definitely put it away, rose and followed her husband. Uncle Ernest was no longer puzzled; instead he said to his sister, "Lettie is your daughter, you know,'' mildly, yet with authority. Chan strolled to the long table against the wall and leaned on it, his ankles crossed, his hands in his pockets and his dark eyebrows peaked up above alert gray eyes. Even Nadine had pink spots in her usually pale cheeks.

Something was happening and Mady didn't know what it was. Larry had instantly rushed after Lettie's mother and the new husband. Lettie linked her hands together and looked at nothing.

Then the two handsomely dressed, perfectly composed people were gone, with Larry struggling hurriedly into an overcoat in order to accompany them. Clarence was rubbing his white hair. ''I thought you'd be pleased, Lettie,'' he complained. ''Why did you let that old coot—I mean your greasy-looking stepfather get away with it? It's your necklace—''

Lettie fumbled for words. ''But he—it's all right—that is, he *is* the head of the family.''

''Not the head of your family,'' Uncle Ernest said gravely. ''I must say I didn't quite cotton to the fellow. Still, to be fair there's nothing specific I can say against him. He seems to have made your mother happy.''

Nadine took a long breath. ''Thank you,'' she said in a low voice to Uncle Ernest, who seemed to understand perfectly why she thanked him. ''I'll be all right now. I'll go, Lettie, and get some night things. Then I'll be back. Let me have your house key.'' She looked so directly at Lettie that it suggested a more important significance. ''So I'll not bother you when I come back.''

''Oh, I don't have a house key,'' Lettie said quickly. ''All you have to do is ring. Chan will be here. He'll let you in or I will.''

''Why, yes, Lettie! You have a key. It's in your bedside table. Shall I get it?'' Mady was on her feet and entering the corridor. She had a dim notion that Lettie had tried to stop her, saying something about forgetting the key, never mind, she'd see to it, something of the kind, and that

Clarence was talking—"and your diamond bracelet, Lettie! I tell you I saw it. At the gallery. To be put up for auction. You really must take steps about that—"

Mady heard no more. She was sure she remembered Lettie's dropping the key in the drawer in the bedside table, and it was still there. She took it and went back to the living room. Clarence was still talking—"and I tell you the girl thought you had caught her and she was going to get as much money as she could for the bracelet and escape—oh, Mady! Got her key?"

"Here it is," Mady said to Nadine and flashed a glance at Lettie. "I remembered where you had put it that day."

"Oh," Lettie said. "Yes. I remember now." Nadine put out a strong hand, took the key and turned away so swiftly that Mady saw only her black hair above the coat into which Clarence had sprung to assist her.

Uncle Ernest put a firm hand on Nadine's arm. Chan said, "I'll just go down with you. Back in a minute."

Clarence skipped out with them.

Lettie rose and began to move about the room absently, picking up used glasses, restoring them to the tray. Mady said, "Really, Lettie, I'd never have dreamed that maid, Gretchen—"

"No. Neither would I. It was odd, Clarence finding my necklace like that. And then saying he saw my bracelet!"

Mady fired up a little. "Clarence didn't take them!"

"No, no! I didn't say he did. I'm so confused. My mother! It's been years since I've seen her. She looks—oh, different. She was so pretty when I was young. Her husband seems to give her everything she wants. Most indulgent. Very rich."

"You have your necklace. And that bracelet. Somebody can bid it in for you."

"Oh, that wouldn't be necessary. Stolen goods. I'm sure there's some law about that. Larry will know—"

The telephone rang.

Lettie had the tray in her hands. "Answer it, will you,

Mady? The library extension. If it's the police again say I'm not here."

Mady went to the sofa, where the bald young man had waded wearily through lists of names, and took down the telephone. Nadine said clearly into the telephone, "I'm glad it's you. Come straight downstairs. Don't tell anyone." She hung up as if someone had approached her.

Nadine must have decided to tell everything she knew, was Mady's only thought. But Nadine had told her not to tell anyone she was to meet her. Even Lettie, she supposed. Lettie had taken the tray into the pantry. She came out as Mady was getting her coat. "I hoped you would stay until Nadine returns."

"I'll be back—in a moment—just an errand—" Mady jumbled it up as she rang for the elevator which for once was prompt.

Her view of Lettie's small black figure was shut off by the doors.

Nadine!

She was just outside on the sidewalk, the lights from the foyer shining down upon her black hair and white, determined face. She took Mady by the arm. She had a grip as hard and certain as a man's, Mady thought vaguely, as Nadine pushed her toward a waiting, throbbing taxi. She heard Nadine give an address that was strange to Mady.

"Your apartment?"

Nadine replied shortly. "No."

After a moment they turned left off Fifth Avenue. "Where's Chan, I thought he was with you?"

"He and Mr. Wilkins went, I think, to the Stanhope Bar. To talk about Lettie, what to do with her. Chan can't keep looking after her forever. Her uncle probably feels that since his sister quite positively refused to assist her in any way, then he is next of kin."

Mady felt a great wave of thankfulness for Uncle Ernest. Perhaps now—Nadine leaned forward to speak to the taxi driver. "We turn here. Now go slowly. I'll watch for the number."

"Nadine! Where are we going?"

"Here we are. All right—" She had a bill for the taximan already in one ungloved hand. "Come on, Mady. You'll see—I think. Oh, yes, I think—"

It was a one-time town house, converted to small apartments. The entrance was dimly lighted. Nadine paused for only a moment, her elegant figure poised as she scrutinized a small plaque of resident names. "Oh, yes. Here—"

Mady hadn't recognized any of the names. Nadine pushed a button and the main door opened, but then she walked coolly up the carpeted stairs. Here were two doors, both of well-polished mahogany—remnants, Mady thought absently, of the former house.

The nearest door swung open as Nadine unlocked it. Mady followed her inside. The place was dark but had a pleasant odor, some kind of light perfume, which oddly at that instant reminded Mady of Lettie.

"Where are we—" she began.

"You'll see." Nadine had found an electric light switch. The little foyer came to life and off it Mady could see a rather bare bedroom, not unpleasant but not pleasant either. It had a feeling of disuse; the bed was made up but looked as if it had never been slept in; nothing at all, not even a brush, lay on the dressing table; there was a mirror above it that was dim and foggy. Mady said, "But surely nobody lives here!"

Nadine said nothing. She stepped across the hall and opened another door on the other side. Mady followed her and here, also, Nadine found a light switch and touched it. Then this room came into being and it had been used. No question of that. It was a charming room, in its way. Thick rugs, one or two comfortable chairs, but a businesslike desk and photographs. Miles of photographs! "Nadine!"

"Yes. Look at them."

"But—but it's Lettie. Everywhere." She went closer to the photographs, some of them framed in silver, all of them showing Lettie with—with some notable, Mady thought amazed. "There's the senator—there's—there's one, no, two—Presidents—"

"In office at the same time as Stu," Nadine replied. She was at the desk rapidly opening drawer after drawer. Papers spilled out. Canceled checks floated onto the floor. Checkbooks, neat in plastic folders.

"Nadine, I don't understand—"

"Neither did I quite until Lettie's precious stepfather tossed her out."

"Her stepfather! I didn't hear that!"

Nadine gave her a look of indulgent scorn. "You weren't listening. It happened right before us."

"How did you know—"

"Because I found and leased this place for Lettie. Not under her own name. I could see why she wanted it—a place of quiet, she said. To rest and—all right." Nadine faced her, head up. "I thought that Lettie expected to meet some lover here. And that suited me. Anything to—"

"To get Stu," Mady whispered. "Oh, Nadine!"

"It wasn't very nice of me. Is that what you think? You are perfectly right. If you wish to condemn me, go ahead. You can't make me feel worse than I have since—since I told Stu."

"*You told Stu!* That isn't like you! You say you helped Lettie. You arranged this apartment as a—"

"Love nest," Nadine said dryly. "Oh, yes. I did that. Hoping. But Stu was never the faintest bit suspicious. He truly loved her, you know. Nothing else in his life was as important. My ugly little plan came to nothing. But then with this appointment to the Cabinet and a Senate confirmation coming up, I knew I had to give him at least a hint of Lettie's love affairs. I was sure of that, you see. Oh, I'm not trying to excuse myself. You see, Mady, while lawmakers may allow for various outside activities, they know that their constituents take a strong moral stand. Suppose the man Lettie was meeting here (or men, as far as I knew) chose to blackmail Stu, or even to leak the facts to the press! A man's whole family is put under a microscope. Some men, I know, have avoided any place in public life for that very reason. Their own little peccadilloes or even some lapse on the part of a family member. I had to warn Stu." Nadine's voice throbbed as if her throat hurt. "I thought I had to. I still think I had to tell Stu what I believed to be the truth. But when I saw and heard Mr. Hadah I knew I had been on the wrong track altogether."

"Nadine—"

"You don't understand. Look around you. All these photographs. Lettie, arm in arm with some celebrity in government. Always in government. On the best of terms. Smiling. Friendly. But she's lost her job. Did Hadah offer Chan a job?"

"Yes. But I don't see—"

"Doing what? Oh, naturally, yes! Chan is a scientist—what is Hadah backing?"

"It's a nuclear research laboratory."

Nadine thought for a second. "A wide field! Yes. That's Chan's field. And Chan refused?"

"Yes, of course. And Nadine, Hadah as good as admitted that Rose's money is helping finance the thing through Chavez et Cie. Rose didn't know it. That's why when she began to suspect or old Mr. Walldon or somebody suspected, she asked Stu to investigate for her and paid him ahead of time—"

Nadine never required anything to be spelled out. "I see. So Lettie's stepfather was behind it all. Yes. Well, now Larry will take over. He's not a physicist but he has certain abilities—yes," she said shortly, "I think Larry will take over Lettie's job."

There were too many things for Mady to say crowding into her mind. Nadine went on. "You were not aware of that. I was when I saw Lettie turn red, and the way this

Hadah told Larry to accompany him. Even the way he slid that diamond necklace into his pocket. The way Lettie— the first time in all these years, put out a hand asking her mother for help and the way her mother deserted her and went along with Hadah. Her bread and butter and luxury. Two of a kind, Lettie and her mother. Poor dear Stu! Don't look like that, Mady. It's obvious that Lettie was making a secret business of lobbying for her rich stepfather. She didn't meet lovers here. I understood that almost as soon as I met her stepfather. She needed this apartment in order to meet her stepfather occasionally or some middleman— whoever he is. Somebody who handed over the money to her. But now Lettie is definitely out of a job. Sounds cruel. But she was cruel. Why do you think she has all these photographs here?''

"To impress her stepfather and his middleman with her friendship to so many—so many important people?" Mady said huskily.

Nadine merely nodded. "There are the records. Check-books, everything will be there. She was right not to keep them where Stu might see them. I'm not just sure how the money was managed, but it seems to me likely that her stepfather had his man pay Lettie. Then Lettie, from the look of those bank statements and canceled checks, simply opened several bank accounts in different names." She scooped up one or two bank statements, and read from them with a satiric, yet sad look in her face. "Here, Mabel Urban, Grace Wells, Helen Skeffington, well, that was Lettie's maiden name. Same address, same apartment, this one. That's why, when her mother tried to phone to her, Mr. Hadah had only the phone number for this apartment. So they stopped at the airport and looked up the big apartment. No wonder Mr. Hadah was surprised. But that's the way Lettie worked the money." She looked swiftly at one or two of the statements. "Yes. Deposited amounts that were large enough, but not suspiciously large and always in a checking account, not a savings account which would report an interest gain. She was very smart about it—she or Mr. Hadah, or the middleman, whoever he is. There must be one. Mr. Hadah must have felt he had fallen into a very rewarding situation when his wife told him of Lettie's place in Washington, her husband a senator. His own stepdaughter able to lobby for him and—'' A telephone on the desk rang sharply, repeating itself while both women stared at it, shocked into immobility. Nadine recovered first and snatched up the receiver. ''Hello—what? —Will you repeat that—Oh, I'm sorry, Mr. Hadah. It seems to be a very bad connection. But I—yes, of course. Right now! But—Oh! Oh, I see!'' Nadine had turned her back to Mady in order to speak into the telephone, but there was something rigidly intent in the set of her body; Mady waited, holding the edge of the desk, scarcely breathing. Finally, at the mumble of the voice at the other end of the wire, Nadine seemed to make up her mind. ''I'll be there, then—yes, at once. Yes, I'll try to—''

She put down the telephone.

''That was Sarim Hadah!''

Nadine nodded, obviously thinking hard. ''He wants me to bring all documents—that's what he said, documents— from this apartment to him. He's at the bar in the Carlyle Hotel.''

''Drinking orange juice,'' said Mady parenthetically. ''Are you going?''

''I want to ask him some questions. But I'm not going to take him any of this mess of checks and bank records. Mady, I brought you here because you are a friend of Lettie's. You like her and I have got to be fair with her. Besides,'' she sighed. ''You are sensible. You'll help with whatever there is to do. I don't know what, but I'll see Hadah now.''

''Mr. Hadah looks as if he could get up quite a storm if he's not promptly obeyed.''

''Obeyed!'' Nadine gave a short laugh. ''That's not why I'm going to see him. I'm going to make him wish himself back wherever he came from. Mady, you phone to Chan. The Stanhope Bar. Chan will come here for you. No sense walking alone—''

''Will you be all right?''

Nadine laughed shortly again. ''I can't see Mr. Hadah shooting me or—murdering me in the sedate Carlyle.''

She flung her coat around her and went through the door of the picture-filled living room, which did not quite close. Mady could hear her swift steps on the stairs, receding until the heavy outside door closed with a slow sigh.

All those canceled checks! The accounts under differing names. All proofs of Lettie's moneymaking affairs! Yet had her stepfather actually been displeased with her? The answer was yes. It was very likely that Lettie had taken all the money she could get, but never accomplished anything at all for her stepfather; certainly he had been in no pleasant mood after Chan's refusal, when he walked out of Lettie's apartment taking her mother with him. And telling Larry to come with him. Nadine must be right; he had fired Lettie, without Mady herself having been aware of it, and demanded Larry's escort—which Larry had accepted with quite evident alacrity. She didn't like this small room where all the photographs seemed to eye her fixedly.

Footsteps were running up the stairs. Not Nadine's; they were heavier; a man was taking, it seemed to her, two steps at a time.

Larry flung the door open wider, stopped and just stared at her, his eyes bright and green.

Nineteen

"What are you doing here?" he said at last.

"I might say the same to you." Mady gathered up the coat she had put down without knowing it.

"But you—what have *you* been doing? Did you get out all those—those checks and everything on the floor?"

"No. Nadine."

"Oh, yes. Of course. Why didn't she take them to—that is, I would expect her to take them to Lettie's stepfather."

An astonishing surmise struck Mady all of a sudden. "Larry! Were you the—Mr. Hadah's middleman? Did you pay Lettie?"

"Now see here, Mady. Well, yes."

"And he gave you money for acting as his intermediary?"

"Why not? He's got plenty." He started across the room.

"Where are you going?"

"I'll get a pillowcase. Shove all these things into it and—"

"Take them to him?"

"Don't be a fool! Destroy them! I don't want anything to connect me with this affair."

"How did you get into it in the first place?"

"Through Sarim Hadah, of course. Good heavens, Mady. He's got business interests all over. Many in New York and—anyway that's how I happened to meet him. Naturally, we got on rather good terms—"

"Naturally, with all his money!"

"Now, Mady. Like a little cat again, huh? Listen, why not? I did nothing illegal. I paid off Lettie. And how she spent the money. And all for nothing."

"Nothing—"

"I don't think she ever even tried to lobby for Hadah. He guessed it this afternoon. Took back her necklace. Now I want to get rid of all these—"

"Larry! *You* phoned Nadine! It wasn't Mr. Hadah at all! She said it was a bad connection."

"I tried to imitate his accent. Didn't do so well, I see. Anyway she left all this stuff here as I knew she would. I only wanted a chance to get rid of them. Didn't expect to find you here. Now then—"

"How *could* you have got Lettie and yourself involved—"

"Oh, I'm not involved!"

"No? No, you would be on the safe side!"

"All right, all right. Now then—"

"I'll not let you take them," Mady said.

"How are you going to stop me?" Larry's green eyes laughed.

"There's always the police. Did you shoot Stu?" Mady said flatly. She hadn't intended to say it. She hadn't meant to accuse him. She hadn't intended to do anything! She was standing at the desk, pressing against it.

Larry waited a moment. At last he said, "No. But I think you may be right about all these things, I mean. I *am* on the safe side. I might tell you that Mr. Hadah offered me the job he fired Lettie for not doing for him. I refused."

"Refused *him!*"

Larry nodded rather unhappily and smoothed back his polished hair. "Had to. I wanted to take it. Money in it—but I'd have to be successful. You saw what happened when Lettie didn't accomplish anything. I don't know enough about Washington, about the people who know the people. No, I couldn't have managed it. I was sorry though. Think of all that money—"

"You did get a fine new car out of it!"

"Why, yes." He smiled frankly. "Yes. I did. And some other little trickles."

I don't know what to do, Mady thought. And actually what can I do? This is evidence but not evidence of Stu's murder. Or is it?

Larry said rather regretfully, "Of course with Rose's money helping to back Chavez et Cie—one of Mr. Hadah's little interests—"

"*Rose's* money backing Mr. Hadah!" So Chan's surmise had been right. "How do you know?"

"Oh, Mady!" Larry was impatient. "Of course I found out. Tried to get it out of you, but either you didn't know or were too smart about evading—"

"I knew you were after something. I didn't know what."

"Well, I thought you might know of—oh," Larry said airily, "this or that. I like to pick up trifles, especially if they show the way the wind is blowing."

"I suppose your girl friend in Mr. Walldon's office told you more than she thought she told you—"

"No," Larry shook his head thoughtfully. "She didn't really know very much. But I could put two and two together. Rose wanted Stu to investigate Chavez et Cie. Hadah was paying Lettie for something. So I asked around here and there. He does have money in Chavez et Cie. Lettie would be expected to influence Stu and his peers in Washington. All easy for me to add up."

She took up the telephone. Without another word Larry whirled around and slid out the door; she heard the light patter now of his footsteps running down the stairs.

She couldn't think of the Stanhope telephone number. She looked around for a directory, found one on a shelf at one side of the desk and began to thumb through it. Chan and Uncle Ernest, and Nadine on a wild goose chase at the Carlyle! She found the number and her fingers were on the telephone dial when she knew that she was not alone in the little apartment.

She listened. All at once her heart was thudding so

furiously that she couldn't hear anything except—yes, except a kind of rustle and click as if a drawer somewhere had been pulled out and then thrust back.

She went slowly to the open door of the bedroom. Lettie was there, standing at an ugly chest of drawers. Her back was turned to Mady. She was busy taking small objects, boxes, from a drawer and thrusting them into a large shoulder bag she carried. Mady must have said something, made some sound. Lettie said, without looking around, "I knew you would come here, Nadine. You've got to help me. You have always helped. Now—"

She was wearing her chinchilla coat. Her lovely curls rose above it. Then she seemed to sense something wrong in the atmosphere, for she turned and saw Mady.

Her eyes opened widely, above the thick fur collar. "What are you doing here?"

"What are you doing, Lettie?"

"What am I—nothing, nothing. Where is Nadine? Why did she bring you here?"

"She's gone—"

Lettie said in a gasp, "But you've been snooping!" She came at Mady with a rush, but whisked past her and then stopped to stare at the debris on the floor. "Oh," she said. Her eyes flashed at Mady. "That's why you gave her the key. You've known all along. You've known and watched me and trapped me and—"

"No, Lettie. No—"

"You gave her the key. You came here—you've been trying to trap me! You stopped me at the door the night of the party! I had the jewels in the grocery bag, enough to support me for years. I could have gotten away and been safe. But you stopped me and you've been watching me—"

"No, Lettie—"

"—and the night that George Shelton was shot, you heard me. You spoke to me. I told you I'd got some warm milk but you waited. You trapped me—" Her eyes above the furs were glazed like those of some small animal, caught and frantic.

Mady edged backward, leaning against the desk.

Lettie was speaking in rapid gasps. "You even knew about your red coat. He didn't tell me the St. Regis. He told me the other hotel. You guessed it."

Mady's voice came out huskily. "What about my coat?"

"I wanted to trust you. But I was never sure. Then you gave Nadine the key to this place. I'd had it in the grocery bag. You knew that. I had had it with me the night of the Valentine party. You saw where I hid it."

"You were coming here then! You were running away!"

"I had to. I hadn't much time. Nobody would know where I had gone. Except Nadine and she would only guess. But you—Mady, *why* did you go and get that key? *Why* did you stick your nose into this? You've been adding things up like—like beads on a string. Catching me Valentine night so I couldn't get away. Finding my jewels and pretending you thought I had only hidden them from the police. I really am sorry. But you can see there's just nothing else for me to do."

She had, incredibly, pulled a gun from her shoulder bag.

Mady stared at it. "You said you'd lost that!"

"I had only hidden it in Clarence's precious Indian." She gave an excited, yet frightening little laugh. "He did find the necklace. That and the bracelet were by far the most valuable of any of my jewels. I meant to get the necklace here, but I had hidden it in the Indian and there were too many people in the apartment. But I got out all my other jewels and brought them here the afternoon of Stu's funeral. Now I—" She gripped the gun hard. "Mady, I've got to get away. I'm so scared and—oh, I am so sorry it must be you. I was sorry about Stu, too. But Nadine had told him about this place and he made me explain. Mr. Hadah and all the money. Stu said I had to return the money, as much as I could. The apartment. The jewels. He would give up the Cabinet post. He would go into law practice. On a junior partner's salary. No more Hadah—no more money—something just went off in my head.''

"No. No, you waited because—why, yes, only the caterers were there. They might have heard a gunshot. You waited for guests and talk and laughter and—then you took Rose's glove to avoid leaving fingerprints, and—how did you get Chan's gun?''

"I didn't! I didn't—''

"You knew where Stu kept it. In the library? When you thought the gunshot wouldn't be heard, you slipped back to Stu and—oh, Lettie, you must have got behind him and told him something, said you were sorry—''

"I wasn't sorry," Lettie said flatly. "Look the other way, Mady.''

Lettie was watching Mady, but she didn't seem to see that Mady had edged closer to the desk so her hip nudged against it. Her groping hand encountered something hard and smooth, a paperweight. She screamed with all her might and flung the paperweight at Lettie. The door behind Lettie crashed open. Chan had Lettie in his arms and the gun went off twice, sounding like a vicious firecracker and filling the air with an acrid odor.

Lettie was struggling. The gun dropped. Chan shouted, "Get the gun, Mady! Get it!''

She scooped up the gun and then just stood there holding it. Lettie all at once dissolved into a sobbing, furry little bundle, clinging to Chan. "I wouldn't really have shot her—''

"You shot my brother," Chan said. He looked at Mady. "Don't feel sorry, Mady. Where is Nadine?''

"I don't know. She had a faked phone call. She's at the Carlyle by now. I'll tell you—'' Now her knees and her voice were shaking. "Oh, Chan, how did you get here when I needed you—''

"Saw Lettie in a taxi, passing the Stanhope door. I waved to her, but she wouldn't stop. I ran a way, then got another taxi and followed. I heard her voice as I ran up the stairs here—"

Lettie sobbed, "Chan, help me! I'm terrified. I'm not guilty—"

"Oh, Lettie," Chan said somberly. "You gave yourself away so many times. From that very first night, the night of the Valentine party. Mady and I met you at the door of the apartment house and you lifted your face for me to kiss—"

And for me, Mady thought.

"—and your cheek was warm. Not cold. If you had actually been out on the street in the storm your face would have been cold."

Yes, yes, Mady thought. I remember.

"You were in a panic, Lettie!" Chan went on. "I wondered about that almost at once, but I couldn't believe you shot him. You were coming to this place, weren't you? When we got up to your apartment you opened a champagne bottle, hoping it would sound like a shot and make us believe someone at that moment shot Stu."

Lettie's sobs rose to a scream. "It's a cruel world! You must help me, Chan."

"I couldn't be sure. Even the room—Stu liked a cool room. Somebody had turned up the thermostat to confuse the time. And then we found that all the papers in Stu's study had been destroyed! You always said that Stu saw to the money you had inherited. You knew that if that were true, the police would expect to find some papers of some kind, some records of money. Actually you handled it all yourself while Stu was busy with government affairs. So you had to destroy everything. But then you got into such a wild panic—"

"I didn't mean to kill him!"

"—that when the guests had gone and you would have had to find and report Stu's death you couldn't face it. You were running—getting out of it—coming here."

No answer.

"You had lied to Stu about the money. Did you ever do any lobbying for—say, your stepfather?"

"No—oh, no! Never once."

"I rather think that is the truth. But your stepfather thought you were because he was paying you until he started to question your results recently and threatened to cut off the money. Was he ever here, in this room?"

No answer.

"We'll take it that he was here several times secretly. Else why all these photographs? You meant to impress him with your friendships. You—"

"But I didn't try to lobby! Never. I wouldn't know how—"

"Who actually paid you? How were you paid? Who was the middleman who handed over money from your stepfather?"

Mady said, "Larry Todd. He was here. He left just now—scared."

"But he'll be made to testify, Lettie. He'll try to keep his own hands clean—"

Lettie surged against Chan's arms. He said, "I began to realize that I had to watch you. Yet the night the impostor was murdered, Mady was with you. So I didn't see how—"

Mady said, "I know how—"

Chan nodded. "I can guess. The police are tracing the person who left the diamond bracelet to be sold. That was you, Lettie? Getting together all the cash you could to help you run for cover—"

"She did panic," Mady said, but sadly.

"She killed my brother."

Nadine opened the door behind him and stood there for an instant. Mady didn't move, but Chan sensed someone's presence and glanced over his shoulder. Nadine came forward. "I'll take her. Chan."

"Oh, yes," Lettie wailed. "Nadine, take me away! Take me anywhere!"

"No," Chan said.

Lettie cried. "He talked about the police—oh, Nadine—"

"I have to take her to the police." Chan held Lettie tightly, almost as a lover might hold her—but a lover wouldn't look as he looked.

Nadine came farther into the room. "All right, Chan. I know—at least, I can imagine how you feel. But you see, I told Stu about this apartment. I had gotten it for her. I thought it was for—another purpose. But I knew that Stu would have to face the most searching and minute inquiry to receive Senate confirmation of his Cabinet appointment. So I knew—I was afraid that anything at all might come out of that. Blackmail on the part of Lettie's lover or lovers. Oh, I didn't care how many lovers she had. And I would never have told Stu if it hadn't been for the Senate inquiry. Really, Chan. I knew, you see—" Her voice had been steady. It now broke a little, but she went on. "I knew what Lettie meant to Stu, which was simply the whole world. It was hard for me to do. But I met him for lunch and told him as gently as I could. He must have gone home and confronted Lettie with it and she couldn't face it. Lying about the money, knowing he'd cut off her supply, make her return what she could, she went into a panic. I told you, Mady, I might as well have taken up that gun and shot him myself. If I hadn't been so sure that he could settle the problem, if I hadn't tried, trying to pave the way as best I could—I'm as guilty as Lettie, you see."

"I see," Uncle Ernest came into the room and spoke very quietly. "Sorry," he said as if apologizing. "Nadine called me, so I had to follow you, Chan. I was going to meet her here. I've been listening outside. I'm not sure I can explain, but you see, Lettie can't face things. She's like her mother, I suppose. Loves luxury, but there is an instability. Not a soldier. Runs away. Let her go, Chan."

"Let Lettie go! She killed him—"

"She'll not kill again."

Nadine cried. "I *must* see to her!"

"I don't intend you or anybody to become an accessory after the fact," Chan said.

"But in a way *I'm* an accessory *before* the fact," Nadine said sadly.

"I'll take care of Lettie. I promise you," Uncle Ernest said.

"No. Call the police, Mady. There's a telephone on the desk."

Mady moved toward it. Lettie screamed a thin, terrified wail. Uncle Ernest moved swiftly ahead of Mady, took the telephone out of her hand and wrenched the wires from the wall.

He said to Nadine, "How long?"

"Give me twelve hours—tomorrow, say?"

"Good." Uncle Ernest was perfectly calm. He and Nadine appeared to understand one another without words, for Nadine said to Chan, "I promise you. She'll never, never again—"

Uncle Ernest said firmly, "We'll see to that. Believe me—"

"The police," said Chan.

Uncle Ernest, oddly, seemed to observe the glass paper-weight and leaned over, his supple athletic figure making a rapid move as he turned to Chan and tapped him, rather lightly, it seemed actually, behind one ear. He caught Chan's sliding figure, eased it into a chair and nodded at Nadine. "Take her. Tickets will be there—"

Nadine put her arm around Lettie and Lettie clung to her, again sobbing, but eager just the same (clutching the big shoulder bag under one arm), her little feet pattering briskly along with Nadine and out the door.

"Don't worry, my dear," Uncle Ernest said to Mady. "You see, Nadine feels she owes it to the senator."

But Mady was intent only in hunting for Chan's pulse.

"He just got a bump. He'll be all right. Now then, when he comes to, tell him that I'll call the police. I don't know just what I'll tell them yet, but I'll think of something," said Uncle Ernest efficiently and left.

"Ouch!" Chan opened his eyes. "What hit me?"

"Uncle Ernest—"

Chan was feeling cautiously behind his ear. "That guy has got a mean wallop."

"They've gone, Chan. Where?"

He winced as he touched his head. "Oh, I can guess. They're going to get Lettie to his place in Australia. And keep her there, I hope." He tried to get up, found his legs wobbly and groped for a chair. "It's not right. It's not even fair to the police."

But in her heart, Mady felt that Nadine and Uncle Ernest were right. Lettie was not, she thought sadly, reasonable or reliable; she did fly into panics. But she would be safe with Nadine and Uncle Ernest. Lettie, as her uncle had said, was not a soldier.

Mady wasn't at all sure that she herself was a very fine soldier, but she had to get Chan home and see to the swelling behind his ear. "Come with me, Chan. I have to get home. Uncle Ernest said he'd deal with the police."

Chan said, "It was hell, you know, with Lettie. Watching her. But she got away the afternoon of Stu's funeral. She took her bracelet to be sold."

And she brought all the jewels she could bring here, Mady thought. Everything but the necklace—there were too many people having that buffet luncheon she had organized; she couldn't get into the wooden Indian. They could and probably would talk it all over later.

Chan went on, "She was afraid of what we might find in the safe-deposit box. So she phoned to us before she returned to make sure that we had found nothing at all that could implicate her. I had to watch and wait and—Mady, it was as if I were a tiger waiting for some lamb to fall into my clutches."

Not exactly a lamb, Mady thought. Only a pathetic, soft, lovely, greedy murderous coward.

"Even that business about the key on the floor inside Stu's study. Remember? She said, 'There's another in the library.' So she had simply dropped the key near the door after she shot him so we would think it had fallen out afterward. She took time to get the key they kept in the library and locked the door with it. Yes—she had the gun, and the key and Rose's glove and—" Chan rose and staggered a little. She took his arm. She turned in the hall to close the door upon the tragic little apartment with all its photographs, still watching her. Larry, of course, would have kept his hands clean. He had made an effort to get rid of all those telltale financial details, but at the same time not one of them really implicated him. So he had shrugged and gone away, sure of his position.

A taxi was waiting. "Miss Smith—" the driver said.

"Why—yes—"

"A gentleman hired me, said to wait, you'd be down with a sick man—" He eyed Chan. "He does look sick."

"No more sick than you are," Chan growled, but permitted Mady and the taxi driver to help him into the cab. And to help him out once they reached Mady's home where there were lights, Clarence and Rose.

Clarence fell upon them. "My dear fellow! Come in— you need a doctor—"

"*No!*" said Chan.

Rose said comfortingly, "It's all over, I think. The police have just left. They came to return your red coat, Mady."

Clarence added, "You remember that somebody at this hotel where that man Shelton was shot said he caught a glimpse of a woman in a purple coat. Well, the police finally figured out that there's a blue neon light over the hotel door and it turns red to purple, so they thought of your red coat and came and got it—that is, naturally, Mrs. Baynes had to let them have it. I suppose Lettie wore it."

"They told you—" Chan said.

"Enough. Didn't have to say much. I told you, long

ago, I guessed Lettie killed him. How did she do it? Simple. She told you he was at the St. Regis. Actually, he was at this other hotel. She went to meet him, got past the desk clerk or elevator man or—a shoddy little hotel as this one seems to be wouldn't be too careful about desk clerks and elevator men and—ladies arriving and not giving their names. Now would it? The point is, Lettie must have suspected this man wasn't her uncle, so she went up to his room—probably he told her his room number over the phone—and just shot him. What did Lettie do with his passport and money? Why, she got away from that little hotel, easy as how she got in, I imagine, and simply dropped all the papers she had found in his room into the nearest trash can. Anything to confuse the case for the police and make it harder for them to track down the dead man. I still don't know exactly where she got hold of a gun, but—''

Clarence looked both shocked and proud of himself. ''I told the police right away about the diamond bracelet at the gallery. So they instantly got out somebody who gave them the information: Lettie herself left it there. Preparing to make her getaway.''

Rose took Chan's arm and guided him to a deep chair. ''Now lean back. I'm sure you ought not to have a drink. Some hot tea with sugar.''

Clarence whisked off kitchenward, Mady knew, for hot tea with sugar. It was a good plan, but it was Rose's suggestion that lent speed to Clarence.

Rose said, ''You see, while the police were here, there was a phone call for them. They've just left, as a matter of fact—''

''The phone call—'' Mady prompted her.

''Oh, yes. They had just told us that Lettie was—well, they were preparing a case against her. But the phone call came from that uncle of hers. He said he had to see them, report something. I don't know his words, but they both shot out of here.''

So Uncle Ernest had already undertaken his role and his story and unless Mady was very much mistaken it would be good enough to insure time enough for Nadine to spirit Lettie away—illegally, perhaps, but away, eventually reaching his ranch in Australia. There was an extradition treaty with Australia, she felt sure of that. She also felt sure that Uncle Ernest and Nadine between them would—as they had said—see to Lettie.

Rose said, "Clarence told me of the scene this afternoon at Lettie's apartment. He had found Lettie's diamond bracelet and the necklace—oh, you were there. You know that." Rose went on smoothly, "A few moments ago Clarence tried to reach her mother by phone at that splendid hotel Hadah is said to have financed—at least partly financed—but they had already gone. They must be over the Atlantic by now. He is said to own a good part of one of the airlines. He always acts, you know, with perfect legality."

Chan had leaned back, his eyes closed. He said, "Rose, do you understand what this man—Hadah—could want anybody to lobby for him?"

Rose sighed. "Oh, yes. A nuclear reactor, but also—"

"Also a cover for atomic warheads," Chan said soberly.

Rose nodded once. "I was afraid of that, Chan. It's been done—or at least attempted. Nothing," she said with sudden vigor, "is too evil for that man Hadah!"

"I'm not certain of it," Chan touched his head gingerly.

"But you are almost certain," Rose said. "Certain enough to refuse to have anything to do with it. Or him. I'll see to him, Chan." There was a serious promise in her voice. She leaned back then. "Now—as to lobbying, Hadah had to get somebody he could trust. Not only for his research but for all kinds of things—coal, oil, minerals. He had many interests that he wished to be represented in Washington. According to Clarence, he was not pleased with Lettie. I suppose he had employed her. She had to get all that money from somebody." Rose added quietly, "This man Hadah has an interest in Chavez et Cie."

Chan sat up. "How in the world—"

"How did I guess that?" Rose almost laughed. "Why, Chan, who would be in a position to employ Lettie except this mysterious person her mother married—with all his money?"

"Larry says—" Mady began.

Rose nodded. "Larry! That settles it! Hadah's money. His various interests. Stu's possible influence. My interest in Chavez et Cie. So, very likely, Hadah's interest in Chavez et Cie. Oh, yes. What Larry couldn't positively know he could guess at. Or track down. Yes. But my glove. I didn't *know!* I only suspected that somebody with a small hand could have snatched my glove. I arrived at the party very early, you see, along with the first arrivals and left my coat and gloves. And I began to think—later on, oh, much later on—that I had heard something being opened in the pantry—champagne perhaps. Or, later, I was afraid it might have been a gunshot. Nobody would have noticed by that time. People were talking and drinking and somehow voices get higher and noisier and—I couldn't remember seeing Lettie for quite a little while. She could have been in the kitchen or pantry or—but I began to wonder. I'm sorry about it. I'll soon get rid of Hadah. But Lettie—oh, there you are, Clarence. Now drink that, Chan."

Clarence had trotted back and now thrust a steaming cup in Chan's hand. "Here, my dear fellow. Lots of sugar. Nothing better for shock."

"It was a shock, all right," Chan said dourly. "Also a bump behind my ear."

Clarence's eyes sparkled. "*Who*—"

"Uncle Ernest," Mady said.

Rose eyed both of them for a second. "I think I see. Yes, much better to get Lettie out of it. She—I can't explain it—but she just was never quite—sound."

"No backbone," said Clarence. "Mady, it's not news to you, but tonight Rose promised—"

"Yes, I did," Rose said and beamed at Mady and flushed like a girl. As Mady and then Clarence and at last Chan had managed to get to his feet and kiss her, Rose left. Clarence said blithely, "I'll just see her to her car," and skipped along with her.

That's one good thing, Mady thought. She said boldly, "Clarence doesn't object to Rose's money."

"Object!" Chan had sunk down again, his hand at his head. "Money is a damn good thing to have."

"Some people—some men—might object to mine." Mady still felt bold. "But of course it's not as much as Rose has—"

It seemed impossible to get him to thinking along the right lines. "I don't know what Uncle Ernest is telling the police," he said. "But whatever it is—this thing isn't over yet, Mady. There'll be news, headlines, all that to go through."

"Perhaps Ernest can prevent some of it. But you'll be at the university."

"We'll have to come back and tell the police everything we know."

Mady gave him a long look and took an equally long breath. "Did you mean what you just said? Or are you still dizzy?"

Chan sat up indignantly. "Good Lord, I've been trying to talk to you. That's why I asked you to meet me at Twenty-One. I've just had a salary boost. Do you mean you aren't going to marry me?"

"I mean—you never asked me!"

"How could I? First the storm, then all those people, then your hair, then the snow and the taxi and then—the sky fell on us—"

Clarence said from the doorway, "Good for you, Mady. I thought you'd never get around to talking him into marriage."

"Go away, Clarence," Chan said firmly.